Copyright © 2022 by Ken Lozito

All rights reserved.

No part of this book may be reproduced in any form or by any electronic or mechanical means, including information storage and retrieval systems, without written permission from the author, except for the use of brief quotations in a book review.

Published by Acoustical Books, LLC

KenLozito.com

Cover design by Jeff Brown

IF YOU WOULD LIKE TO BE NOTIFIED WHEN MY NEXT BOOK IS RELEASED VISIT

WWW.KENLOZITO.COM

ISBN: 978-1-945223-52-5

INFINITY

KEN LOZITO

1

THE COMMAND DECK of the *Infinity* was almost silent but for the soft background sounds of environmental recordings. The bulkheads were invisible beyond the projection of star-speckled space and the grayish landscape below the lunar shipyards. Noah glanced about, going through his own mental checklists for the hundredth time.

"Cargo shuttle has departed, Captain. Shipyard control has cleared us to leave," Markovich said.

"Thanks, Chief," Noah replied. "Secure all moorings. Let's put some distance between us and home."

"Yes, Captain."

"Comms, send our current flight plan to COMCENT," Noah said.

"COMCENT has confirmed receipt of flight plan, Captain," Jessica Yu replied.

Noah's stomach didn't quite do a full flip-flop, but it was damn close. This wasn't the first ship he'd been on, but it was the first one he'd commanded. The old adage about being careful what you wished for had been banging around his head since he'd gotten approval.

A large portion of the crew was former CDF, but the *Infinity* wasn't part of the colonial military. With a crew of a hundred spacers, the civilian exploration ship, *Infinity*, was the first of its kind.

The *Infinity*'s main engines engaged at five percent power, and they slowly left the lunar shipyards behind. Once they were far enough away, the power draw of the main engines increased as they settled into cruising speed.

Markovich turned toward him, eyebrows raised.

"This was the easy part," Noah said.

Markovich smiled. "Nothing fell off."

Noah grinned. "I think we can set the bar a little higher than that."

Reconfigured over the last year, the *Infinity*'s hull was an appropriated CDF frigate that massed at seventy thousand tons, had a length of three hundred twenty meters from tip to stern, and was fifty meters across the beam. The entire ship had been reconfigured by removing primary weapons systems, adding a hangar bay, and expanding the sensor array to accommodate a more robust platform. They'd removed all the systems that made it a warship, turning it into something more suitable for long-term exploration that met the Infinity Drive's power requirements.

"Agreed. I was just trying to take the edge off," Markovich said.

Noah stood. "We've got several hours before we really depart. I'm going to check on our last-minute additions to the crew. You have the con."

"Aye, Captain, I have the con."

Noah walked off the bridge toward the main hangar, entering

the lift and selecting H deck. The brightly lit corridors were a pale gray, and his internal HUD marked the hangar's location in front of him. He disabled the guide function of his HUD. He knew every bit of the ship.

He palmed the door controls to the hangar bay, and they opened onto a space that was nearly the width of the ship. Two Pathfinder shuttles were secured off to the side. A platoon of CDF soldiers in blue uniforms were moving several platforms of equipment that had been offloaded from the cargo shuttles.

His deck officer, Peter Blood, was speaking with two of the soldiers. Noah recognized one of them instantly, even if he didn't quite believe he was here.

"We'll need them stored in accessible locations near the standard comms drone-deployment tubes," Colonel Sean Quinn said.

Blood frowned. "I need to know what's in those crates before I can approve their use in the deployment tubes. Whatever's in there is shielded, and I can't get a reading on my scanner."

"You won't. They're shielded for your protection. I can take this up with your captain."

Blood saw Noah walking toward them. "Excellent. Captain, Colonel Quinn has something he'd like to discuss with you."

Sean turned toward Noah and smiled a little.

Noah arched an eyebrow and looked at the metallic crates for a few seconds. "Well, you didn't get demoted to be here," he said, ignoring the crates.

Sean shook his head. "I volunteered."

Colonel Sean Quinn commanded the CDF fleet. He'd served in two wars and was a decorated hero in both of those wars. He had short dark hair, was of average height, and had an athletic build. He was also one of the bravest men Noah had ever met, and he was a friend.

"Uh huh," Noah replied. "Are those new toys?"

Sean nodded. "They're new attack drones."

Noah's eyebrows raised, intrigued. "A prototype ship needs a prototype weapon?"

Sean shrugged. "You need something more than a pair of mag cannons and some point-defense systems. The ship doesn't have any missile tubes, so this is the next best thing."

Noah looked toward the dark crates again. Several soldiers stood next to them, waiting. "Let's have a look," he said and strode toward the crates.

The nearest soldier looked past Noah, confirming whether he should stop him.

"Open one of the crates," Sean said, following him.

Two soldiers lifted one of the long dark crates off the pallet and set it on the ground. The locking mechanism flashed green, and several latches appeared on the side. The soldiers opened the crate.

Noah peered inside. The attack drone was two meters in length with an elongated, bronze-colored head. The bronze color became black toward the opposite end, and the drones were as thick as one of his thighs.

"I can detect multiple energy signatures. It's almost as if they're individual power cores, but they're not active?" Blood asked.

"You'd know it if they were armed," Noah said, and Sean flicked his eyebrows. Noah regarded his friend for a moment. "I didn't think these were in use anywhere."

"R&D has had a lot of success reverse engineering them, but it was the subspace comms that really gave us an edge. Targeting can be maintained from your ship's nav computer," Sean said.

Blood held up his hand. "I've heard about Krake attack drones. They burn as hot as a yellow star and can penetrate armored ship hulls. How are we supposed to launch them without damaging our own ship?"

"First, you won't be launching them at all," Sean said, and held up his hand when Blood began to speak. "Not without training and certainly not without one of my people with you. To answer your question, they launch in stages. They have a passive active state, which will be used as part of the arming sequence. Once they're away from the ship, we can arm them fully."

Blood considered this for a second and looked at Noah. "Captain, given what we're about to do, should we really increase the risk to the ship by having these aboard?"

Sean didn't respond but instead waited for Noah to speak.

"It's a risk, but there's no evidence to suggest we're in more danger by having them aboard," Noah replied.

Most of his officers knew how the Infinity Drive worked, but that didn't mean they trusted the technology. He *could* reject clearance to allow the attack drones on his ship. It was an option, but he'd anticipated the arguments raised in support of bringing them along. Since the I-Drive hadn't been installed on any CDF warship, Sean had chosen to bring at least *some* weapons capability with him. If Noah chose to reject them, Sean would report this to COMCENT. Then the CDF brass would report a lack of cooperation from a certain civilian mission commander, and Noah would be told to accept the cargo or possibly be relieved of command. He didn't know exactly why Sean was here, leading one solitary platoon of soldiers, but the CDF hadn't sent one of its most decorated commanders without certain contingency plans in mind.

Noah looked at Blood. "Give them our full cooperation, Mister Blood."

"Understood, Captain," he replied.

"Excellent," Sean said. "Mister Blood, you can work with Lieutenant Jesse Rhoades." He gestured toward a nearby soldier, who gave Blood an agreeable nod.

The soldiers closed the container and set it back on the pallet.

Noah looked at Sean. "I think you and I need to talk."

Sean nodded. "That would be a good idea."

Noah led them out of the hangar bay and headed toward the lift. Once the doors were shut, he regarded Sean. "So, if you're not demoted, then what are you doing here? I was told Captain Davis was leading the platoon."

"He was, but I wanted to come."

Sean was toying with him, and he wasn't in the mood for it. "Sean, give me a break. You command fleets—multiple-ship engagements. You're not here simply to lead a platoon of soldiers on my ship. Why are you really here?"

"I'm the most qualified for the mission."

Noah scowled but didn't say anything. The lift doors opened.

Sean looked at the corridor beyond and frowned.

Noah waved a finger at him. "You thought I was taking you right to the bridge. We'll get there, but I figured you'd want to see main engineering first."

They stepped out of the elevator and Sean lingered behind.

"Noah, I know this isn't easy. I'm here to help you with the mission."

"You're here to take over the mission if I mess things up."

"If it comes to it, I *am* to take command."

Noah exhaled a long, resigned sigh. "What are your orders?"

"They're confidential."

Noah gritted his teeth and rolled his eyes.

Sean grinned. "I'm kidding. Geez. You're the one who always liked joking around. I'm just trying to loosen up the tension a little bit."

Noah lifted one of his hands into the air. "I don't think this is funny."

Sean shrugged. "It's not funny. Noah, I'm here to help you. I'm not going to take command away from you. You're still the mission commander. I'm here in case the situation becomes hostile."

"We lost contact with the *Ark II*, but that doesn't mean they were attacked," Noah said, praying that wasn't the case.

"They might not have been, but I'm here in case they were. I'm to do a tactical assessment and then help you return home."

"I don't need a babysitter."

A grin bubbled out of Sean's chest and became a full-on laugh. "When did you get so uptight? No, hear me out. You convinced Governor Mullins that this ship should remain under civilian control, and this was *after* you appropriated one of our ships to be fitted with the Infinity Drive. You're venturing out into the unknown. Take it from someone who's done it before— you can never bring enough fire power with you. This is a compromise between the CDF and the colonial government."

Noah considered it for a few moments. "What about you?"

Sean pursed his lips. "Me," he said and smiled. "I'm the bonus."

"Bonus! Are you serious?"

Sean sighed. "You're starting to make me feel like I'm not welcome."

Noah frowned and gave a quick shake of his head. "It's not that. I'm glad you're here. It's just that I had to jump through so many damn hoops just to get this mission off the ground."

"I know. It was quite impressive to watch." Sean smiled, which came easier for him now. It hadn't always been like that. War with the Krake had taken a toll on him.

"I guess I should thank you for coming along."

"That would be a good start. It's Oriana you have to worry about."

"Your wife loves me."

"She does, but you're taking me three lightyears away from New Earth. She said you better get me back in one piece. Plus, it's not fair that Kara gets to come."

Noah exhaled forcefully and rubbed his palm through his hair. "You can't be serious. There was no way she was going to miss this. She helped me build the I-Drive."

"Oh, I know. I got an earful about that."

"It's the price we pay for marrying brilliant women."

"So, 'I-Drive'?" Sean asked.

Noah nodded. "It's less of a mouthful than Infinity Drive." They walked down the corridor. "I really am glad you're here. I had no idea who Captain Davis was, and sometimes you just don't know how capable someone is until they're in the thick of it."

"He would have been fine, but you need the best. And lucky for you, you got it."

Noah shook his head. "Are you going to be like this the entire time?"

Sean shrugged. "I don't remember the last time I was on a ship that wasn't in my command. This is going to be like a vacation for me. I'm going to enjoy being a passenger."

Noah sighed heavily. "I hope the *Ark II* is okay. Even if their subspace comms suffered some kind of failure, they should have been able to fix it by now. It's been months since we lost communication."

Sean nodded grimly. "We need answers."

Over ten years ago, the *Ark II* had left New Earth with five thousand colonists aboard. During that entire time, the ship's computer system had checked in regularly, but shortly after they arrived in the Zeta-Alpha star system, communications had stopped. They had no idea why or any indication of what had happened.

Noah had made several breakthroughs with faster-than-light technology. The *Infinity* was the first ship to be fitted with what he called the Infinity Drive. Some of the engineers had begun referring to it as the I-Drive, and it stuck. The I-Drive enabled them to travel many times faster than the speed of light. The only problem was that he'd only successfully tested it with test drones. No human-crewed vessel had ever made the journey. When Noah learned about the loss of contact with the *Ark II*, he worked himself tirelessly to finish construction of the *Infinity*. This ship would give him the answers he needed. He had friends who were part of the second colony mission aboard the *Ark II*, and he would never accept that five thousand of his fellow colonists had simply disappeared.

2

Noah led Sean into main engineering. If the bridge of a ship was the brain, then main engineering was the heart and soul. A young man with short, curly hair and the barest hint of a mustache spotted them and walked over.

Sean snorted a little so only Noah could hear him. "Does he know that fuzz of a mustache makes him look even younger than he probably is?"

Noah twitched his eyebrows once and threw a nod toward the young man. "Mister Leiter, this is Colonel Sean Quinn of the CDF. He and his team will be joining us for the duration."

An easy smile lit up the young man's face and he extended a hand toward Sean. "Xavier Leiter, Colonel Quinn. It's a pleasure to meet you."

Sean shook the proffered hand and gave him a cordial nod.

Xavier looked at Noah. "Is there anything I can help you with, Captain?"

"I'm looking for my chief engineer."

Xavier nodded and gestured toward an adjacent corridor.

"She's at the computing core. They were getting the last of the processing arrays installed."

"Thank you, Mister Leiter. Carry on," Noah replied.

Xavier waved and returned to his workstation.

Noah looked at Sean as they walked down the corridor. "You'll get used to it."

"You mean the nomenclature of a civilian ship? It'll just take a little while. The jobs are similar, anyway. When will we be far enough away to use the I-Drive?"

"In theory, we could use it right now. We don't need to be that far from any planets or moons to use it. The probes we tested with were much smaller and didn't need much clearance to engage the drive."

"I remember when probes were only good for a one-way trip."

Noah nodded. "First, we were sending probes through a larger gateway," he said and shook his head. "Never mind that. Yes, we did use smaller probes with smaller drives. Once the concept was proven reliably, we built them for multiple trips."

Sean chuckled. "It's all right. I know it was way more complicated than that."

Noah blew out a breath. "Thanks. I had to dumb it down for the governor and his staff. We're bending space in front of the ship and expanding it behind. The bubble in the middle isn't affected at all. It sounds so simple, but we had to go through thousands of iterations to figure that out. And getting it to maintain normal space—n-space—wasn't easy."

"I bet."

"What we haven't tested is how long we can maintain the bubble and just how fast we can really go. We could in theory make the journey to Zeta-Alpha in about twenty-five days, but even if all goes well, it'll take us closer to forty days."

Sean frowned for a few seconds. "Navigation. That's it, isn't it?"

Noah bobbed his head with a small smile. "We've got to crawl before we walk, so I've broken the journey up into smaller chunks in the beginning. We know space is vast, but that doesn't mean I want to bump into anything out here."

"Don't worry, Noah. We wouldn't even feel it," Sean said and grinned.

Noah did as well. "Or anything else for that matter."

Sean made his voice deeper. "I laugh in the face of death."

Noah's eyebrows pushed forward and he tipped his head to the side. "This isn't a joke. I thought you'd be more serious about it."

Sean stopped walking and regarded him.

"I am serious about this, but I also have a good idea about what you did to put this together. I wouldn't be here if I thought we were all gonna die. I also know that at some point we've got to take the leap. Now, granted it's a bit sooner than you would have liked. I agree with you on that, but like you, I want to know what happened to Lars and everyone else who was aboard the *Ark II*. We'll stumble, but if there's anyone better than you to get us there, I haven't heard of them."

Noah regarded his friend for a moment. "Thanks for that."

"It's all part of the service. I do have a question, though."

"All right, what?"

"The mission clock has us leaving in about five hours."

"That's right."

"Any chance we can move that up?"

Noah was about to answer when he heard his wife.

"I thought I recognized that voice," Kara said, quickly walking over to them. She gave Sean a hug and a peck on the cheek, then tipped her head to the side. "What are you doing here?"

"Officially, I'm here to assist with the search and rescue operations once we reach Zeta-Alpha-5," Sean replied.

"And unofficially?" Kara asked, moving to stand next to Noah.

They'd all been part of the CDF. Though Noah and Kara had retired from the military, their R&D projects had overlapped with some of the CDF initiatives over the years.

"I'm to evaluate the presence of any hostile forces that could be a threat to the colony." He gave Noah a wry glance. "Also, I'm to assist the mission commander in any way possible."

Kara looked at Noah.

"He's got to do what I say unless we encounter hostile aliens. Then he's authorized to take command."

Kara nodded once. "So, I guess we need to be nice to him. Don't work him too hard. And give him quarters in officer country."

Sean laughed.

"Is Oriana with you? I could really use her help," Kara said.

Sean shook his head. "No, she couldn't be here."

"Oh, okay. I'll contact her through ship comms then."

Sean's eyes widened for half a second. "Uh, hold off on that, would you?"

Kara frowned and then her golden eyebrows raised. "She doesn't know you're here!"

Noah felt his mouth slacken as he stared at Sean.

Sean leaned against the wall, looking as if he'd gotten caught doing something he shouldn't have. "There wasn't time." He pressed his lips together in a small smile. "And if we can move up that launch window, that would be great."

"Oh my God," Noah said, his gaze narrowing. "You're not supposed to be here."

Sean lifted his hands in front of his chest. "No. No," he said, bobbing his head with each word. "I'm authorized to be here. It's just that not everyone knows about the authorization just yet."

Noah shook his head and grinned a little. "Sean," he said as he rubbed his forehead for a couple of seconds, "last I heard you were being considered for promotion to Brigadier General. What are you doing?"

"I know. If they'd gone through with it, I'd never have been able to come."

"Who else knows you're here? Does Connor know? What about Nathan?"

"They will, just not yet."

"And you want us to get underway sooner so they don't have the option to recall you if they don't approve."

Sean shrugged. "Better to ask forgiveness than permission. How many times did we watch Connor and Nathan do the same? Besides, this is where I need to be. If I could, I'd bring a fleet of CDF warships with me."

Kara's eyebrows drew down in concern. "The CDF is everything to you. They could dismiss you for this."

"They won't."

Noah sighed explosively. "Maybe Connor and Nathan won't, but just hear me out now. If this goes before a review board and they determine that you're abusing your authority, they'd have grounds to dismiss you."

"Which is why we need to get out of here as soon as possible."

Noah's shoulders slumped a little and he looked at Kara. "Can we push up the timeline?"

"How much?"

"Under an hour?"

"An hour!"

"Yeah, an hour. If we increase our velocity, we'll be far enough away to engage the I-Drive. By then, there wouldn't be much anyone could do about it."

Kara considered it for a few moments, and Noah could see her mind flashing through the mental checklists they both maintained.

"I'd much rather have Sean with us than someone else. I know we can do it, but I won't do it without your consent. You're the Chief Engineer. I actually need your consent," Noah said.

Kara was silent while she thought about it.

"Wait," Sean said. "It would be great if we could leave sooner, but if you're not ready, then that's the way it is. I'll deal with the fallout."

Kara looked at them and rolled her eyes a little. "Look at both of you with your hopeful glimmer that I'll allow this recklessness to go on. Don't make me the mom here."

Noah smiled. "We all have our roles to play. But if I'm right, I don't see why we couldn't move things up to say, ninety minutes."

Kara narrowed her gaze with severity, but her eyes twinkled a bit. "Are you trying to make me feel better?"

Noah smiled but not too much. He didn't want to push it. "Is it working?"

The edges of her lips twitched. "Yes, yes. We can move things up. Quicken the system testing times. Provided that everything checks out, we'll get underway as quickly as possible."

"Great, I can have my team assist with whatever you need," Sean said.

"That'll depend on what they're qualified to do, but I'm sure the captain can get them assigned appropriately."

Noah leaned over and kissed her cheek. She goosed him and hastened down the corridor, calling out to her own team.

Noah and Sean went back the way they'd come.

"She's right. What can your team do to help?"

They went to Noah's ready room near the bridge and assigned the CDF soldiers where they could help. Word quickly spread about moving up the timeline to engage the I-Drive. They increased the power output for the main engines, increasing the ship's velocity.

Noah waited as long as he could before sending an update to COMCENT. They'd probably already noticed the increased velocity but hadn't contacted them yet. Noah glanced at Sean, but his friend didn't give anything away. He suspected that Sean had covered all his bases prior to coming aboard, including certain key personnel on duty at COMCENT.

Ninety minutes seemed to pass in a fraction of the time. No sooner had they moved onto the bridge than the crew of the *Infinity* began to go through their extensive checklists, and all systems were green across the board. Noah sat at the command workstation on the bridge, and Sean took the auxiliary workstation next to him.

Noah scanned the readiness reports one more time, more to set himself at ease than to double- or triple-check what his senior officers had already gone through. He authorized the mission plan update be sent to COMCENT and opened a broadcast channel to the ship.

"Crew of the *Infinity*, this is the Captain. We're about to embark upon a journey of unprecedented importance, a true landmark in our history. Not since our first trips into space have we taken a leap like we're about to take. But this is only the first step, and we wouldn't be here if it weren't for the work of so many who aren't able to be here with us. For hundreds of years, faster-than-light travel has remained elusive, beyond our grasp, and it might have remained that way if three hundred thousand brave colonists hadn't decided to journey through interstellar space to make a home on New Earth. We stand upon the shoulders of the great people throughout our entire history, and we honor our legacy here today by embarking upon this massive undertaking. The fact that in just over forty days we'll be making a journey that took the *Ark II* over ten years is astounding. There have been so many firsts since the colony was established. There are those among you who have traveled throughout the multiverse, and now we take the next step in our legacy to keep pushing the limit, to keep exploring, to keep learning, while holding onto what makes us a species worth striving for. All of you serving on this ship are volunteers. You dared to step forward into the unknown, and I'm proud to share this moment with you."

Noah closed the broadcast comlink.

Sean stood up and snapped him a crisp salute while the bridge erupted into cheers.

When things settled down, Sean leaned toward him. "I'm not the only one to pick up a few things from Connor Gates."

"He always seemed to know how to motivate us," Noah replied.

Sean tilted his head to the side once and then sat down.

"Helm, cut main engines."

"Aye, Captain. Cut main engines," Myers replied.

"Ops, divert power to the Infinity Drive," Noah said.

"Diverting power to Infinity Drive, Captain," Delta Mattison replied.

Noah watched the status window on the main holoscreen as the central ring around the middle of the ship began to charge. The ring was a heavily modified spacegate.

"Nav, confirm course has been accepted by computing core."

"Course has been confirmed and accepted, Captain. I-Drive to be active for twelve hours," Caleb Reid replied.

"Very well," Noah said and watched as the Infinity Drive was brought online.

The Casimir power core was capable of producing energy beyond anything that their fusion power core had been capable of. The foundation for the technology had been taken from Krake warships and further refined by the colonists. The Krake had inferior containment systems because they hadn't devoted any of their vast resources to developing more resilient alloys capable of handling the amount of energy produced. Humanity, on the other hand, had superior ceramic and metallic alloys that could. They'd even improved on the Casimir power core, increasing the power yield.

"I-Drive is charged and ready, Captain," Delta Mattison said.

Noah shared a look with Sean, then said, "Engage."

There was a burst of energy from the Infinity Drive as space contracted in front of the ship while expanding behind them at the same time. The bubble that the ship resided in was considered normal space (n-space).

"Power levels are constant. I-Drive is performing within acceptable limits, Captain," Delta Mattison said, her voice high with excitement. "All systems are still green, sir."

Noah smiled and looked around the bridge.

"You did it," Sean said. His voice carried a note of amazement that Noah had rarely heard from him.

Noah opened another ship-wide broadcast channel. "Congratulations, crew of the *Infinity*. We're now moving twenty-seven times the speed of light. Stand down from active status. Normal ship status authorized."

He closed the comlink and the people on the bridge cheered

and clapped. Noah stood up and shook hands with everyone present. When he returned to the command chair, he looked at Sean.

"It almost doesn't feel real."

Sean nodded. "It doesn't. The scanners and sensors reporting in confirm it, but I get what you're saying."

"Captain," Jessica Yu said, "COMCENT forwarded their congratulations on this momentous occasion."

"Thank them for me," Noah said. He looked at Sean. "I guess they don't want us to turn around and send you back to New Earth."

Sean chuckled. "I guess not."

3

GENERAL CONNOR GATES had just wrapped up an operations meeting when he received news of the *Infinity*'s successful departure from the star system. He checked his schedule and saw that the ship had departed several hours earlier than planned.

Major Jeffrey Stinnet cleared his throat. "I thought the *Infinity* was departing later today."

"So did I," Connor replied. He checked the logs and saw that Noah had sent an updated schedule. He pursed his lips in thought.

Stinnet's wrist computer chimed, and he answered the comlink. "Yes, General Hayes, he's right here." Stinnet looked at Connor and then made a passing motion toward a nearby holoscreen.

"Thank you, Major. That'll be all," Connor said.

Major Stinnet quickly left the conference room and closed the door.

Connor turned toward the holoscreen. "Hello, Nathan."

"Hi, Connor," Nathan replied. "Did you know about this?"

"Could you be more specific?"

Nathan snorted. At some point, both of them instinctively assumed the other knew what was being referred to. "*Infinity*'s early departure."

Connor shook his head. "I didn't. Noah must have been able to move up his schedule."

"It's odd that he didn't let us know until right before he left."

Connor frowned. Something didn't add up. He brought up a sub-window and checked a few deployment schedules, then chuckled and shook his head.

"What is it?"

"It looks like there was a last-minute change to his crew and the platoon we insisted be added to the roster. Here, take a look," Connor said and made the data available.

Nathan's blue-eyed gaze scanned the data. "Colonel Quinn. It looks like he authorized himself a mission."

"It looks that way," Connor replied and couldn't decide whether he was irritated with Sean or not. "Sean timed this all so we wouldn't find out until the *Infinity* had already gone."

Nathan nodded. "We trained them too well," he said and leaned toward the camera. "I blame you, Connor."

Connor raised his hands in front of his chest. "Guilty as charged."

"You didn't make Sean disobey orders. No matter how you slice it, he's abandoned his current command."

"He did. I'm trying to figure out why."

"I thought that was obvious. Noah is his friend."

"I know that, but why didn't he come to us first?" Connor asked.

Nathan considered it for a few seconds. "It's because then he would have disobeyed orders. I've just been notified of a temporary leave request from Sean."

Connor chuckled and Nathan did the same. "He's good. You're right, we trained him too well."

"Indeed. Either I grant the request in which his jaunt aboard the *Infinity* is authorized, or I deny it and he'll be charged with dereliction of duty," Nathan said and shook his head. "I don't like either of those options."

"I understand. You know, Sean has the most experience exploring the unknown. He can evaluate whether there's any threat at Zeta-Alpha."

Nathan's eyes flicked skyward. "That's quite a spin, Connor."

"I know him. That's what he was thinking."

Nathan nodded. "We teach them these things. I know *you're* no stranger to doing what's necessary."

"Yeah, I'm just not used to being on the receiving end of it."

"At least we're in agreement about that. What do you suggest we do?" Nathan asked.

"Unless you want to disclose this to Governor Mullins, I say we handle this off the record after Sean gets back."

Nathan sighed. "I have to agree with you." He paused for a few seconds, considering. "This thing got put together so fast that I can almost forgive Sean's lack of judgement."

"Same here. Almost," Connor agreed. "But at the same time, I keep thinking this is something we should have proposed ourselves."

"Sean commands fleets, but I understand what you're saying."

"They're like brothers. All of them—Noah, Sean, and Lars."

Nathan raised an eyebrow. "Are you regretting not going with them? Don't let Lenora hear that."

Connor laughed. "I'm always tempted, but no. I can't think of anyone better than those two making that journey together."

Nathan nodded and gestured off screen. "Well, I just

authorized Sean's leave. I should make you update Governor Mullins about this."

Connor shrugged. "We get along just fine now. Do you want me to take this off your plate?"

Nathan smiled. "Nope, I'll handle it. It *is* remarkable, isn't it?"

"I know Noah's been close to making this work for a long time, even with the success of the test probes."

"It makes me think of all the other places we'll get to travel to. Maybe not us but certainly our children. We've become a people of multiple worlds. Theirs will be a world where interstellar travel is something as regular as us exploring this star system," Nathan said.

Connor thought about his daughter and son and felt a pang of fatherly protectiveness rouse inside him. "Not yet."

Nathan smiled knowingly. "The time does go by quickly. We'll soon be toasting Noah and his team's success."

"We will," Connor replied.

The video comlink closed and Connor stood there for a few moments, thinking about the world he'd help build for his children. Nathan was right. Time did indeed pass by too quickly. He powered off the holoscreen and left the conference room.

4

Noah watched the wavering gray and black, as well as the pulsing purple and green of traveling at FTL. It glowed and throbbed, beckoning to him, starless and shifting, as infinitely beautiful and mesmerizing to him as anything he'd seen in his life.

Kara stood next to him and sighed, leaning her head on his shoulder. "I never thought it would look like this. It's so amazingly beautiful that even after fifteen days, I can't look away from it."

Noah nodded, catching the rose-and-lavender scent of her lustrous blonde hair. "I know what you mean. The probe sensors didn't do it justice."

They stood alone in a dimly lit conference room, awash in color from external sensor feeds on a wallscreen that took up the entire side of the room. The door to the conference room opened and the lights flicked on.

Sean walked in. "Am I interrupting cuddle-by-the-window time?" he asked with a wry grin.

Noah chuckled and lifted his chin in greeting. "I was just thinking the only thing that could make this moment even more perfect was if you were in it, so thanks for coming."

Sean laughed and walked over to them, looking at the colorful display on the wallscreen. "It's an impressive sight to be sure, but enough is enough already."

Kara arched an eyebrow toward Noah and pursed her lips. "Would you look at who has a pouty face. I think someone is missing their better half."

Sean gave her a sidelong glance and leaned closer to her. "We really need to stop playing all these games. When are you going to dump this guy and run away with me? He probably wouldn't even notice. Just get him sidetracked on a technical problem with the I-Drive and he'll be occupied for hours, maybe even days. What do you say?"

Kara laughed and pushed him away.

Noah regarded Sean with mock severity. Then he brought up his personal holoscreen. "That's it. I'm opening a comlink to Oriana right now and confining you to quarters."

Sean grinned. "You can try. I just spoke with her."

"So," Noah said, drawing out the word. "She's speaking to you again?"

Sean nodded. "Of course. She knows the two of you would never let anything happen to me."

Noah frowned and looked at his wife for a second. "That's strange because I thought he was here to keep anything from happening to *us*. Isn't that what he told you?"

Kara rolled her eyes and brushed her fingers through her long blonde hair, regarding both of them for a few seconds. "All right, that's enough. It's funny for a minute or two, but if I don't say anything now, you'll just keep it going."

Sean looked at Noah for a second, but then his gaze sank and he shrugged a little. "I guess it's time to work now."

"Yes, it is," Noah said and sighed.

"Speaking of which, are you joining us for PT this afternoon?"

"I'll be there."

Sean looked at Kara. "I don't know if it's such a good idea if you come with him. He tends to get distracted when you're around."

"I doubt it after being married for as long as we have."

"Now, you know that's not true," Noah began and stopped.

Kara smiled and looked at Sean. "That's all right. I heard the grav emitters were flaky in the hangar bay. I thought I'd take a look and run a few tests," she said, tilting her head and narrowing her gaze inquiringly. "You're training at 14:30, right?"

Sean laughed and shook his head. "All right. I'm really done now. I should tell you what Oriana did to some of my soldiers with gravity emitters."

The rest of the *Infinity*'s senior officers, along with other team leaders, arrived at the conference room at the top of the hour, and Noah started the meeting.

"The I-Drive has been active for ten days now, and by all reports, it's functioning flawlessly. This appears to have been a smooth jaunt through interstellar space."

Kara nodded. "Power consumption levels have been constant. We've adapted the field containment protocols to bleed off the energy that builds up on the bubble."

"We didn't come across that in testing because the flight durations with the I-Drive were so short. How'd you bleed off the excess energy?" Noah asked.

Kara gestured toward the holoscreen, and a data analysis window appeared. "Initial analysis of the sensor data showed that the buildup of energy was somewhat random, but we think that the region of space we're flying through has a big influence on it. We'll learn more as we go, so it's going to take some time. Bleeding off the energy requires precision power bursts to expel the energy safely."

Delta Mattison, his operations officer, raised her hand to speak. "Excuse me, but wouldn't that alter our velocity and take us off course?"

Alissa McGinnis shook her head. "Our course hasn't changed. We would have noticed it during our watch standings."

"The I-Drive isn't like our main engines," Noah said. "While the bubble is maintained, there are fluctuations that the computing core compensates for." He looked at Kara. "We need to understand why the energy builds up in the first place."

"Agreed," she replied.

Noah leaned forward, propped his elbows on the table, and steepled his fingers in front of his lips. Exhaling, he regarded the others. "It sounds like we're managing the issue, but we don't fully understand why it's happening. We could reduce our speed and allow the ship's AI more time to analyze the sensor data. Alternatively, we can stop and do a full sensor sweep of our heading and our previous course. There could be something we're just not seeing while the I-Drive is active."

Kara considered it for a few moments. "We're scheduled for an 'all stop and evaluate' in three days. I'm fine with waiting until then. We'll continue to gather data and then compare it with the most recent sensor sweep of the area."

Noah nodded and looked at Markovich. "I agree with Kara, Captain. If we've managed it for this long and the systems are stable, there's no reason we shouldn't keep going."

Noah looked at Sean. "What do you think, Colonel Quinn?"

The others around the conference table turned toward Sean.

Of everyone in the room, he had the most experience commanding spaceships, some of which had also carried unproven prototype technology.

"I'd echo what the others have already said regarding the current state of things. However, I'd be remiss if I didn't ask whether your watch-standers are familiar with emergency procedures if these anomalies get out of control. Has that been defined? At what point would the buildup of energy be a cause for concern?"

"Everyone is familiar with emergency procedures," Noah replied. "There's a threshold for escalation to the senior watch-stander on duty, who has the option to change our readiness status. It's not that much different from procedures followed on a CDF ship."

"Plus," Kara said, "we've also updated the monitoring systems to show the current field status of the I-Drive. Anomalies would generate alerts for the watch-standers to investigate."

Sean nodded once and looked at Noah.

"All right, I think we can put that matter to the side for now. Dr. Lachlan, have there been any updates about Zeta-Alpha-5? What do we know about the planet?" Noah asked.

Carter Lachlan was of average height, and his thick, dark eyebrows and prominent nose made his face seem more angular than it probably was. "I see some new people at this meeting," he said with a nod toward Lieutenant Rhoades from the CDF, Sean's second-in-command, and the senior watch-standers, Delta Mattison and Jeremy Markovich. "I'm Dr. Carter Lachlan, planetary scientist. Unfortunately, we don't know much more about the Zeta-Alpha star system than the data the initial probe sent back years ago. The scout ship sent ahead of the *Ark II* was to catch up with the initial probe about a year prior to the *Ark II*'s arrival into the star system. But the scout ship went offline before it reached its destination. It suffered some kind of equipment failure. I can't remember off the top of my head, but there's a report available for anyone who wants to review it." He paused for a few seconds and then continued. "The data we have available was collected by the *Ark II* en route to the star system. The probe sent to the star system doesn't have subspace communication capability and didn't have the capacity to build a transceiver. There are a few rocky planets in the Goldilocks zone, with at least one of them being near the size of Earth—about .78 Earths is the current estimate. It does appear to have an atmosphere, but we're not sure of the exact chemical composition. Wobble indicates a healthy, stable star system with eleven planets. This was confirmed by the telescopes and sensors on the *Ark II*."

Sean cleared his throat before he spoke. "So, we don't know any specifics about the star system, and we won't know anything until we actually get there."

"That is an accurate assessment, Colonel Quinn. We'll continue to monitor Zeta-Alpha throughout our journey. Once we reestablish contact with the *Ark II*, we'll have all the data it has collected, which given the amount of time the ship has been in the star system, should be considerable," Dr. Lachlan replied and looked at Noah.

"Thanks, Carter," Noah said and then looked at Sean. "There's been no indication of an advanced civilization in that star system—not fifteen years ago when we received the initial data burst from the probe and nothing from the *Ark II* during its ten-year journey."

Sean regarded him for a few moments and looked at the others. He pressed his lips together and nodded in a way that reminded Noah of Connor when he was about to turn things on its head. "It's my job to be suspicious even when there's nothing to be suspicious about. I'm not going to dispute the current facts, but those facts assume that we've conceived of every possible way a civilization could evolve. Now, just hear me out. We've been a spacefaring species for hundreds of years. The Krake were at it for even longer. There were some similarities in our technological capabilities, but there were also significant differences. My point is that we just don't know what's going to be waiting for us at the Zeta-Alpha star system, and we should be extremely cautious in our approach to anything we do there. Sometimes it's worth questioning the things we think we know just to see if something doesn't add up." He smiled and tipped his head toward Noah and Kara. "We wouldn't be here if it wasn't for you two doing that."

Noah's eyebrows twitched. "I agree that we should take nothing for granted. That's why I want to change how we're going to explore Zeta-Alpha once we get there by assuming there's some kind of hostile force that we want to avoid, at least until we can confirm there isn't. We need to account for as many scenarios as we can think of given our current capabilities."

Kara's eyebrows pulled together in concern. "What about reaching the *Ark II* as quickly as possible?" she asked. Her eyes darted toward Sean for a second. "We can fly the ship right to the interior planets. It doesn't have to take weeks or even days after we arrive at the star system."

"But we'd be flying blind," Noah said. "I want to get there as much as you do."

Kara inhaled explosively. "Look, I don't believe we lost contact with the *Ark II* because of some hostile alien force that we can't detect. I think there's a more reasonable explanation."

"Okay, like what?" Noah asked.

"They're more than likely having a mechanical issue that they're working through. I know it's been months since we've lost contact, but sometimes things can take months to repair. Or something else could be interfering with subspace comms. The ship could be on emergency power because of some kind of issue with the reactors. Sending a distress signal would be a lower priority if they're working through multiple problems. A distress signal wouldn't help them anyway, since by their reckoning, it would take us a decade to get there to help."

"That's fair, and all of those are valid scenarios," Noah replied. "I don't propose taking more time than we need to make sure it's safe for us to go there, but we need a plan to make a comprehensive assessment of the star system before we head to Zeta-Alpha-5."

"Okay, but what if the people on the *Ark II* don't have that kind of time? I'm not saying we don't assess, but we can certainly restrict our assessment to the regions of the star system that the *Ark II* went to," Kara replied.

Noah knew they were up against the clock, but he knew better than to rely on a passive scanner sweep.

Sean leaned forward. "I have a couple of ideas on how we can speed up scanning the star system once we get there. You could say it's something I've had to do more than a few times over the years." Several people grinned, and Sean continued. "While we won't have the convenience of multiple spacegates to work with, we should be able to leverage one of our most valuable assets."

Noah nodded in understanding. "You mean this ship."

Sean snapped his fingers. "Yes, that's exactly what I mean."

Kara looked away, frowning in thought. Then she shook her head. "I hadn't thought of that. We definitely have some options to work with."

Noah rapped his knuckles on the table. "This is why these meetings are so important. Okay, let's come up with our best options and take it from there."

The meeting ended and they left the conference room. Kara went to main engineering and Noah watched as her brisk pace carried her down the corridor away from him.

"I think she's annoyed at me," Noah said.

"Nah, she's worried about the people on the *Ark II*. You told me she helped with its design," Sean replied.

Noah nodded a little. Kara turned a corner and disappeared from view. "She had concerns with how fast things were going. Building the ship. Getting the stasis pods ready. Supplies. All of it. She thought they were rushing."

"They were. They had to. We didn't know if we were going to survive the war with the Krake." Sean eyed Noah for a few seconds. "The loneliest job on the ship is the captain or mission commander, if you will. We can all make our recommendations, but it's you who has to make the decisions."

"Yeah, I know. And then when you get back home, there's a committee review where every decision you made is scrutinized."

Sean shrugged. "It's how we improve from one mission commander to another. You're doing fine. Better than fine, really."

Noah regarded him for a moment. "Thanks."

"I mean it, Noah. There isn't anything I would do differently. I'd tell you if there were."

"Coming from you, that's a real compliment."

The edges of Sean's mouth lifted. "Come on. We've been sitting around long enough."

More years ago than Noah wanted to count, he'd been recruited into the first Search and Rescue platoon. The rigors of physical training had been the hardest thing he'd ever experienced. Then, when the Colonial Defense Force was officially formed, he'd been recruited for that, too. Connor and former members of an elite military platoon had worked at breakneck speeds to build a colonial military to protect the colony. Noah had retired from that more than a decade earlier, choosing instead to lead different research and development initiatives for the colony and the CDF.

Now, with sweat pouring off him, he questioned his decision to do PT with the CDF soldiers. As he struggled to do a million push-ups, he became firm in the knowledge that Sean was some kind of maniacal taskmaster who could give Connor a run for his money.

"Feel the burn, Noah," Sean said. He blew out puffs of air as he labored next to him.

"I shouldn't have let you talk me into this," Noah replied with a gasp.

His arms shook with effort, and he was pretty sure his back was arching more and more as he struggled to keep going. Then he sank to the floor, gasping, and his arms refused to do anything else.

Sean kept going and then stopped. Twelve CDF soldiers trained with them, along with ten people from Peter Blood's salvage team.

Sean stood up and Noah glared at him for a few seconds before doing the same. Sean accessed his wrist computer and Noah's eyes widened as he brought up the artificial gravity controls.

"That's why this was so hard. You increased the gravity twenty percent higher than Earth norm," Noah said.

Sean smiled and nodded. "It's fun, isn't it?"

Several of the others groaned a bit. More than a few rotated their arms in slow, concentric motions.

"In spite of popular opinion, I didn't increase the artificial gravity here just to torture you. We train for all kinds of environments. Tomorrow we'll be doing drills with the fields configured for low-gravity worlds. We'll be both in and out of Pathfinder suits for the *Infinity*'s team and the Nexstar combat suits for the CDF. Now go on and hit the showers. I can smell several of you from here. Oh, and Butler," Sean said to Jessica Butler, SAR specialist on the *Infinity* crew, "I heard what you said about women not generating the same amount of odor as a man. That's completely untrue. You're as ripe as the rest of them."

Butler smiled. "Keep telling yourself that, Colonel Quinn."

Sean grinned and looked at Noah. "You've got a good crew here."

Noah nodded. "They are. They're all volunteers."

"So are mine," Sean replied evenly.

"I didn't know that. That's… something." He regarded Sean for a moment. "You're kidding me, right?"

Sean laughed. "Yeah, of course I'm not serious. Since when has the CDF ever asked its highly trained soldiers whether they'd like to participate on a dangerous mission? Never. But they're still a good group."

"How well do you know them?" Noah asked, following a hunch.

"Rhoades has served under me before, but the rest I hadn't met until we were on the shuttle on the way here."

Noah snorted a little and shook his head. "I'm glad you can use this mission to hone your team-building skills."

Sean blew out a breath and grinned a little. "Yeah, that's what I'm doing. Come on. Let's go get cleaned up."

Over the next several days, the crew and passengers aboard the *Infinity* settled into a routine. Sensor logs were checked and monitored. Systems performance continued to be reviewed to ensure they were working properly. It was all perfectly routine, until it wasn't.

A klaxon alarm roused Noah from sleep. He sat up and then sprang out of bed. Kara was seconds behind him. He grabbed an envirosuit and dressed himself, then snatched a helmet from the hook and pulled it over his head. The auto-locks engaged, and he was on his own life support. He looked at Kara, who had just donned her own helmet.

They hastened into the corridor, each of them running in opposite directions—Kara heading to main engineering and Noah running toward the bridge.

He headed toward the flashing lights of the bridge doors, using his implants to send his authentication. The doors opened and he went through, heading straight for the command station.

"Sitrep," Noah said.

Chief Markovich's eyes were focused on the holoscreen in front of him. "The I-Drive's field integrity has been compromised, Captain. We're unable to hold the field."

Noah's eyes widened and he swung his gaze toward the main holoscreen. The deck lurched to the side, and Noah grabbed onto the nearest handrail for support. The field wasn't just destabilizing; they were off course and were almost out of control.

"Helm, disengage the I-Drive," Noah said.

"It's not responsive, Captain," Myers replied.

Noah hastened toward the command station, using the handrails to steady himself.

Markovich looked at him. "There was some kind of gravitational anomaly detected and then the field started to destabilize. I ordered an emergency stop, but the computer core hasn't been responding. It's sluggish."

Noah nodded. "It's struggling to compensate." He opened a comlink to main engineering.

The deck lurched again as if some great unseen force had swatted the entire ship like an irksome bug. Metallic straps burst from their chairs, locking Noah and the rest of the bridge crew in place.

Kara acknowledged his comlink.

"We've got to get the I-Drive offline or we'll come apart," Noah said.

"I'm at the controls and it's not responding. The damn thing won't acknowledge any commands I give it."

Noah gritted his teeth and tried to think of a solution. "Cut the whole damn thing. Get to the power core and do an emergency reset."

There were a few moments of silence. The ship would be destroyed if she couldn't get it done.

"Noah—"

The comlink severed and a barrage of damage reports appeared on the main holoscreen. Then it flickered and went offline.

The ship shuddered violently, and Noah clenched his teeth, swallowing hard. He wanted to race down to main engineering. He knew what needed to be done, but so did Kara and the rest of the crew there. They were much closer to the problem, but that didn't mean the powerful urge to do something about it wasn't in him.

"What do we do, Captain?" Markovich asked.

The ship lurched again, and this time it felt as if the ground had fallen away from his feet and he was free-falling. He grabbed onto the armrests.

"Hold on!" Noah shouted. "Just hold on!"

5

Noah swallowed against a sudden ripple of nausea as the visual display on the main holoscreen altered abruptly. The endlessly shifting patterns of hyperspace flickered, jumping about with a chaotic cadence like a poorly executed animation. His readouts flashed steadily downward as the entire ship wobbled out of the bubble in space created by the I-Drive. A pattern of bright flashes raced past the external feeds on the main holoscreen, the I-Drive bleeding transit energy in curtains of azure glow. The flashes of lights cycled downward as their velocity decreased until the ship was once again in n-space.

Noah's readouts stopped blinking. The visual display was suddenly still, filled once more with unwinking pinpricks of normal-space stars. He sagged against his restraints and the sense of nausea faded almost as quickly as it had come. He looked at the helm and navigation readouts. The *Infinity's* velocity had dropped from 27c, or just over 29 billion kilometers per hour, to just under ten percent of c. It hadn't been a smooth transition and they were tumbling through space.

Noah's mouth was dry, and he cleared his throat. He lifted his head and turned toward Markovich. "Are you all right?" The chief nodded. "Everyone sound off. Is anyone injured?"

The bridge crew had only suffered some bumps and bruises. They'd all been strapped into their seats, but Noah knew that probably wasn't true for everyone, and certainly not for anyone who hadn't reached their emergency stations in time.

"We've got emergency power, Captain," Markovich said.

Noah nodded. "Helm, we should have maneuvering thrusters. Get us out of this tumble and level us off. Ops, are any of our scanners working?"

Delta Mattison rubbed her face and blew out a breath. She reached toward her holoscreen and cycled through the menu of options. "Negative, Captain. Scanners are offline. I'll review the logs and get the current status from engineering."

"Understood. Everyone else, we need to find out what shape we're in. I want to know what systems are operational and what needs to be repaired. Ms. Yu, are shipboard comms working?"

"Yes, Captain."

That was something at least. Otherwise, he'd have to rely on limited comlink capabilities in the envirosuit.

Noah brought up the critical-systems readout on his personal holoscreen. Life support systems were only working on the bridge, but there were several areas that had been sectioned off. Believing it was better to conserve his suit's life support reserves, he removed his helmet. After a few moments, the others on the bridge did the same.

Noah opened a comlink to main engineering.

"Engineer Duckman here, Captain."

Kara hadn't answered. His stomach sank and he scrunched his face into a tight frown as his heart rate spiked. She might not have been near any of the comlink terminals in main engineering. "What's your status? We're still on emergency power. When can main power be restored?" Noah asked.

"We have some injuries, Captain. Dr. Hathaway is on her way here with two of her aides. Uh, she's just arrived," Duckman said, sounding as if he were gesturing. "Chief Roberts was near the computing core. Captain, it's going to take us some time to get things sorted down here. We need to do a full system purge and reset for the main reactor, but the main power relays have been overloaded. I can put together a schedule, but I need to show Dr. Hathaway where our injured spacers are."

Noah heard the strain in Duckman's voice. They were shaken up. "Understood. I'm going to make my way down to you."

He severed the comlink and Markovich raised his eyebrows inquiringly. "We need to get damage-control teams deployed. I'm going down to main engineering. There are several people injured down there. I want you to take a team and check the forward sections. We need to account for everyone onboard."

"I'm on it, Captain," Markovich replied.

Noah tried to open a comlink to Kara, but there was no response. He shook his head and chided himself. He needed to focus.

He walked toward the helm station.

Myers looked up at him from his console. "I've managed to reduce the tumble, but with the main engines offline, it's going to take a lot of time."

"Smooth us out as much as you can, and I'll see what I can do about getting the main engines back online."

"Aye, Captain," Myers replied.

The inertia compensators and the artificial gravity still worked throughout the ship. At least those systems were still online. They could run off emergency power, but with the ship still tumbling through space, those systems were going to drain the power reserves before long. He might need to reduce the artificial gravity field to fifty percent of Earth norm if this kept up.

"Ms. Mattison, you have the con. I'm heading down to main engineering. I'll conduct a deck sweep on my way down," Noah said.

"Understood, Captain," she replied.

Noah grabbed his helmet and headed for the door. He opened a comlink to Sean. The bridge doors opened, and he saw Sean striding toward him. He killed the comlink.

"Are you all right?" Noah asked.

"Yeah, I'm fine. I have a couple of teams conducting a sweep of the decks below," Sean said and shrugged. "That is…"

"Good, thanks for that. I have Markovich leading a team checking forward of the bridge. I'm heading down to main engineering."

Sean nodded and fell into step beside him. "Is Kara okay?"

"I don't know. I can't reach her via comms. There are some people injured. Main power is offline, along with four major systems that are causing a cascade of systems failures throughout the ship," Noah said with an edge to his voice.

"When it rains, it pours."

Noah hastened past the elevator and entered the stairwell. Elevators would remain offline until he knew the extent of the damage to the ship.

"Are any of your people injured?" Noah asked as they turned a corner and descended another flight of stairs.

"Yeah, seven have been taken to sickbay to get checked by the doctor. Mainly impact trauma but nothing life threatening as far as I can tell."

They reached main engineering and Noah heard Kara's screams echoing through the corridor to the computing core. He ran, swinging off his helmet as he sped toward her voice. There were several people being carried out on stretchers. The lights flickered nearby, and Noah smelt acrid smoke from a recent fire.

"I can't reach her like this. I need the pressure jack to lift this thing off her—Captain!" Duckman said. He'd been speaking to Dr. Hathaway.

"Kara!" Noah called out.

"Noah," she answered in a gasp of pain.

He couldn't see her. There were several processing unit towers smashed together over the entire work area in the computing core.

"We're going to get you out of there. Just hold on," Noah said. He scanned the area, searching for a way to get to his wife.

The walls of the towers had torn open, exposing numerous metallic shafts that made up one of hundreds of the *Infinity's* central processing units. Long metallic rods pierced the towers' shield walls like spears. They were bent into a tangled mess, and his wife was somewhere inside.

He stepped to the side and leaned around, careful not to put any of his weight on the towers. He couldn't see her face, but there was blood on her legs. A chunk of a tower had her pinned to the floor.

Noah looked at Dr. Hathaway and spoke before he lost his nerve. "She's wedged to the floor by the rods. There's some blood."

Hathaway leaned over to take a look. "The rods might be what's keeping her from bleeding out."

"If I can get them off her, will you be able to save her?"

Hathaway blinked a few times. "I'll need a path to her as soon as you clear the debris. I can't even examine her to see what the extent of her injuries are. If you're seeing blood, that means her envirosuit has been breached."

Noah clenched his teeth and nodded.

Duckman came over to him. "I have two pressure jacks on the way here. We can get her out of there as soon as they arrive."

Kara cried out in pain as the entire mass of debris shifted. "Noah!"

"I'm here, Kara! I'm here. We're working on getting you out of there."

"My legs. Oh God, my legs… ahh! There's so much pain. So much pain—" she bit off the last of her words with a gasp.

Noah swung his gaze around, hoping someone could help, but all he got in return were sympathetic looks.

Kara cried out again, and it tore at his heart.

Noah clenched his teeth and growled in frustration. He spun around, frantically searching for something he could use to get her out of there. "We can't wait for the pressure jacks. Duckman, I want you, and…" he paused, searching for someone else, "you, Xavier, come over here. Get ready to lift. Sean, I want you on the right side with me."

"Captain," Duckman said, "all of us here can't lift even one of those towers, let alone three. We have to wait for the jacks—"

"Do what I say!" Noah snarled, startling them to silence. He turned toward the doctor. "I can see her legs from the right side. We'll get this up and you can reach her."

Hathaway glanced at the others for half a second, then moved toward the right side and squatted. She clutched her med kit to her side.

Sean moved into position, grabbed a section of metal, and waited for him.

Noah accessed the ship systems for the area through his wrist computer, bringing up the artificial gravity controls. "Engage the magnets in your boots," he said. The others clicked their heels together and the boots of their envirosuits became active.

Noah reduced the artificial gravity field to ten percent. "Okay, together now. Lift!"

The four of them lifted the tangled mess of processing units off the floor.

"Hold it right here," Hathaway said and scrambled underneath. "She's clear!"

"All right," Noah said. "Let's move this away over here," he said and tipped his head to the side in the universal gesture indicating the nearest clear space.

They carried the remains of the processing units off to the side and lowered them to the ground.

"I don't believe it," Duckman stammered. "I'm such an idiot. I didn't even think of lowering the artificial gravity field."

Noah hastened over to Kara.

Hathaway had placed trauma packs on Kara's legs and was running a scanner over her waist toward her chest.

Kara winced. She was in so much pain. Noah froze at the sight of her. He stood there blinking, not knowing what to do, but he wanted to do something to take away her pain more than anything. Every instinct inside him urged him to hold his wife in his arms, and through sheer force of will, make her better. He waited. He had to. He couldn't give in to his primal protective instincts, and he hated not being able to do more.

Dr. Hathaway pushed a metallic cylinder to the side of Kara's neck and pressed the button. "This will dull the pain. You're bleeding internally, and your legs, pelvis, and back have been crushed. We'll give the medical nanites a chance to reach the problem areas, and then we'll move you to sickbay."

Noah swallowed hard, his throat as dry as a barren planet. He sank to the deck by Kara's side. She looked up at him, and her lips trembled as her eyes seemed to lose focus and her blinks became longer. He reached out, took her hand in his own, and leaned closer. "You're going to be all right. You hear me? You just lay there and relax for a minute. You're going to be all right. Don't worry about anything."

"Noah," Kara said softly. Her eyes were open, but she seemed to be staring past him. "Is the baby okay?"

Noah's mouth slackened and the breath caught in his throat. His gaze darted toward Kara's stomach.

"Did she say baby?" Hathaway asked.

Noah's thoughts flatlined, and his mouth refused to form any words.

Is the baby okay?

Hathaway brought up her scanner and made circular motions above Kara's stomach, staring intently at the small holoscreen.

Sean squatted across from him, his eyes wide. "She's pregnant?"

Noah shook his head, his breath coming in gasps. "I don't know. I don't know," he said and looked at the doctor. "Is she?"

Hathaway closed the scanner, the edges of her lips drawing downward grimly. She looked at Noah. "I'm so sorry. There was too much trauma. I can't detect anything. I'm so sorry."

Sorrow closed his throat and he looked at his wife, going blind for a few seconds before blinking away the tears. Her eyes were closed, and she was breathing evenly.

He let go of her hand, laying it down gently by her side. Then he opened his wrist computer and accessed Kara's biochip records.

"She *was* pregnant. She just found out. Her chip sent an alert to her earlier today." He lifted his gaze toward Sean. "She was pregnant, Sean." The words caught in his throat and his mind went numb as waves of emotion threatened to overwhelm him. He just sat there. Kara was alive, but their baby…

Noah rocked back and forth. "I don't know. I don't know what to do. I don't…"

Sean reached out and grabbed Noah's shoulder. "Hey," he said, firmly. "Hey, just breathe. Okay, just breathe. One second at a time. Just breathe, Noah."

Noah nodded and closed his eyes.

He inhaled a breath, held it for a second, and then released it. It was all he could do, but what he wanted to do was scream.

6

Connor was descending the stairs of the colonial administration building in Sierra when his wrist computer buzzed a warning for his upcoming appointment, and he dismissed it. It had been seven hours since they'd lost contact with the *Infinity*. He reached the seventy-fourth floor and palmed the door controls, striding down the hallway heading toward the governor's office. A security agent looked at him and waved him through the checkpoint.

"General Gates."

A young man came from a nearby workstation. He had short red hair and pale blue eyes. Connor wasn't sure if he was just getting older or if everyone else was getting younger, but this admin looked so young that he wasn't sure whether he should still be in school. Connor was part of a small minority of people who hadn't been born on New Earth. With a population of over one million, only around twenty-eight percent of that number had been born on Old Earth.

"Governor Mullins is expecting you. Please, if you'll follow me, General Gates, I'll take you right to him."

"Thank you," Connor replied.

The young man led him through a crowded work area. Several people looked up as he approached.

"Do you have a name?" Connor asked.

The young man frowned for a second and then smiled. "I'm sorry, General Gates. My name is Michael Holland, sir."

"Nice to meet you, Michael."

Holland's eyes widened for a second, a bit awestruck. "I don't mean to stare, General Gates. I've just heard so much about you. I believe you know my mother, Dr. Blake Alison."

Connor smiled in recognition. Had so much time really passed? He remembered when Dr. Alison had been a medic in Field Ops. "Oh yeah, I do know your mother. How is she?"

"She's good. She and my father live in New Haven. They're about to have another baby."

"That's great. How many is that?"

"This is their fifth. A boy. They're going to name him Alex."

Michael led him to the governor's office and Connor stopped.

"Please congratulate them for me and tell your mother I said hello."

Michael smiled—a dead ringer for his mother, especially around the eyes and mouth. "Quick question, but would you tell me her nickname when she was a cadet in Field Ops?"

Connor arched an eyebrow.

"I have a bet going on with my father and... well, it's a family thing with all of us."

Connor considered it for a second and then smiled. He leaned toward Michael conspiratorially. "You didn't hear this from me."

Michael nodded vigorously.

"Babyface, that was her nickname. She was probably the same age as you are now."

Michael grinned. "Thank you, General Gates. I really appreciate it."

Connor chuckled and opened the door. Governor Bob Mullins sat behind a large wooden desk that had been built by the first governor of the colony, Tobias Quinn, who'd been a friend. He thought Tobias would have loved the progress the colony had made.

Mullins had short-cropped, curly hair that had an oily shine to it, and his face was leaner than when Connor had first met him. He looked away from the holoscreen and gestured for Connor to come to his desk.

Mullins looked back at the holoscreen with video comlink. "That's fine. Just get back to me when you've heard back from them."

He closed the video comlink and stood up.

"Hello, Connor."

"Bob," Connor replied.

Mullins gestured toward one of the chairs near the desk and then sat in the one across from it. He regarded him for a moment. "Almost the end of my second term. Just six more months."

"Are you looking forward to it?"

Mullins shrugged and tilted his head to the side. "Yes, and no, I suppose. It wears on you here and there, but thankfully most of my time as governor has been peaceful."

Mullins had become acting governor when Dana Wolf had become sick and couldn't serve anymore. He'd been thrust into a leadership position when war with the Krake had nearly destroyed the colony. He and Connor had bumped heads a lot when he'd been an advisor to Dana Wolf, but through the years they'd learned to work together for the mutual benefit of the colony.

"What do you think you'll do after your term is done?" Connor asked.

"I'm really not sure. Probably an advisory role somewhere. I can't serve as governor again until two terms have passed."

"I'd heard about that. Think you'll campaign for another five-year term?"

"I could. I'd only be a hundred years old, but I'm really not sure. Dana always said that two terms as governor was enough. Let someone else take the reins. Anyway, what about you? You've been in the CDF for twenty-five years and you spent over twenty years in the NA Alliance military before that. Think you'll ever retire from it?"

"I retired from the CDF for a few years after the Vemus Wars."

"I bet if you were to put your hat in for the governor's race, you'd be a frontrunner for sure."

Connor shook his head and chuckled. "No thanks. Dana used to say the same thing. I was mayor of Sanctuary for a couple of years before rejoining the CDF."

The door to the office opened and Michael carried in a tray with a carafe of coffee. He poured them each a cup and then left.

"Is the CDF all you ever wanted?" Mullins asked.

Connor added some cream to his cup and sipped. "There was a need, and it just grew on me. It's more of what I know, but… I'll just wait and see how things go before I think about making any changes."

"Most of us came to New Earth with an idea of what we'd be doing, but not you." Mullins set his mug down. "Thanks for indulging me for a few minutes. Tell me about the *Infinity*."

Connor finished his coffee and set his cup down next to the other. "We stopped getting updates about seven hours ago. There wasn't a distress beacon and there have been no responses to any communication since."

Mullins nodded. "What do they think happened?"

"They hadn't reached the Zeta-Alpha star system, so this is likely unrelated to whatever happened to the *Ark II*. Their last known location was just over a lightyear away from New Earth."

"Beyond our ability to help them."

"We were hoping it's just a communication issue they need to fix. Normally, we'd wait a few days to see if we received a distress beacon. However, we're building another I-Drive, but it's going to take some time."

"We can't adapt a spacegate? Convert it somehow?"

Connor shook his head. "I'm afraid not. I wish it was that simple."

Mullins sighed and eyed Connor for a few moments. "What do you need from me?"

"Permission to put an I-Drive on a CDF cruiser."

"What does this give us?"

Connor had anticipated the question. Mullins wouldn't promise assistance without a good understanding of the costs and benefits. "First, a cruiser can meet the power requirements for the I-Drive. Second, CDF crews are familiar with emergency rescue operations above and beyond any civilian crew. Third, a cruiser carries enough crew and cargo capacity to bring equipment needed to repair the *Infinity* if that proves necessary. Fourth, sensor capabilities on our warships are superior to anything we have on any ship currently able to support an I-Drive."

Mullins nodded slowly and then frowned at the last.

"I don't think this is a simple loss of communication.

According to Dr. Oriana Evans, it's more likely that something has happened with the I-Drive itself and that's the reason we lost contact."

"I thought you said this was equipment failure. A malfunctioning transceiver or something."

"I said that, and initially we hoped that's what it was. The *Infinity* has redundant comms systems in place, but Dr. Evans shared some very good scenarios that we should consider as well."

"Dr. Evans," Mullins said thoughtfully.

"She's Colonel Quinn's wife."

Mullins blinked a few times and whistled softly. "I understand." He paused for a second, considering. "Is there someone more objective who's an expert on the I-Drive?"

"Besides Noah Barker and Kara Roberts, she's as much an expert as we have in the development of the I-Drive. I'd trust any theories she chooses to put forth concerning what happened. Her record speaks for itself, Bob."

"She has to be worried. More than worried. I'd be going out of my mind and would need someone like you to keep me grounded."

"Oh, she's worried. We all are, Bob. But she worked with the CDF through the Krake War. She knows how to perform under pressure. Like I said, I trust her opinion. She figured out how to use the spacegates. Target other universes. She's as brilliant as they come. The only other people I trust as much as her are on the *Infinity*."

"How long before another I-Drive is ready?"

"I don't have a definite timeline for that yet. Before we lost contact with the *Ark II*, we were months away from having one of those drives. Noah created a miracle getting the first one ready, but it came at the expense of a second one."

Mullins considered it for a few moments and then looked at Connor solemnly. "Assuming everything goes in our favor, how fast can we send another rescue team?"

"If we had another drive today, we'd be more than fifteen days travel time to even reach the same location where we lost contact with the *Infinity*. To test the drive, they used it for shorter bursts. It was during this longer duration that we lost contact with them. Preliminary reporting indicated that the drive was stable and that we could travel even faster than what the *Infinity* was going, but we'll need to wait on a recommendation from the engineers. I don't want to create more problems by pushing the limits on something we're still learning about ourselves."

"Understood. What can I do to help?"

This is what Connor had been working toward. Mullins wasn't all that difficult to work with provided he had the right information from which to base a decision. "We'll need access to senior engineers outside the CDF, resource allocation, and processing priority at the lunar shipyards."

Mullins smiled. "I'm happy to help, but I'm not going to just give you a blank check across the board. Have your team put together a proposal and I'll see that it's pushed through the appropriate channels. You'll get what you need."

He would have liked a blank check, but priority treatment would have to suffice. "That will be fine. Just make sure your team knows about the high-priority request that's coming."

Mullins smiled. "They will. Good luck, Connor." He paused for a moment, considering. "Will you be going on the rescue mission?"

"That hasn't been decided yet. Nathan will have the final say."

"I understand that, but if Nathan approved?"

Connor pressed his lips together for a few seconds and exhaled. "I'd be lying if I said I didn't want to, but it's not that simple. We have plenty of senior officers who would be well suited to conducting a rescue mission."

Mullins regarded him for a few moments. "It doesn't get any easier—balancing family and a career like yours."

Connor nodded but felt his neck tense up. He'd served on a lot of dangerous missions, both planned and otherwise. But when his friends or family were in danger, his first instinct was to go. He doubted he'd ever change, but he'd had to learn to balance those risks.

"No, it doesn't. Regardless, I'm not making any decisions now. Nathan and I will work it out, and you'll be the first to know."

Connor left Mullins's office and headed back to the roof of the colonial administration building. He opened a comlink to the lunar base.

Oriana answered. Her eyes were tight with worry, but otherwise she looked fine, considering.

"We're cleared to proceed. The *Phantom* is on its way to the lunar shipyards. How's the I-Drive coming?"

"Not fast enough. I'm trying to figure out how to condense what should take months to build into weeks. I just wish we had more information. On the one hand, we need to take our time to make sure things are done properly, but on the other hand, if something *has* happened to them, we need to get done as soon as possible."

"You're doing everything you can, Oriana. Sean, Noah, and Kara know how to take care of themselves."

Oriana winced and looked away from the camera feed.

"I'm going to come up there in a few hours and we'll take it from there."

Oriana's eyes widened. "You're coming up here?"

Connor nodded. "Absolutely. I know how to motivate people to get things done. I wouldn't leave you alone in this."

Oriana nodded and sighed. "Thank you, Connor. That's going to be a big help."

"We'll get them back, assuming they don't contact us first. Regardless, we'll still push forward with that second I-Drive. Hopefully, this is just a small hiccup."

"Let's hope so," Oriana said, sounding only half convinced.

Connor was only half convinced himself, but he had absolute faith in both Noah and Sean. He just hoped they hadn't bitten off more than they could chew with all this. He'd do everything he could to help them, but sometimes even his best efforts weren't enough.

7

NOAH WOKE with his head on his desk, his wrist tingling from where his forehead had rested on it. Pushing away his sleepiness, he sat up and yawned widely as he glanced around, bleary-eyed, trying to remember how he'd gotten to his ready room. He inhaled deeply and then sighed. He'd only meant to check on a few things, but once he'd sat down... He must have rested his head for a few seconds and then—nothing.

Noah glanced at the clock and saw that he'd slept for nearly three hours, which explained the dull ache he felt on the right side of his neck. It hadn't been enough time to make up for lost sleep, but it would have to be enough to get on the move again.

Over the past fifty hours, Noah and the rest of the crew had succeeded in restoring main power to the ship, even though they were shorthanded in some areas because of injuries.

He rolled his shoulders a few times, stretching his neck to work out the stiffness.

A text message chimed on the holoscreen above his desk,

which had become active. He tapped it, and a message from Dr. Claire Hathaway replaced the alert.

Captain, please come to the medical center on E-Deck to review Kara's condition.

Noah acknowledged the message and shot to his feet, exhaustion forgotten as he rushed out the door. The medical nanites had stabilized Kara enough that she could be moved to the medical center, but she wasn't out of the woods. Her legs had been crushed by the heavy processing unit inside the ship's computing core. He'd seen Dr. Hathaway's preliminary assessment, but he couldn't wait around at the medical center. There was too much work to be done with repairs and figuring out what had happened to cause the cascade of failures that almost destroyed the ship in the first place. He hastened down the corridor at a fast pace and took the elevator down to E-Deck.

A comlink chimed on his wrist computer, and Noah acknowledged it.

"Captain," Chief Markovich said, "full functionality of our sensor arrays has been restored. Leiter's team is on their way back inside for a shift change."

"Good work. Thank Leiter and his team. What's the status of subspace comms?" Noah asked.

"That's next, sir. Xavier reviewed the repair drones' preliminary analyses, and it looks as if we just need to replace a few components and recycle what's left."

Noah nodded, stopping briefly to bring up the repair schedule. He had neither the skill nor the luck to read and walk at the same time without tripping or bumping into something.

"Okay, it looks like there will be a main engine test at sixteen hundred. I'll be on the bridge for that." He regarded Markovich with a thoughtful frown. "When was the last time you slept?"

"I had a block last night, sir."

A block was four hours, while a solid block was eight. No one was getting a solid block of sleep right now.

"All right, check in with Duckman. He's been running diagnostics on the I-Drive. See if there's anything he needs."

Markovich looked away from the video feed with lips pressed together.

"What is it?" Noah asked.

Markovich exhaled through his nose. "Duckman blames himself for what happened to Kara."

"It wasn't his fault."

Markovich shrugged. "He still blames himself, sir."

Noah nodded. "All right, I'll speak to him about it when I have a chance. Am I missing anything else?" he asked and then shook his head. "With the sensors back up, get McGinnis and Reid back at astrogation. We need to figure out where we are and how far off course that is. We also need to look for any anomalies that might have caused things to go sideways."

Markovich nodded. "Understood, Captain. I'll get them on it." He paused for a second. "How is she? How is Kara doing?"

Noah started walking again. "That's what I'm about to find out. Heading to the medical center right now. I'll check in with Duckman after."

"Understood, sir. I hope you get some good news."

Noah grimaced. "Me, too."

He closed the comlink and quickened his pace. He needed Duckman to focus. With Kara in sickbay, Duckman had to step up and fill some pretty big shoes. Noah couldn't have an unfocused chief engineer. Duckman was a good man, but he was a little shaken by what had happened.

Noah entered the medical center. Just beyond a small waiting area were beds along each side of a larger room, separated by privacy curtains. Additional bedding had been brought in.

Twenty-three people had been injured, and five of them were in critical condition.

He started walking toward the back of the medical center where the critical care units were located.

Emily Lockhart, a nurse, met him halfway. She was in her early twenties, with long black hair and an easy smile. "Captain, Dr. Hathaway is in 3A. At the end of the corridor to your right."

"Thanks," Noah said. He was about to keep going but stopped.

Lockhart frowned. "Are you okay, sir?"

"I'm fine. I just wanted to make sure you guys have everything you need here. With so many people injured, you must be feeling stretched a little thin."

Lockhart smiled. "Yes, Captain, but we're pretty well stocked here, and eleven people will be discharged tomorrow morning, so that will help ease things quite a bit."

Noah nodded. "That's good news. Keep up the good work."

"We will, Captain," she replied and went to check on another patient.

Noah walked the length of the medical center and then entered the critical care unit. Separate rooms held trauma patients who'd sustained extensive injuries. He walked to 3A, inhaled deeply, and then entered.

Kara lay seemingly asleep. Most of her body was surrounded by a gray medical capsule with an amber glow emanating from inside. The air in the room was warm, almost pleasant. Forest sounds and birdsong could be heard from nearby speakers.

Dr. Hathaway sat on a stool at a counter off to the side. "Hi, Noah, thanks for coming down. I know you've been very busy."

"How is she?"

"She's making good progress. Come over here so I can show you."

Noah started to walk past the bed where Kara was lying but stopped to watch the rise and fall of her chest, just to reassure himself that she was breathing. The last time he'd seen her, her thighs and stomach had been swollen and bruised as if she'd sustained a severe beating. Her haggard expression seemed burned into his memory. He exhaled softly and turned away from her.

Hathaway waited patiently, giving a sympathetic lift of her lips. She gestured toward a nearby holoscreen. "We recreated what happened based on her injuries. Honestly, Noah, Kara is lucky to be alive."

Noah watched as an animation began recreating the incident. One tower broke loose from its holdings and crashed into another. The humanoid model that was supposed to be Kara scrambled to get out of the way but had gotten pinned down instead.

"If she'd been a little bit to the left or right, those towers might have done a lot more damage. I know it may not look like it, but I'd say she had a guardian angel watching out for her."

Noah blinked and watched the animation again. His brain slipped into calculation as he pieced together the mass and force with distribution. He barely suppressed a shudder. "She would have been cut in half."

Hathaway nodded. "Like I said, she's very lucky."

Noah looked at Kara again and felt a wobble in his stomach. He'd almost lost her.

"Her recovery is going to take some time. We'll keep her asleep for part of it while the nanobots work with a skeletal regrowth protocol that will speed up the healing process."

"How long will she be unconscious?"

"A few weeks at the very least, possibly a month." Noah's eyes widened. "It's better if she's unconscious for this. Her body is stressed, and she'd be in a lot of pain if she were awake. Basically, her knees, femur, pelvis, and lower back have sustained crush injuries. We can repair the bones, but we'll need to reconstruct the nerves as we go. We'll monitor her closely."

Noah's throat thickened and he clenched his teeth a little. "Will she be able to walk?"

"Eventually. She'll need physical therapy."

Noah exhaled and shook his head.

"What?" Hathaway asked.

He sighed. "I've been through something like this before. Severe head injury. I was in a coma for almost a year. When I woke up, I needed PT to be able to walk or do just about anything."

Hathaway's eyebrows raised. "I had no idea. Well, then you definitely have an idea of what she's in for. You'll be able to help her."

"I'll try. Kara hates sitting around. She won't like being off her feet. Not one bit. I just wish I could talk to her." He wanted to know that she was okay, and in spite of understanding everything Hathaway had said, he wanted to hear it from Kara. He wanted to hear from her how she was feeling.

"Okay. But I also need to warn you, or more like set your expectations. Spinal injuries are a delicate matter. There will be gains and losses as she recovers. It's important that she doesn't lose faith that she *will* recover. A lot of that is going to depend on you."

Noah nodded. "I understand."

"I also encourage you to visit her regularly. Talk to her. She's in a medically induced coma, but there's strong evidence that she'll be aware of your visits."

Noah smiled a little. His fragmented memories from his own

coma experience had left him firmly aware that she would know he'd visited. "I will."

"Good," Hathaway said and regarded him for a few seconds. "I've reviewed Kara's biochip. It looks like she was overdue for her regular birth control treatments."

Noah swallowed hard and blew out a breath. "We've been so busy getting the *Infinity* ready that... will she be able to get pregnant again?"

"Yes. Her ovaries are intact. There shouldn't be any issue with her eggs."

Noah leaned back against the wall in relief. For all the medical advances they'd made, they couldn't replace a woman's eggs.

"Thank you so much. That's a huge relief."

Dr. Hathaway smiled.

"We intended to start a family someday. I just wasn't expecting it now, and I feel like I've lost something I never really had in the first place."

Hathaway nodded and stood up. "It's completely understandable and normal for you to feel that way. Don't worry, you'll be able to try again before too long. I'll leave you alone with her for a few minutes and then see you tomorrow."

She gave his shoulder a squeeze and it seemed to steady him. People often underestimated the power of a simple touch.

Noah grabbed the stool and brought it over to the bed. As he sat, he reached over and took Kara's hand in his own. Her skin was warm to the touch.

"You're going to be fine, Kara. You'll see. You'll be running around in no time," he said and stared at her. He studied every curve of her face, from her delicate cheekbones to the shape of her mouth. She looked oddly serene, but if she were awake, she'd be in unbearable pain. Kara had visited him many times while he'd been in a coma. She must have felt so alone, not knowing whether he was going to wake up. At least she wasn't like that. He knew she would survive this.

He inhaled deeply and sighed. She'd been pregnant with their child. He knew the science. It was the earliest stages of pregnancy, but it had happened. They would have become parents. Were they supposed to become parents now? Over the years, he'd seen many friends start families, and it had always seemed like one of those things that they would do later on. He leaned close to her ear and whispered. "Maybe it's time we started doing the stuff we've been putting off, too." He squeezed her hand a little. "After you get better."

He kissed her cheek and smoothed her hair away from her forehead.

"I'll be back to see you as soon as I can," Noah promised.

Taking one last glance back at his wife, he left the room.

Noah sat in the command chair on the bridge. In front of him were two active holoscreens with various sub-windows open.

"Main engine test is complete, Captain," Delta Mattison said.

A main engine performance report appeared on one of his holoscreens. "These are good scores. Well within acceptable ranges. Let's run this set of tests one more time. Schedule a full power cycle and diagnostic suite of tests for the overnight shift. If those performance reports match this one, I think we'll be in good shape."

"Understood, Captain. I'll put it on the schedule."

"Thank you, Ms. Mattison."

Noah had expected the main engines to perform well, but he

knew the value of double and sometimes triple checking critical systems for consistent results, regardless of what any diagnostic computer told him.

Noah left the bridge, already late for a meeting he'd scheduled. He hated being late for anything. It wasn't something anyone had drilled into him. Kara liked to joke that he'd been born with an innate sense of timing.

He saw Sean walking down the corridor, coming from the elevators. Sean mimed checking his wrist computer.

"What's your excuse?" Noah asked.

Sean grinned. "I have a list if you want, but it's not going to change anything."

Noah chuckled.

They walked into the conference room. Senior officers were already gathered, and they quieted down. The mood was definitely lighter than the first few times they'd met since the incident.

"All right, let's get started. Last meeting of the day and it's just before dinnertime. I'll try not to keep you any longer than necessary," Noah said and looked around the conference table. "First thing, we're going back to normal watch standings from here on out. Emergency watch rotations are hereby suspended. Also, I was at the medical center earlier today and eleven people are scheduled to be discharged tomorrow morning, so we'll have more help then."

Pete Duckman raised his hand. "How's Kara?"

All eyes went to Noah. He'd been expecting the question.

"She's in a medically induced coma while they repair the broken bones in her legs, pelvis, and lower back. The doctor told me she'd be kept in that coma for at least a month."

Duckman's eyes sank to the table and his shoulders rounded.

"She was very fortunate. Dr. Hathaway showed me an

animated recreation of the accident, and I watched it about twenty times. Kara is lucky to be alive."

Duckman kept staring at the table.

Sean cleared his throat. "I've been meaning to ask you, but what made you think about changing the artificial gravity setting?"

"She was being crushed and we couldn't wait for equipment to get her out of there. Changing the artificial gravity field in the area seemed like the quickest solution."

Sean nodded with pursed lips. "I've seen my share of ship damage and people trapped, but I've never seen anything like that. I think we might need to update our emergency procedures."

Noah tilted his head to the side. "I don't know if it should be the standard, but with a medic or doctor present and the ship relatively stable, then yeah, the idea definitely has merit."

Duckman lifted his gaze and looked at him. "It's just so obvious, sir. I should have thought of it. I could have gotten her out of there much quicker."

Noah shook his head. "You can't beat yourself up about this. There was so much going on. We learn and we move on. That's all there is to it."

Duckman regarded him for a few seconds and then nodded.

Noah looked at Alissa McGinnis. "What did you find?"

"Captain, you were right. The I-Drive didn't malfunction per se. Caleb and I went through the sensor logs both pre and post incident. The sensors detected multiple powerful gravity waves, which the I-Drive had difficulties compensating for. These waves caused severe turbulence," McGinnis said.

"Turbulence," Sean said. "That can't be right. Unless we were near a black hole, a gravity wave wouldn't be powerful enough to do anything."

"Actually, it wouldn't take as much force as you think," Noah replied. "The effects are compounded given our velocity. The I-Drive bends space in front of the ship and expands it behind, but we're still traveling through space."

Sean frowned and glanced at McGinnis for a second before turning back toward Noah. "This is usually when Oriana explains things to me."

Noah smiled. "Since she's not here, I'll do my best. The *Infinity* exists in a bubble when the I-Drive is active. We bend space in an area in front of the ship. The drive doesn't care what's in front of the ship. We must have been close enough to those waves for it to throw us off course. Then we have the cascade of events after that."

Sean considered it and shook his head. He wasn't the only one who looked confused.

"Think of it this way. If you're flying a ship and you collide with something else, you get knocked off course if the object you hit is of sufficient mass. It's a little more complicated here, but the principle is close enough to get a high-level understanding. Duckman, what did the diagnostic of the I-Drive reveal?" he said and then held up his hand. "Wait. I predict that after we encountered the wave or turbulence, if you will, the field the I-Drive creates destabilized."

Duckman nodded. "That's right. The field did destabilize. The system tried to compensate and correct it, but that made it worse."

"How?" Sean asked.

"Because it couldn't make all the corrections at the same time," Noah replied with a thoughtful frown.

Sean pressed his lips together.

Noah chuckled and shook his head. "It's not you. I just like finding logical explanations to things."

He nodded for Duckman to continue.

"The more the system tried to compensate, the worse it performed."

"Why didn't the emergency shutdown procedures fix the problem?" Sean asked.

Duckman glanced at Noah for a second before he replied. "It's not a clean cutoff. The system is designed to first bleed off the transit energy before reducing the field back to normal space."

"We're all lucky to be alive," Noah said. "Now that we know what happened, we need to focus on solutions. What can we do to mitigate the problem?"

Sean's eyebrows raised. "You intend to keep going?"

"As long as we can come up with real solutions. Since Ms. McGinnis was able to identify the cause of the turbulence, we might be able to avoid those conditions altogether. We'd have to come up with an acceptable error ratio to be on the safe side. The question that remains is whether we can detect those waves in time to do anything about it," Noah said and looked at McGinnis.

"We can detect them, Captain. It wasn't a single gravity wave that caused the turbulence. It was a buildup of waves that caused the issue."

Noah pursed his lips in thought.

"Detection gives us something, but how can we prevent what happened from occurring again?" Sean asked.

"We'll need to run some simulations through the computing core. We could try altering our speed and trajectory. We know the waves had an effect, but we need to dive a little deeper and determine the source of the waves, as well as the angle at which they entered the field. I think the key here is to prevent a situation from spiraling out of control. Once we can work out the protocols to alleviate the issue, we should be able to move forward."

"You sound confident that we'll be able to figure this out," Sean said.

Noah nodded. "We'll figure it out. We didn't come all this way just to turn around and go back to New Earth." He looked around the conference room. "I know we're tired, but we *can* do this. The people on the *Ark II* are depending on us. Also, we're making history here. We're the first humans to ever do what we're doing. Exploration is part of our legacy. We're all pioneers on the edge of the unknown."

He looked around at his senior officers, specialists, and friends. They were exhausted, but there was a spark glinting in their eyes. No one was going to give up. Not now. Not when they'd come so far.

Duckman leaned forward and cleared his throat. "I'll work with Alissa on this, Captain. Figure out when those waves started affecting the I-Drive's performance. If that's okay with you?"

"Absolutely. That all right with you?" he asked Alissa McGinnis.

She smiled. "Of course, sir." She turned toward Duckman. "We can start tonight if you want."

Duckman nodded.

"All right. I don't want to keep us here any longer than necessary. It's been a long couple of days. Go on and get out of here," Noah said.

Everyone walked out of the conference room except Sean.

Noah raised an eyebrow toward him. "I figured you'd have more to say."

Sean leaned his head to the side a little and crossed his arms in front of his chest. "Assuming that Duckman and McGinnis can sort this out."

"They'll get it worked out, and I'll look it over."

He wanted Kara to look it over… He just needed her. She knew as much about this ship as he did, and they balanced each other out. He knew she would recover. He hadn't lost her, but it had been such a close thing. Noah banished those thoughts from his mind, willing himself to focus on what needed to be done.

Sean tapped his fingers on the table absently while he considered. "Okay, so it gets your stamp of approval. What are you going to do if COMCENT tells us to return home?"

Noah blinked several times and frowned.

Sean snorted and looked at him wryly. "You didn't even think about that, did you?"

He shook his head. "No, I didn't."

"They might, you know, once comms are restored and they review the report you'll send."

Noah pressed his lips together while he considered it. His friend watched him but didn't say anything else.

"What do you suggest?" Noah asked.

"Officially, I can't suggest anything."

"Fine, unofficially then."

Sean shook his head. "Not even unofficially, Noah. It's better if whatever decision you make is wholly yours."

Noah regarded Sean for a few seconds. He imagined that Sean would follow direct orders unless he had a very good reason not to, but sometimes a situation wasn't so clear-cut. Sean was right. He couldn't lean on him for this. The colonial government could recall them after learning what had happened. This wasn't a military ship, but it wasn't an independent ship either. Noah didn't own this ship; the colonial government did. He wouldn't lie on the report and bury the incident. That just wasn't how he did things.

"I think I've got a way to deal with COMCENT. Do you need plausible deniability?"

The edges of Sean's lips quirked up and he shook his head. "No, they'll see through that. We're in this together."

"I'll file the report right before we get underway. We'll be in transit and well on our way to the *Ark II* before they can recall us, if that's even what they decide to do," Noah replied.

Sean smiled. "Now you're thinking like a commander."

Noah laughed. "I'll tell them you told me to do it. They know how persuasive you can be. 'Colonel Quinn has dominated this whole operation from the beginning.'"

Sean grinned. "If they thought I could roll right over you, they wouldn't have made you commander of the mission. And anyway, I'd tell them you altered the logs to make it look like it was me, but you were the mastermind behind the whole thing."

"I guess we'll both pay the price then. But for now, come on. I'm starving, and I could use a drink. I've got a bottle of Nathan's Reserve Bourbon in my ready room. We'll get dinner brought to us, and there are a few more things I'd like to discuss with you."

He walked toward the door.

"You had me at Nathan's Reserve. That's the best bourbon I've ever tasted."

8

Connor stood in one of the observatories on the lunar surface. The CDF heavy cruiser *Phantom* was on its final approach for entry into the lunar shipyards. Navigational control would have been passed to the lunar docking authority.

The heavy cruiser had a mass of four hundred and eighty thousand tons. The hull was roughly cigar-shaped, though flattened to provide a narrower profile, but was wider at the top and bottom to support the superstructure and the mag cannon turrets. Between the turrets were missile tubes. The warship had bronze-colored accents along the gray battle-steel hull, with special ports near the main engines that were used to connect to a spacegate. The *Phantom* had been part of a battlegroup used to patrol the multiverse to monitor for any resurgence in Krake activity. The Krake homeworld had been destroyed, crippling its support structure for off-world operations.

He spotted the areas of replaced hull plating from the damage the ship had taken during the Krake Wars. It had been over eleven years since the end of the war, and there were still

CDF warships with battle scars. He carried scars of his own that he'd collected over the years.

The nearby doors opened and Oriana walked over to him. Her long dark hair was tied back in a loose ponytail, and she looked a bit less worry-worn than she'd been when he arrived on the lunar base a week ago.

Connor jutted his chin toward the *Phantom*. "There she is."

Oriana came to stand next to him and folded her arms. "I'm sure the ship is more than adequate for our needs, but is all this effort moot now that we've heard from them?"

Connor shook his head. "Absolutely not! I'm glad they're okay. We can both rest a little easier now, but the report confirms that it's more dangerous to travel FTL than we'd anticipated."

"They're very lucky. I've only read through the incident report once and haven't had a chance to review the log data."

Connor snorted. "Only read through the incident report..." He shook his head. "Pace yourself, Oriana. That report isn't even a day old."

"I don't like that comms are still limited."

Connor frowned in thought. "Don't like or don't believe?"

Oriana raised a dark eyebrow, looking around to be sure no one was close enough to listen. "I'm not telling you something you don't already know, but doesn't it seem a little too convenient? They repair comms enough to send a data burst just before they get underway again."

"I think it's fairly obvious what they're doing."

"You approve of this?"

"I'm still reviewing the data they sent, too, but they've put protocols in place to prevent what happened. They analyzed the incident and made a decision."

Oriana eyed him for a moment and sighed. "I see where they learned it from."

Connor chuckled. "If they wait around asking for permission to do what they intend to do anyway, they'll never get anything done. Sean and Noah know better than that."

She pursed her lips in thought. "It's just so different from what we do in R&D. I've been around it enough, thanks to Sean, but I'm worried they're pushing too far."

"We have to trust their judgement. They're the people who're there and who have to live with the consequences."

"I suppose you're right," Oriana admitted. She unfolded her arms and leaned toward the window. "This doesn't have to change our timeline."

They were still two months away from finishing the I-Drive. "Unless you've figured out a way to accelerate the deliverables faster than you already are."

Oriana shook her head. "No. We're going as fast as we can. If anything, we might shave off a few days, but that's it."

"All right, so we can't build it any faster, but what about traveling faster? We could make up the time that way. The reports from the *Infinity* indicate that they were nowhere near the limits of what the drive is capable of."

"We'd have to test, but you expected that, didn't you? Anyway, it's possible. We'll have to do our own testing and make determinations based on those results."

Connor nodded. "Fair enough. At least we have updated protocols to avoid the same incident they encountered."

"Yes, but it also frees us to discover more on our own."

Connor regarded her and didn't reply.

Oriana shook her head. "I'm sorry. I don't mean to sound so negative. I'm just worried about that. I wish I was there with them."

"I understand, but I'm glad you're here to help us with this," Connor said, gesturing toward the CDF warship.

A comlink chimed from Connor's wrist computer. "It's Lenora. I'm going to take this."

"I should be getting back anyway. Tell Lenora I said hello," Oriana said and walked away from him, heading back toward the elevator.

Connor acknowledged the comlink and his personal holoscreen appeared in front of him. Lenora gave him a tight smile.

"What's wrong?" he asked

She arched an eyebrow. "Your son," she replied.

Connor grinned. "I can't take full responsibility for him. You were there, too."

Her smile was a bit easier this time, and she shook her head. "I'll start over then. *Our* son. You like that better?"

Connor nodded, satisfied.

She inhaled and regarded him for a moment. "I can't. This is you. Sometimes he's my sweet little boy, and other times he's like a miniature version of you, but with a temper."

"Okay, what did he do? Has he been fighting again?"

"You could say that, but it was more of an organized retaliation with multiple groups. You'll appreciate this. He only told the smaller groups the things they needed to know to get the job done." She'd made air quotes around the last bit.

The edges of Connor's lips quirked up in amusement. Lenora didn't seem to notice and kept going.

"It's not only the one-upmanship, but also the humiliation. He's starting to get a reputation as a troublemaker, and he's only eleven, Connor."

"Just Ethan?" he asked.

"He's an organizer. I've tried reasoning with him, but he either doesn't listen or he just forgets. Or he doesn't agree."

"He listens to you," Connor assured her. "I just want to

understand. Whatever it is that he's done was retaliatory, right? What happened to the instigator?"

Lenora leveled her gaze at him. "He didn't initiate it, but his response is over the top. What happens when he's older and the consequences are higher?"

Connor nodded. "No, you're right to be concerned. So am I, but I'm also a little proud, too. I can't help it, Lenora. I wouldn't want either of them to be pushovers."

"Neither Ethan nor Lauren are pacifists, and I wouldn't want them to be, but we need to find a way to rein in Ethan's exploits."

Connor sat down and exhaled, trying to think of what he could do to help. "Send him up here with me. Lauren is visiting Ashely in Sierra. Maybe he just needs to be removed from the situation for a while."

Lenora considered it with a thoughtful frown. "It sounds like a reward for poor behavior."

Connor chuckled. "It's not going to be a vacation. He can keep up with school from here, and I'll find ways to fill up the time for him."

"Fill the time?"

He nodded. "Yeah, put him to work. Look, he's all boy. He's active and has a lot of energy. All he probably needs is for it to be channeled into something constructive. Also, it would be a change of pace for him. Let's try it out for a few weeks and see how it goes. What do you think?"

Lenora tipped her head back and looked at the ceiling for a few seconds. "I'm worried we're setting a precedent. He needs to learn how to appropriately respond to situations."

"I agree with you, love. But, in his mind he *is* responding appropriately. As crazy as that sounds, he's thinking several moves ahead of everyone else."

Lenora chuckled a little. "He's too smart for his own good sometimes. It's just so surprising."

"I wish you could have met my mother. I'm sure she'd have a few things to say about me at his age."

Lenora's gaze softened. "I'm sure she would."

Connor's father had died during an armed conflict while in the NA Alliance Navy when Connor was about Ethan's age. He hadn't taken it well, and it had started him on a troubled path that almost ended badly for him. Ethan wasn't on that kind of path, but Connor did see a lot of himself in his children. He saw a lot of Lenora in them as well. Both Lauren and Ethan were an interesting mix of his and Lenora's personalities. They had Lenora's keen intellect, but with a healthy dose of Connor's cleverness and adaptive determination. In addition, Lauren and Ethan dealt with conflict differently, which Connor believed had more to do with their gender than personality traits. Neither of them would be considered shy or gentle, and he wasn't sure how he would have dealt with it if they had been. He'd love them just the same, but both he and Lenora had strong personalities, and the thought that either of their children would be anything other than headstrong was a bit of a stretch.

"I wish I could have met her, Connor."

He smiled. "She would've loved you. You would've gotten along well."

"How's Oriana doing?"

"She's fine. Less worried now that we've reestablished contact with the *Infinity*."

"Good, I'm glad. Noah is determined to make this work."

"Yes, he is. You know, if we get tired of New Earth, there are other planets to explore. Other mysteries to unravel."

Lenora's full lips lifted, and she gave him an alluring look. "Do you have a place in mind?"

"No, but if you keep looking at me like that, I might have to take a shuttle back home."

"Oh well, let me bat my eyelashes at you then." She giggled.

They regarded each other for a few seconds.

"I miss it sometimes," he said.

"Me?" she asked.

"Always, but I meant exploring New Earth, back when we didn't know anything about the planet or the Ovarrow."

Lenora nodded. "Their tragic history aside, this planet has been an archeologist's dream. Maybe one day we'll get to explore another planet."

"Yeah, one day."

They were both quiet for a few seconds.

"I'll make sure Ethan is ready to go," Lenora said.

"I'll contact the base there."

"Do *not* send him up there with a squad of soldiers. I'm not ready for him to get that kind of education."

Connor grinned. "Understood. Loud and clear. I'll have Bradley set something up with the vetted escorts. She's good."

"Okay, Connor. I hope you're right about this."

"All we can do is try. If not this, then we'll come up with something else."

Lenora kissed her fingers and pressed them to the screen, watching expectantly. She knew public displays of affection made him uncomfortable sometimes, but he returned the gesture. She smiled and then severed the comlink.

Connor returned to his office and called Lieutenant McClintock in. McClintock had been assigned to him as part of the CDF base personnel serving on the moon.

He entered Connor's office and stood at attention.

"My son will be joining me here for a few weeks. There are a couple of things I want arranged beforehand," Connor said and told McClintock of the list of things he'd put together on his way.

"I'll get started on this at once, General Gates. There are student field expeditions on the lunar surface that he might like. They're popular among the students visiting the base."

"That's a good idea. Thanks for letting me know. If you think of anything else as far as activities, I want to hear about it. Not all entertainment, but skill-building exercises would be ideal."

"I'll do some research and come up with a list for you to review," Lieutenant McClintock said.

Connor believed that Ethan was just going through a phase. He was sure his friend Diaz could relate. Maybe he'd contact Juan. The man had raised six kids, and according to him, he was just getting started.

Connor attended a security council meeting, which had once been considered a nail-biting affair by some. Those had been different times.

"Article 571 is up for review," Mullins said. He looked at Nathan Hayes, Connor's commanding officer, and then at Connor, who was attending the meeting remotely. "This is regarding allowing the Mekaal to serve in the Colonial Defense Force."

The Mekaal were part of a species known as Ovarrow and were indigenous to New Earth.

"Yes, this was put forth by my office," Nathan said. "Mekaal soldiers have served on joint task forces both on New Earth and beyond. Since they're now considered colonial citizens, the next step is to allow them to join the CDF."

"The Mekaal *are* considered colonial citizens, but they still have their own military and police force that protect their city," Mullins replied.

"That's true, but eventually these two forces will merge.

While it may take many years for this to occur, there's no reason to delay or deny entry to Mekaal who petition to join the CDF," Nathan replied.

Mullins nodded and looked at Connor. "General Gates, do you have any concerns you'd like to offer about this?"

"There will be an adjustment period for both humans and Mekaal, especially as Mekaal rise through the ranks and take on more responsibility. We'll do our best to make the transition as painless as possible, and there is potential for friction. But of all the assimilation involving the Mekaal, the CDF integration will be an easier transition than other things like Field Ops and Security. The enforcement of laws, that sort of thing. Very few of the Mekaal live in colonial cities, but that may change over time."

Mullins considered this for a few moments. "You raise some very important points. I agree with you regarding the ease of integration. The Mekaal are, or were, more of a militaristic society, but they have become more open to peaceful coexistence, even among the other Ovarrow groups."

Nathan nodded. "After over a decade since the Krake were defeated, they're finally thinking of themselves in the long term rather than just surviving."

"The Mekaal have been our allies for a long time," Mullins said.

"The Konus are a different matter. They're still a militaristic society, and building trust with them may not ever occur."

"Eventually they might come around, especially after watching how the Mekaal adjust to being part of the colony," Mullins said. "There aren't going to be perfect solutions, but I think your proposal will be a shining example for the colony. My thanks to you and the rest of the CDF who are always willing to take the first step, even when governments are hesitant to align."

Nathan shared a look with Connor. Mullins had become more tolerant of the CDF as he matured as a colonial leader, but he'd also be the first to point out their shortcomings if there were issues integrating the Mekaal into the CDF. Both Connor and Nathan knew that and were prepared to deal with whatever came their way. No military in their history had multiple species serving in it, and yet as the first human interstellar colony, it was something they had to embrace.

The meeting ended, but Mullins asked both Connor and Nathan to stay behind. "We've been reviewing the mission status update from the *Infinity*. I wanted to know if either of you had any thoughts on it," Mullins said.

"Is there anything specific you wanted to discuss?" Nathan asked.

"The fact that they kept going without consulting my office. They almost lost the ship. They should have consulted with us about their proposed actions," Mullins said.

"There is a significant risk in what they're doing, but what would have changed if they had checked in with your office? What's the real issue here? The fact that they kept going, or that they should have asked your permission to keep going?" Connor asked.

Mullins blinked a few times. "Straight to the point as always. However, I don't feel I'm off the mark by expecting a little more input regarding how this mission is carried out."

"If that's how you feel, you could inform them of that," Connor replied.

Mullins regarded him for a few moments and then looked at Nathan. "Am I wrong?"

"We have to trust their judgement. It's *their* lives on the line," Nathan replied.

"That's just it. I'm considering whether to have Colonel

Quinn assume command of the ship and the mission," Mullins said.

"I would advise against it," Connor said. Mullins raised his eyebrows and gestured for Connor to continue. "If Colonel Quinn believed the mission and the ship were in danger because of Noah's actions, he would've taken command of the mission already. He hasn't, which means he agrees with the decisions Noah has made."

"Connor's right, Bob. This isn't something that can be micromanaged from here," Nathan said.

Mullins looked at each of them and sighed.

Connor leaned toward the camera. "Noah knows what he's doing. You wanted a civilian commanding the ship, and he's got CDF backup with him. They're two of the best people I know, and they're well suited for this. The only thing that would come from us ordering Sean to take over would be a demoralized crew that would view the CDF soldiers as something to contend with rather than work with. That's not what we want. That's not what the mission needs."

"Okay, you've made your point. We'll stay the course then."

"Good," Connor said.

He disconnected from the meeting and leaned back in his chair. It was only a small possibility that both Noah and Sean were being reckless, but Mullins was very concerned about the mission. It would reflect poorly on him if it failed, but Connor had as near absolute faith in Noah and Sean as he possibly could. They knew what they were doing.

9

Noah watched as Kara stumbled a little before she grabbed hold of Dr. Hathaway. She gasped and took several shallow breaths.

Kara scowled. "It still hurts."

She'd only been awake for a few days, but she expected to be able to do all the things she could do before she'd gotten injured.

"It's going to hurt," Hathaway said. "The pain is a good thing."

Kara glared at her. "Since when is pain a good thing?"

"Since it means that you can actually feel your legs," Noah replied.

Kara rolled her eyes and gritted her teeth. She grabbed the railing and lowered herself into a chair.

"He's right," Hathaway said.

Kara groaned and exhaled forcefully. "He usually is," she said, massaging her thighs.

"It's the new nerve endings. They're hypersensitive, and the only way to get them to stop is to stimulate them," Hathaway said.

"There has to be an easier way."

"There isn't, at least not until your brain accepts the new nerve endings. The pain will reduce, but it's going to take some time."

Kara muttered a curse and shook her head.

Noah looked at Hathaway. "Why don't I take over for a little while?"

Hathaway nodded. "She needs to do another lap. Then you'll have to stretch her legs like we did yesterday."

"I remember," Noah assured her, and Hathaway walked out of the rehabilitation room.

Kara eyed him with the hint of a scowl about to return at any moment. She tapped her foot and winced a little.

Noah smiled.

"What are you smiling about?"

"I'm just happy you're awake. It's been over a month, and I was starting to get lonely."

Kara stared at him for a moment. "You think this is funny—"

"No, I don't think this is funny," Noah said, but a grin bubbled up from his chest.

She shook her head. "You are unbelievable. Get away from me."

"Come on, don't be like that."

"How am I supposed to be, Noah? Tell me. Everything from here down hurts," she said, gesturing from her stomach to her knees.

"It's only been a few days. You've got to give yourself some time to heal."

Kara closed her eyes and inhaled a steadying breath. When

she opened her eyes, he saw that fear had replaced her anger and frustration—the fear that she'd always be in this much pain. Pain could wear away at anyone, no matter what their tolerance for it was.

Her face crumbled and she reached for him. Noah rushed to her side and held her, rubbing her back with one hand.

"I'm here," he said soothingly.

Kara leaned into him, shivering a little. "What if they're wrong, Noah? What if something is wrong and I don't heal? I can hardly walk. How am I going to… What if they're wrong?"

"Then we'll figure it out, Kara, like we always do." He paused for a moment, and she wiped away her tears.

"I don't want to think they're wrong, but I'm scared, Noah. What if I can never walk again? What if there will always be this much pain?"

"I don't think they're wrong. You were badly hurt. You just need time for your body to heal, and everything will fall into place."

She looked at him. "It happened so fast. I went down to the computing core to try to reset it. Then the next thing I knew I was thrown to the side and pinned down. I didn't even feel it at first. People were screaming. The ship kept…"

Noah watched her, knowing that her injuries went beyond what had happened to her body. They were both engineers to their core. They liked knowing how things worked. Kara was trying to figure out what had happened to her, and if there was anything she could've done to avoid it.

"That'll take time, too," he said.

She frowned. "What will take time?"

He gestured at his head. "Getting everything right in here. There was nothing you could've done. We're just lucky… sometimes that has to be enough. I'll leave it at that."

She looked away from him, her head tilted to the side. She looked so vulnerable. "I'd only found out that morning. I got the alert from my biochip." She swallowed hard.

"Kara, it's all right. You didn't do anything wrong. It's not your fault."

"I know," she said, softly. "But it feels like it is, like I should have done something. I should have told you right away, as soon as I learned about it. I should have told you. Maybe it would've changed what happened."

Noah went blind for a second as the tears built up, and he rubbed his eyes. "I wish I could change what happened, too. Believe me, I do."

They were silent for a little while. Kara seemed to relax, leaning against him. He'd had a month to rationalize his feelings about what they'd lost, but for Kara it had only been a few days. She needed time.

He waited a few silent minutes. "Are you ready to try again?" he asked.

Kara groaned. "Can't you just carry me?"

Noah chuckled. "I could, but that wouldn't help you much now, would it?"

He stood up.

Kara gritted her teeth and did the same with a determined glint in her eyes. For the next half hour, he helped her with her physical therapy exercises, then watched as Emily Lockhart guided Kara through stretching her legs. After that, she got to soak in a small therapy pool. The water was at a subtropical temperature that Kara loved.

"I'm tempted to join you in there," Noah said.

Kara arched an eyebrow.

"I know what you mean," Emily said. "Any chance that we can have a pool in the next ship?"

Kara sighed contentedly. "I wish we had one of these in our quarters."

Noah grinned. "I'll see what I can do."

An alert chimed on his wrist computer. He eyed it as if it had betrayed him.

"Duty calls, Noah," Kara said with the hint of a sigh.

"I know. I have to get to the bridge," Noah replied, dipping his hand into the water. He wouldn't have minded some time in there either—something to soothe his sore muscles.

The alert chimed again, and he pulled his hand out of the water. "Next time," he said.

He kissed Kara's forehead and left the medical center.

THE *INFINITY* HAD SETTLED into a routine. Days were spent ensuring it was in tip-top shape. All other efforts were devoted to preparing for their arrival at the Zeta-Alpha star system. Kara continued to make steady progress with her recovery and wasn't in as much pain as she had been, which was a relief for both of them.

Since they'd added the protocols to detect gravity-wave interference with the I-Drive, the rest of the voyage to the Zeta-Alpha star system was uneventful. Noah had been able to increase the I-Drive's efficiency, which reduced the amount of time it would take them to reach their destination.

He met up with Sean on his way to the bridge.

"Did you tell her?" Sean asked.

Kara had made steady progress in her recovery from her injuries. She could walk for short distances without assistance, and she'd just been released from the medical center, so she could at least sleep in their quarters.

He nodded. "She wasn't happy about it."

"I wouldn't imagine she would be."

"She's not cleared for duty. That's just the way it is."

Sean snorted. "Good luck with that."

Noah looked at him. "What's that supposed to mean?"

"She's not going to ride this out at the medical center or even in your quarters."

Noah glanced behind them, almost expecting to see Kara heading toward the bridge.

"No, she won't come to the bridge. She knows you'd just make her leave. She's going to go down to main engineering."

"No, she wouldn't."

"She's been cooped up for a while, Noah."

"Yeah, but... she better not."

"Do you really think Duckman is going to turn her away when she shows up down there?"

Noah already knew the answer to that. Duckman was in charge of main engineering, but Sean was right. He wouldn't turn her away.

He stopped just outside the doors to the bridge and brought up a security feed on his personal holoscreen. He saw Kara getting off the elevator and slowly walking toward the engineering deck.

"I don't believe this."

Sean's eyebrows waggled once. "Wait for it."

Noah frowned and then looked back at the security feed.

"There they are," Sean said. Two CDF soldiers followed Kara down the corridor. "If we get into any trouble, they'll look out for her."

Noah shook his head. She wasn't ready to be back in engineering. He had half a mind to go down there and... but he let that train of thought go. He closed the security feed and sighed. "Thanks, Sean."

"How does it feel to be on the opposite end of it? Did you forget all those times you weren't compliant with doctor's orders during your own recovery?"

"No, but there was a good reason for what I did." Noah paused, realizing the futility of what he was saying.

Kara had been making progress and was getting better, but he was still worried about her.

"She wouldn't be who she was if she didn't push it. Neither would you."

Noah scowled at his friend. "One day, Sean, I'm going to be there to give you some sage advice like you just gave me. I expect you'll take it like I am right now."

Sean grinned and bobbed his head once.

Noah palmed the door controls and walked onto the bridge.

Markovich stood up and vacated the commander's chair, going to the aux workstation nearby.

Noah sat in the commander's chair and Sean took the workstation next to his.

"Ms. McGinnis, put our time to destination on the main holoscreen," Noah said.

A HUD overlay became active on the main holoscreen. The view from external video showed a wavering gray and black with pulsing purple and green waves as if they were riding ribbons of light amid a celestial backdrop. In the past two months, he hadn't tired of seeing the mesmerizing beauty of what they'd achieved. They stood upon the threshold of the entire galaxy, and this journey to the Zeta-Alpha star system was only the first of many steps.

Noah looked at Sean and shared a proud moment with his friend. This was where they thrived, pushing the boundaries of what was possible. It was what allowed the colony to survive, and it was how they would flourish into a bright future. He believed it to his core.

The I-Drive cycled down, and the *Infinity* transitioned back to normal space. They were well within the Oort cloud of the Zeta-Alpha star system but were far enough away that light from the star still took over eight hours to reach them.

"Begin active scans, Ms. McGinnis," Noah said.

"Yes, Captain."

The Oort cloud contained leftovers from when the star system had formed billions of years ago. Icy proto-planetary debris was detected by the ship's systems as an image of their region of space began to appear on the main holoscreen. The *Infinity* was still in interstellar space, but they'd travel into the heliosphere eventually.

"Still no contact from the *Ark II* over subspace comms, and no emergency broadcast beacons detected, Captain," Jessica Yu said.

"Understood," Noah replied.

"That's not surprising," Sean said.

"No, it's not. If subspace comms were working on the *Ark II*, we'd never have lost contact, but if something did go wrong, I would have expected an emergency broadcast beacon at the very least."

Sean regarded him for a few moments. "Unless they didn't have time to broadcast a distress beacon or even launch a comms drone."

"Or they had a distress beacon working, but it stopped for some reason."

Sean nodded once.

"Captain," Jessica Yu said, "I'm getting a response from one of the *Ark II*'s exploratory probes. It's located near one of the Jovian-type planets."

A new icon appeared on the main holoscreen, showing the probe's location. "If it's this far out, it was likely launched as the ship headed toward the star system's interior."

"Would they have launched multiple probes?" Sean asked.

"Yes, they would have, but…" he said and paused.

Noah started to bring up a data window and stopped, giving Sean a wry look. "Ms. Mattison, can you extract the logs from the probe and determine the last time it had a successful check-in with the *Ark II*?"

"Yes, Captain," Delta Mattison said.

As she looked for the data, Noah watched the main holoscreen. The tactical plot was populating with data from their scanners.

"Captain," Jessica Yu said, "I've gotten replies from three other probes. All of them are located farther in the star system."

"Thank you, Ms. Yu," Noah replied.

Delta Mattison turned away from her workstation to look at him. "Last successful check-in was within days of when COMCENT last reported getting a status update, so six months since the last successful check-in."

"Understood, continue to get a full data dump from those probes. Maybe there's something they've detected that might shed some light on what happened here," Noah said and looked at Sean. "If there was a hostile alien force here, why would they allow the probes to continue to explore the system?"

"I could venture a couple of guesses, but there's no way to be sure if I'm right until we head on in there."

"We still have a few minutes before our next move, so guess away."

Sean watched the main holoscreen for a few seconds and

then looked at Noah. "We're assuming they're hostile if there is, in fact, a 'they' at all. Anyway, the probes aren't a threat, so they didn't see the point in wasting resources to hunt them down. They don't have the resources to venture this far into the star system. They haven't detected the probes. They're waiting to see if anyone comes to look for the *Ark II,* and leaving the probes alone allows them to function as some kind of trap."

Noah held up his hand. "Okay, I get it. I bet you haven't even really gotten started."

Sean raised his eyebrows. "I can keep going, but I don't think it's going to help."

"Probably not. We'll stick with the plan to explore the outer star system and then decide when we go to Zeta-Alpha-5," Noah replied.

"It's a good plan," Sean agreed.

Noah looked at the main holoscreen for a few seconds and then leaned forward. "Nav, do we have a course ready?"

"Yes, Captain," Alissa McGinnis said.

"Ops, ready the I-Drive," Noah said.

This was where things would diverge from their voyage here. The I-Drive would be brought online, but at less than ten percent power. They only needed to cross to the other side of the star system, and they'd scan the area before moving on. This would give them an accurate picture of the outer star system within the capabilities of the ship's scanners.

"I-Drive is online, Captain," Delta Mattison said.

"Engage I-Drive."

The I-Drive was engaged for a few seconds, and the only indication on the external video feeds was a bright flash before they emerged back into normal space. The sensors were temporarily blinded, but after a few moments they began to pump data into the computing core.

Sean blew out a breath and Noah looked at him. "We just crossed forty percent of the star system in a few seconds."

Noah frowned. "We crossed three lightyears to get here."

"I know that. It's impressive, but this is just as impressive. This capability would have been extremely useful during the Krake War. We had to sneak across star systems, essentially running blind to avoid contact with enemy ships."

"Someone could detect what we did. We're still traveling through space."

Sean nodded. "We just need to do this a few more times, gather what data we can, and find out where the *Ark II* is."

10

For the past twelve hours the *Infinity* had flown to different locations along the outer Zeta-Alpha star system. In all that time, they couldn't confirm whether there was an advanced alien civilization located among the habitable planets, but by all appearances there didn't seem to be.

Noah sat in the command chair on the bridge and rubbed his forehead for a few seconds. "Unless this is the most well-hidden advanced civilization no one has ever seen, I think it's time for us to head straight to Zeta-Alpha-5."

"Agreed," Sean replied.

Chief Markovich looked at Noah. "I agree, Captain. We've learned all we can from here."

Noah lifted his gaze to the main holoscreen. The tactical plot displayed a star map of the planets they'd detected. The Zeta-Alpha star was categorized as a common G-class main sequence star, but it was over 1.2 solar masses, which had placed it on the edge of an F-class star. The star blazed at a higher luminosity and had a surface temperature of about 6400 degrees

Kelvin, hotter than the star of New Earth and the Old Earth sun.

The star system was highly populated, with over eleven planets orbiting it. The outer system hosted five Jovian-type planets, each with dozens of moons, with quite a few being planet-sized themselves. The exploratory probe data indicated that the moons of at least two of the Jovian planets were rich in metals. Noah expected that the inner rocky planets were also rich in resources. Three of the inner systems of planets were within the habitable zone, but only two of them were near Earth-sized.

There were two asteroid belts in the star system. One of them was among the outer system of planets. The Jovian's had prevented a large planetary mass from forming, but for some reason it hadn't been pulled into orbit around them. The second asteroid belt bordered the inner system just beyond the habitable zone. That asteroid field was likely the victim of a celestial tug-of-war between the nearest Jovian planet that prevented the rocky planets from forming.

All the planets were in a stable orbit around the star, which indicated that the star system had been here for a while. There'd been no recent events that had disrupted the system.

Zeta-Alpha-5 was the fifth planet from the star. In terms of interstellar travel, they were so close, but they still knew so little about the planet. At this range, they could determine that there was liquid water on both near Earth-sized planets, and that they had a substantial atmosphere, which was a strong indicator of an ecosystem. Zeta-Alpha-5 was right in the heart of the habitable zone, which was why the *Ark II* would have traveled there.

Noah tried to think of anything they might have missed. Had he ignored some small piece of data that would later have extreme consequences? The entire crew was focused on what they would find. No one was throwing up any red flags for him to consider, but he still wanted to take a few minutes to go through the plan in his mind. The crew was depending on him to make the best decisions he could. Once they traveled to the planet, there would be no turning back.

"Okay, I think we're ready now," Noah said. "Ms. McGinnis, I want emergency secondary coordinates ready to execute if we need to leave quickly."

"Secondary coordinates are programmed into the nav computer and ready to execute on your orders, Captain," she replied.

"Very well," Noah said. He opened a broadcast com to the rest of the ship. "Crew of the *Infinity*, we're about to voyage to Zeta-Alpha-5. We know that the *Ark II* did arrive in the star system, and it did make it to the inner system of planets before contact was lost. We don't know what we'll find once we get there, but five thousand of our fellow colonists are depending on us, and everyone back home is waiting to learn what we're about to do. As a good friend of mine used to remind me in times like these, stay focused and stay vigilant. Captain Barker out."

Sean gave him a knowing look and leaned forward. "It's almost as if Connor is here with us."

Noah smiled and then replied quietly. "He is."

Sean tipped his head to the side in acknowledgement.

"Ops, ready the I-Drive," Noah said.

"I-Drive is online, Captain," Delta Mattison replied.

"Take us in."

The I-Drive became active with a precision that could only be accomplished by the *Infinity's* powerful computing core. Over the span of a few seconds, the ship traveled to within five hundred thousand kilometers of Zeta-Alpha-5. The external video feeds showed a planet that had two moons orbiting it. Its atmosphere had large areas of reddish-violet color, with some areas gleaming amid greens and blues. It wasn't like any planet Noah had ever seen before.

"Would you look at that," Markovich said with awe in his voice.

Noah stood up and stared at the image on the main holoscreen as the ship's scanners began feeding data about the planet.

"With an axial tilt like that, it's got to have more extreme weather patterns," Noah said.

"There are oceans down there, but they're not as blue as what we have on New Earth. I've never seen a planet like this," Sean said.

Noah looked at him. Sean was among a cohort of soldiers and scientists that numbered in the thousands. They'd traveled through the multiverse, seeing many different versions of the New Earth star system.

"Comms, anything from the *Ark II*?" Noah asked.

Jessica Yu peered at her screen as she navigated the holointerface. "Nothing on subspace comms, but I'm getting something on a general hailing frequency. It's a return ping from the *Ark II!*"

"Where?" Noah asked.

Jessica Yu frowned as she listened to something from her earpiece. Then she typed into the data window on her holoscreen. "It's coming from an area near the closest moon to the planet."

"Ops, get me a fix on them," Noah said.

"I'm on it, Captain," Delta Mattison said.

Noah glanced at Sean.

"Captain, the initial hails put the *Ark II* in a lunar synchronous orbit."

"Yes!" Noah said, pumping his fist. "Comms, hail them back."

"No response, Captain," Yu said.

Noah frowned, considering. "Nav, put us on an intercept course."

They were too far away to get a visual of the *Ark II*, but at least the ship was there.

"Comms, do a sweep for other comms signals. There might have been an issue with the *Ark II*'s subspace transceiver."

The *Infinity*'s main engines engaged, and they were slowly making their way toward the planet.

Sean exhaled through his nose. "Why wouldn't they answer our hails? It doesn't make any sense. The *Ark II*'s computer systems should have replied to a colonial signal."

Noah frowned. "You're right. We should have gotten more of a response."

"Comms, are you still able to reach the probes in the outer star system?" Sean asked.

"I'll initiate a check-in," Yu replied. A few moments passed and she shook her head. "That's odd. I'm not able to reach the probes anymore. None of the ones we detected before are reachable now."

"Run a diagnostic on our subspace comms," Noah said.

"Systems reporting fully functional, Captain."

Markovich cleared his throat. "Could someone be jamming our communications?"

Noah looked at the data on the main holoscreen and shook his head. "I suppose it's possible, but who? There are no installations detected on either of those moons except for the *Ark II*."

A new icon appeared near the planet.

"It looks like those are observer satellites deployed from the *Ark II*. Standard deployment for studying a planet," Sean said.

Noah nodded. "That means Saul Ashworth must have woken up from stasis and ordered them deployed, but why wouldn't he respond to us?"

Sean shook his head with a thoughtful frown. "I don't know."

"Comms, are you able to establish a comlink to any of those satellites?" Noah asked.

"Yes, Captain. I can initiate a data connection," Yu replied.

"Do it. Those satellites must have been orbiting the planet for at least six months. There has to be data that we can use. Ops, make the data available to Dr. Lachlan and his team. They can start their own evaluation of it," Noah said.

"Will do, Captain," Delta Mattison said.

After coming so far so fast, the last leg of the journey seemed to take the longest. Slow and steady, they were closing in on Zeta-Alpha-5's primary moon. The moon had a three thousand kilometer diameter and orbited the planet, maintaining a distance of three hundred fifty thousand kilometers. The secondary moon was much smaller, with a diameter of twelve hundred kilometers, but its orbit was over four hundred thousand kilometers from the planet. There were significant ice formations at the polar regions of the primary moon that they'd begun calling Alpha. Alpha was tidally locked, meaning it took just as long to rotate around its own axis as it did to revolve around the planet. The secondary moon, or Beta, was not tidally locked and had a relatively quick spin on its axis.

"Captain," Sean said, and Noah turned toward him. Sean's formal address wasn't lost on him. "I think we should enable some of the CDF detection protocols."

"On what?"

"The *Ark II*."

Noah considered it for a few moments and then nodded.

"Ops," Sean said, "enable CDF scanning protocol suite seventy-four. Keep it active."

"CDF scanning protocol seventy-four," Delta Mattison confirmed. "Protocols are active, sir."

A new data window appeared on the main holoscreen, and Noah noticed that a similar window appeared at Sean's workstation.

They had visual confirmation of the *Ark II*. The ship was still intact and didn't appear to have suffered from damage of any kind.

An alert appeared and took prominence on the new data window.

"Weapons detection?" Noah asked.

Sean's hands flew through the interface. "It's accurate. The *Ark II* was equipped with light mag cannons and a few grasers, as well as a seventh-generation guardian point-defense system."

"Helm, all stop," Noah said.

"Aye, all stop, Captain," Myers said.

"Alter course to increase our distance from them," Noah said.

The *Infinity* didn't have weapons of any kind. The hull was comprised of light-armored ceramics, which gave them enough protection from what they'd encounter in space but wasn't meant to repel actual weapons.

Another alert appeared.

"They're locking onto us," Sean said.

"Comms, any reply to our hails?" Noah asked.

"Negative, Captain."

"Why the hell are they shooting at us? We're broadcasting a colonial signal that should register as a friendly to the *Ark II*'s threat-management system," Noah said. He paused for a moment. "Helm, go full emergency. Get us out of here. Best speed!"

"Aye, Captain," Myers replied, his voice sounding tight.

"They're firing," Sean said.

"Helm, evasive maneuvers! Ops, set condition one," Noah shouted.

Klaxon alarms sounded throughout the ship.

"Action Stations. Action Stations. Set condition one throughout the ship," Delta Mattison said.

Noah tightened his grip on the armrests of his chair. The *Infinity's* main engines burst with energy and the ship moved away from the *Ark II*.

Sean looked at Noah. "Fly us closer to Alpha. We can use the moon as cover."

Noah ordered Myers to alter their course again. Maneuvering thrusters controlled by the guidance computer organized the main engines to put the *Infinity* on a smooth arc away from the *Ark II*.

Noah looked at Sean. "Are they going to hit us?"

Sean watched his holoscreen for a few moments, then shook his head. "They're going to miss, and they haven't fired any more of their weapons at us."

Noah swallowed hard and sighed. "Ops, stand us down from Action Stations."

A general announcement was broadcast over the ship-wide comms.

Noah looked at Sean. "We need to figure out what's going on. They shouldn't have fired on us."

11

Noah had the *Infinity* maintain a lunar orbit that matched the *Ark II* but kept a distance that put the ship on the other side of the moon. He then called up his reserve watch-standers so he could meet with his senior officers in the conference room near the bridge.

"Never a dull moment, is there?" Kara said.

She'd been cleared for light duty, which made her extremely happy. As many times as Noah had been injured over the years, it was sometimes the most burdensome the closer he'd gotten to getting back to normal. He'd just wanted to be over and done with it, and Kara was reacting the same way he had.

Noah smiled. "I guess it would've been too easy otherwise," he said and nodded a greeting toward Duckman.

Peter Blood, who led the *Infinity's* salvage and repair operations, entered the conference room, followed by Lieutenant Jesse Rhoades. The CDF officer was lean and average in height, but his large hands looked as if he could crush a grapefruit. Sean had told him that Rhoades was quite good at playing acoustic guitar and knew a whole bunch of very old folk songs from the heart of the old NA Alliance. As part of Noah's recovery from a head injury that left him in a coma for months, the neurologist had encouraged him to learn a musical instrument—something that involved hand-eye coordination—and he'd chosen the guitar. After months of practice, he could play more than a few songs. He found that it helped him in ways he hadn't anticipated, but it also remained a mystery. Brain injuries were mysterious like that. His guitar was in storage, along with everything else he'd left back on New Earth.

Noah walked to his place at the conference table and sat down. The others did the same.

"Okay, there's been no shortage of surprises on this trek, but I think we can all agree that no one had anticipated the *Ark II's* defense systems firing its weapons at us. Would anyone care to offer a guess as to why?" Noah asked.

Chief Markovich cleared his throat. "Sure thing, Captain. COMCENT gave us all the communication protocols we would need before we left, so the issue cannot be with that."

Delta Mattison leaned forward, jouncing the curls of her long tawny hair. "This wasn't a lack of response. They determined that we were hostile and opened fire on us."

Noah looked at Sean. "It has to be some kind of security lockdown, but we don't know why or how to disable it," Sean said.

Kara nodded. "I have a few things I can try to remotely override the lockdown."

"It's worth trying, as long as we can maintain a safe distance. The automated defenses were reactionary and won't hesitate to fire on us again," Noah said.

"They were," Sean agreed. "But I'm not sure a remote override is going to be possible."

Noah frowned. "Why not?"

"Connor sent me the security protocols he'd recommended while they were building the *Ark II*. They were further refined by Major Wesley Samson."

"I remember Samson. He was Connor's friend. Part of the original Ghost Platoon from the NA Alliance Military," Noah replied.

Sean nodded. "That's right. The Second Colony effort was meant to be independent from New Earth. Essentially, it's a separate entity."

"So, they limited our access?" Kara asked.

"Yeah, basically. No one thought we'd send another ship here. The *Ark II* was our backup plan in case the Krake won the war. It was our failsafe if the worst happened to the rest of us left on New Earth."

"Yeah, but the *Ark II* didn't leave until after we'd defeated the Krake. Why wouldn't they have changed it?" Noah said.

"Why *would* they have changed it?" Sean replied, the edges of his lips lifting. "The number of checks done for the computer systems and protocols that the ship's onboard AI follows had already been approved. Changing everything so the *Ark II* was an extension of New Earth would have set the entire effort back with no real gains."

Noah considered it for a few moments and nodded. "I see your point. For all intents and purposes, the second colony was always going to be separate from back home. But there still has to be a way for us to access the *Ark II*'s systems."

"I'm sure there are multiple ways, but it's not going to be as easy as a simple data comlink with an override protocol," Sean said.

"Saul Ashworth is the mission commander for the *Ark II*. The security lockdown protocol had to have been initiated by him or a member of his senior officers. But that doesn't explain why they haven't responded to our hails or why subspace comms stopped working," Noah said.

"They worked farther out in the star system," Kara said. "Perhaps there's some kind of interference that's unique to this planet."

"We're going to need to figure that out, but our first priority is to find out the status of the five thousand colonists on the ship," Noah said.

Markovich cleared his throat and raised his hand. "Just a quick question. Would COMCENT have some kind of override protocol we can use? I mean, they have the source code for the system."

"We already spoke about this," Sean replied. "The system is self-contained."

"I understand that, but if we trick the *Ark II* into believing that the *Infinity* is part of its fleet, it wouldn't fire its weapons on us," Markovich said.

"It's a good thought and something we might pursue, but I'm not sure it's going to work," Noah replied.

"Why is that?" Markovich asked.

Noah smiled. "Can *you* find something you worked on more than ten years ago?"

Markovich chuckled. "I see your point, sir."

"We could send a team to infiltrate the *Ark II*," Kara said.

Noah looked at Sean.

Sean shrugged. "Maybe. We'd need to review the capabilities of their point-defense systems. Lieutenant Rhoades can look into that for us."

"Yes, Colonel. I'll get right to work on that," Lieutenant Rhoades replied.

Noah felt a couple of ideas tugging at the edges of his

thoughts. He activated the holoscreen and could feel Sean's gaze on him. He was the mission commander and should delegate what he was about to do.

Noah held up his hand but kept his eyes on the holoscreen. "I know what you're going to say."

Sean grinned. "I wasn't going to say anything."

"You can take the techie out of the engineering lab, but you can't take the engineering lab out of the techie," Kara said, and others laughed.

"Have a good laugh," Noah replied and smiled. "But guess who found out that the *Ark II* sent an away team to the surface of the planet?" He jutted a thumb towards his chest. "This guy."

Sean arched an eyebrow, looking mildly amused. "How did you figure that out? Did you bypass the *Ark II*'s security systems somehow when we weren't looking?"

"No, that would be too easy. Instead, I queried the access logs from the observer satellites. The *Ark II* might be under a lockdown, but not the satellites. They're not secure at all. It appears that there were two away teams sent from the *Ark II*," Noah replied.

He put up the log entries for the two shuttles that had accessed the satellites and watched as Sean scanned the data.

"Eagle 7s. Those are heavy-duty shuttles. They weren't just going for a quick aerial reconnaissance. They were bringing equipment to scout wherever they ended up going," Sean said.

"How do you know the type of shuttles they used?" Markovich asked.

Sean smiled with half his mouth. "It's part of the log entry. It has the abbreviation of the shuttle manufacturer type."

Markovich nodded and pursed his lips, impressed.

"They were probably setting up a forward operating base,"

Noah said. "But the time stamps for these log entries are months old. They might still be down there."

"That doesn't make much sense," Sean said.

"That's where the evidence leads."

Sean nodded. "I know, but I don't like it. Saul Ashworth would have woken up enough people for two teams to do an extensive scouting mission, which means they'd intended to begin colonial operations on the planet. What changed?"

"You guys would know better than all of us," Kara said, gesturing toward Noah and Sean.

Some of the others regarded them in confusion.

"We were part of the early risers when the *Ark* arrived at New Earth," Noah said. He looked at Sean. "You were brought out of stasis before me."

Sean nodded. "I was, but that was after they'd already established a base. They'd had a seed ship in orbit around the planet that arrived twenty years before the *Ark*, so the situation was a bit different from what we have here."

"Yeah, but would your father have gone down to the planet and put the entire *Ark* in lockdown until he came back?"

Sean's father was Tobias Quinn, the first governor of the colony and the leader of the Ark Program that had brought over three hundred thousand colonists to New Earth.

"No, I don't think he would've done that. I don't know for sure, but I doubt it. He'd want support from the *Ark* in case anything went wrong with establishing the base."

Noah nodded and leaned back in his chair, rubbing his chin for a few moments.

"What if they weren't sure about establishing a colony here?" Kara asked.

"It's possible," Noah replied.

"More than possible. I think it's probable. I was just looking at the observation data from those same satellites you used to figure out that an away team was sent down to the planet. You're really quite clever."

Noah raised his eyebrows. "Well, thank you for noticing."

Kara smiled. "You're quite welcome. The atmospheric composition isn't compatible with humans. It's denser than what we're used to, but there's twenty percent less gravity. The atmosphere is a mixture of nitrogen, oxygen, carbon dioxide, xenon, methane, hydrogen sulfide, and the list goes on, but the levels aren't ideal for our survival. There's an extensive ecosystem on the planet, so terraforming it to match our needs would be unethical."

"So, you're saying they might have just been doing a small scouting mission to determine the long-term viability of establishing a colony here," Noah said.

Kara nodded. "That might explain why there was no one on the *Ark II* to greet us. It doesn't explain the lockdown protocol, though."

"One thing at a time," Noah said and looked at the others. "Since we can't get answers from the *Ark II* at the moment, we'll need to send our own reconnaissance mission to retrace the steps of the *Ark II* teams."

Sean cleared his throat. "It sounds like I finally get to earn my keep around here."

Noah nodded. "It'll be a joint effort."

Kara's gaze darted toward him, her eyebrows drawing down in concern.

"We need to do our own analysis of the data we have available, as well as figure out what is interfering with subspace comms. We'll need to rely on radio transmissions, which means we'll need to deploy comms drones of our own. I still want to get access to the *Ark II*'s computer systems, but the answers we need are likely down on the planet. They could be stranded down there, so we'll need to be prepared for that. Let's start putting together a plan for each of those efforts and meet back here for a status update by tomorrow morning."

The meeting ended and people began leaving the conference room until only Noah and Kara remained.

"What's wrong?" Noah asked.

"Tell me you're not going down to the planet."

Noah chewed on the side of his lip for a second. "I can't because I'm going down there with Sean and the others. The science team as well."

Kara started to reply but stopped. "Just let Sean go and report back what he finds."

"They could miss something. They're soldiers and good at their jobs, but sometimes they miss things you and I wouldn't."

"Fine, then I'm going with you."

"No, you're not," Noah replied. "Kara, you've only just been cleared for light duty in main engineering. *Light* duty."

Kara cursed and looked away from him. "I can't believe… This stupid damn recovery is taking too long."

"It's not like I don't want you to come with me, but you're not ready for this."

Kara glared at him, her eyes searching his.

"I mean it. We've done enough crazy stuff together that trying to sideline you at this point in our marriage is just foolhardy, but you were hurt. You were severely injured, and like it or not, you're still healing."

Kara exhaled forcefully. "You know damn well that I can't argue with any of that."

Noah smiled. "I know, but that's why I want you to focus on bypassing the *Ark II*'s security lockdown."

Kara narrowed her gaze. "Oh, now you're redirecting me so

I'll have something to do. Quite the mission commander you've turned out to be."

Noah raised an eyebrow innocently. "Is it working?"

The edges of Kara's lips twitched, her eyes flicked to the ceiling, and she chuckled. She put her hands on his shoulders and stared up at him. "You better be careful, Noah."

"I will."

"No unnecessary risks from you. There is a platoon of CDF soldiers who are here to take those risks."

"I promise. No unnecessary risks."

She stared at him for a moment, and Noah felt a tinge of guilt for how much he'd caused Kara to worry about him over the years. All the risks he'd taken had been unavoidable and vital. He wasn't some kind of thrill-seeker or adrenaline junkie. Kara just wanted assurances that he would be careful, which was something he could give her. He hugged her close, feeling the warmth of her body against his. After almost losing her a little over a month ago, he didn't want to waste any of the time they had together. He wouldn't take any foolish risks, but he was venturing into the unknown. Takings risks kinda went with the territory.

12

Days and nights on the lunar base took some getting used to, but over the years, Connor had lived in so many different places that adjusting to life there wasn't difficult. Over the last decade, his internal clock had settled into a predictable rhythm. On the other hand, Ethan had never been to the lunar base before.

The wide viewport in Connor's office showed a gray lunar landscape. The pockmarked surface boasted a veritable city of white surface domes that only hinted at the vast network of living space beneath. As an extension of the colony, the base supported thousands of people who lived and worked there. An extensive series of interconnecting tunnels joined the various major colonial centers that had begun as a CDF outpost.

Connor's gaze sank toward the chessboard with cool calculation, but his attention was really on Ethan, who wore a thoughtful frown, focusing all his attention on the few remaining pieces. He sucked in his lower lip a little while trying to think his way out of his current predicament. Over the past month, they had begun playing chess, and Ethan had improved greatly since they'd first started. It was interesting watching him learn the game. Ethan could think through the possible moves, and he wasn't afraid to take risks. Within the past week, he'd begun to grasp the concepts of which pieces were best suited for early game play as opposed to later game play. Connor occasionally made a careless mistake just to see how Ethan would react. Sometimes, Ethan pounced without hesitation, and other times he was cautious, as if he was looking for a trap. They limited themselves to two or three games a day. The first one was a warmup match, and the second or third was the main event. The later games usually took longer, and this one was no exception.

Ethan leaned back in his chair and sighed. Then he reached out and placed his king on its side. He looked at Connor with a lopsided smile, his mother's blue eyes gleaming. "I almost beat you that time."

Connor smiled. "Almost."

"One day I will. If I hadn't put my knight… I should've made sure he was covered."

Connor pursed his lips and tilted his head slightly. "I used my rook to distract you."

Ethan nodded. "And you pressured my queen to distract me from my knight."

"It's your favorite piece. What would she think if you didn't rescue her?"

Ethan regarded him for a moment. "You know I'm not a little kid anymore. The queen doesn't have feelings. They're just pieces on the board."

Connor's eyebrows raised a little and his lips curved. "Then why did you feel so compelled to protect her?"

Ethan propped his chin on the heel of his hand, thinking. "She's the most powerful piece on the board. She can do anything."

Connor nodded and regarded his son for a moment. "She's still only one piece."

Ethan thought about it and stared hard at the chessboard. "You're talking about me having my knight camped out in the middle of the board. He was the real threat."

"You could have done a lot of damage."

Ethan blinked several times, his eyes studying the board. Then he raised his gaze, mouth slightly agape. "You were bluffing!"

Connor chuckled. "There it is."

Ethan shook his head and rolled his eyes. "I don't believe this. You were bluffing, and I fell for it."

Connor shrugged. "It was a gamble. Sometimes you win and others you lose. There's a lesson to be learned either way."

"Bluffing won't work on me again. I'm going to watch out for it."

"I'm sure you will. You'll probably try to fool me, too, I expect. Goad me into doing something I wouldn't have done otherwise."

Ethan frowned, sensing that the conversation had shifted to something else. "You're talking about what happened."

Connor's eyebrow raised. "I was talking about the game, but I suppose the same applies to what happened, too."

Ethan looked away and leaned back in his chair. "It was just a prank. We were having fun."

Connor cocked his head to the side a little and gave him the "dad" look. Ethan squirmed in his seat.

"*Maybe* we went a little too far," he finally admitted and looked at Connor as if trying to determine whether he'd said enough to end the uncomfortable conversation then and there.

Connor watched his son in silence, letting the tension build. Sometimes silence really could speak louder than words.

Ethan's brow furrowed and his jaw set for a few moments of sheer determination. Connor calmly met his son's gaze and continued to wait.

Ethan blinked. "Dad, it was a challenge. If I'd let it go, then I'd have to deal with Marcus, Andrew, and Isabela."

Connor softened his gaze a little. "What do they do?"

Ethan looked away and glowered. "They make trouble. They say things. Comment on stuff. Like every little thing is put under the microscope. They try to get the others against me." He looked at Connor with all the seriousness that an eleven-year-old boy could muster, and Connor thought he glimpsed the teenager Ethan would become. "If I let it go, then it just gets worse. I know Mom wants me to ignore it, turn the other cheek. I've tried, but it's…"

"Not right," Connor said.

Ethan stared at him for a second before nodding. "No, it's not right. Why should they be allowed to do whatever they want to people? Say whatever they want, and there's— Nothing ever changes."

"So, you thought you'd teach them a lesson."

"Yeah, I did."

"Show them that you're better than they are."

"I *am* better than they are."

"Smarter. Tougher," he said evenly.

Ethan grinned with excitement, eager to share what he'd done. "You should have seen their faces. I got my other friends to help. Planned the whole thing. They never knew what hit 'em. We didn't fight. We just scared them a little. Lured them to the maintenance shed at school, the one on the far side of the field. Then we locked them in the storage compartments. They thought they were going to be locked in there for the whole weekend."

Ethan giggled and looked at Connor, but then his smile slipped away.

Connor leaned forward. "I understand wanting to get back at someone who's bothering you. It can be frustrating. You thought you were giving them what they deserved, and it must have felt good to finally get them back for a change. Am I right?"

Ethan blinked, uncertain how to respond. "I know you're going to tell me I was wrong. Mom already did. Mr. Lopez at school did, too, but I don't care. I wouldn't take it back if I could."

Connor nodded a little. "No, I don't expect you would."

Ethan swallowed, looking uncertain. "Are you going to yell at me?"

Connor suppressed a grin and shook his head. He'd never really yelled at either of his children.

"Then what are you going to do? I know I've been here for the past month because of what happened. I kept expecting you to bring it up, but you didn't."

"I wanted to give you time to think about it."

"Why?"

Connor regarded his son for a moment. He recalled a conversation with Juan Diaz, who told him that kids were way smarter than we gave them credit for.

He exhaled through his nostrils. "Relax Ethan, I just want to talk to you about what happened."

His son leaned back in his chair for a second but kept his back straight. Connor thought he would rather be standing, but it was time his son learned a little bit of patience.

"Did you know that if an incident happens on the base where soldiers get hurt, the investigation can take days to resolve? Sometimes longer if it's really serious. The reason is that when we're angry or frustrated, we don't think clearly. The same thing happens when we're scared. Sometimes people need a few days to get the events straight in their minds."

"I *have* thought about it," Ethan began.

Connor held up his hand. "Hold on a second. Just listen. Sometimes it's not the thing that makes us angry that needs to be fixed."

Ethan's shoulders slumped and he sighed. "I don't understand."

"Look, that stuff with those other kids has been going on for a little while, right?"

Ethan nodded.

"Would you say it's kinda like a competition?"

Another nod. "But I had to get them back. The others—"

"There it is," Connor said. "The others. You didn't want to lose their respect. Were you afraid that if you didn't retaliate, they'd think you were afraid?"

Ethan nodded vehemently. "A coward. I'm not a coward."

"No, you're not, and you'll never be."

Ethan perked up at hearing this.

"These pranks have escalated—each one more devious than the previous one."

Ethan frowned thoughtfully. "Devious is such a strong word, Dad."

Connor felt a chuckle start to form and quickly smoothed his features. Instead, he gave his son the "dad" look again.

"All right, fine."

"Were people watching these things that you and the others did?"

Ethan's eyes widened and he nodded.

"So, you had an audience."

Ethan chewed on his bottom lip for a couple of seconds, and Connor wondered how long this mental tick would stick around.

"I guess—Yes, yes we did."

Connor smiled. Ethan knew better than to give him non-committal answers.

"Okay, there's a difference between standing up for yourself and performing for an audience. If this was just about getting back at someone, then why humiliate them with an audience? When does it stop? What's the end game?"

Ethan squished his lips together for a second. "When they stop antagonizing us."

"So, you want to have the last word. You want to get them back in such a way that they won't ever retaliate in kind. That about sum it up?"

His son shrugged. "Maybe."

"Ethan," Connor warned.

"Yes! Come on, Dad. We wanted to win."

Connor shook his head. "No, you wanted to dominate. You wanted them to know you're better than they are, and you wanted everyone else to know it as well."

Ethan looked away, gritting his teeth, and didn't respond.

"Look at me," Connor said gently.

Ethan lifted his gaze.

"There's a time when you have to make a stand. Believe me, I understand that, but there's also a time when it's just as important not to give the group what it wants. It becomes a cycle otherwise. You perform and the group approves. They *love* the performance. They're entertained. But that doesn't mean they like you, otherwise they wouldn't approve when the inevitable retaliation happens. And sometimes when you make a stand, it's *against* the group. It might cost you a few would-be friends, but you'll gain something far more valuable in the long run."

Ethen blew out a breath. "What would I gain?"

Connor stared at him for a moment. "Integrity, son. Self-respect. Never put passions above principles. You know what right and wrong are. You need to learn when to draw the line. When simple retaliation becomes something more."

Ethan blinked several times, frowning thoughtfully. "You want me to let them win?"

"No, but if there has to be a competition, then choose a better outlet that doesn't involve taking prisoners and locking them in a storage shed. You mentioned three kids' names before."

Ethan nodded. "Marcus, Andrew, and Isabela."

"Who's the leader?"

"Marcus mostly."

"Take on the leader first."

"How?"

"Run the obstacle course."

Ethan shook his head. "The ones at school are too easy."

"Fine, run the obstacle course on fire."

Ethan smiled.

"We can work on the challenge, but the question becomes whether you can live with the outcome."

"What do you mean?"

"What if you lose?"

Ethan hadn't considered it before. "I could challenge him again."

"Sure, and that's fine, but there are going to be times when you can't win."

"You've never lost."

Connor winced and then sighed. "Yes, I have, Ethan. No one wins all the time. The difference is that there are those who get up when they're knocked down, and those who don't. I just want you to think very carefully about what you'll do next time something like this happens again."

Ethan regarded him in a way that reminded him of Lenora

when she was trying to figure out a piece of Ovarrow history they'd brought back from some long-forgotten, uninhabited city.

"This is a lot like playing chess."

Connor grinned. "Yes, it is."

Ethan smiled.

"Okay, this next part is important."

Ethan's expression became serious.

"I know you want to solve your own problems, but sometimes you need to know when to get help. You can always come to me, son. No matter what. You can come to me or your mother. Even Lauren."

"Dad, she's a girl," Ethan said, as if that explained everything.

"She's your big sister. We're family. We stick together. That's the way it will always be."

Ethan smiled and nodded.

A priority comlink alert chimed from the holoscreen at his desk.

"Please put the pieces and board away while I take this," Connor said.

Ethan began cleaning up the chess pieces.

Connor went to his desk and acknowledged the comlink. Lieutenant McClintock's face appeared.

"I'm sorry to bother you, General Gates, but there's been an issue with the construction of the *Phantom's* I-Drive. It's affecting the project's critical path."

"You have the report there?"

"I do. I've just added it to the session, General," Lieutenant McClintock said and looked away from the screen. "General, I have a comlink request from Dr. Evans."

"Put her through," Connor said.

Oriana's face appeared. "Connor, I know it's your time with Ethan, but this couldn't wait."

"It's fine," Connor assured her. Oriana would never have contacted him if it wasn't important. "What happened with the *Phantom's* I-Drive?"

"The production run from the fabricators weren't configured properly. Entire sections of the I-Drive rings have to be taken off and replaced."

A spark of irritation seemed to heat his face and neck. "They're not salvageable at all?"

"We won't lose the material, but we can't use them as they are now. They don't meet specifications. The I-Drive won't function properly if we don't get this right," she said and scowled offscreen. "I just happened to run an integrity check of a sampling of sections."

Connor grimaced and resisted the urge to clench one of his fists. "Let me get this straight. You did your own due diligence and found something wrong."

"Yes."

Connor looked away while he considered it for a few moments. "That means we have to inspect every piece of the drive since construction began. These…" he began and shook his head again. "This is going to set us back—a lot."

Oriana nodded and bit her lip. "I know. I don't know how to fix it. I mean, I don't know how we can make up the lost time, Connor. I don't think we can."

"We might not be able to. In fact, we should accept that we're probably not going to be able to, but we can fix what went wrong. We had a quality assurance process that completely failed. I keep thinking, what if you hadn't checked anything? We could have lost the *Phantom* and her entire crew."

"Connor, this isn't my first time through something like this. It would be great if we could trust the process, but I've always been one to trust but verify."

"Same here, but I didn't expect a delay like this," Connor said. He shook his head again. "Unbelievable! This is what I want you to do. Assemble your team and get anyone else you need to do an integrity check of all the construction that's been done to this point. I can assign CDF personnel to you, but they'll need a procedure to follow. I'd say save the most critical systems for your team, but with the I-Drive..."

Oriana nodded. "The entire system is critical. We'll put together a process to figure out what's wrong. Then we can focus on what we need to do next," Oriana said.

Connor couldn't believe this was happening. Until that day, he'd thought they'd gained a few weeks, but this setback was going to push them beyond what they'd anticipated at the start. And the worst part of it was that he didn't have an actual end date for completion.

He glanced across the room where Ethan was checking his personal holoscreen.

"I'm going down to the fabricators and hand out some aggressive motivation," Connor said.

Oriana nodded. "I've seen Sean do the same thing. I guess he learned it from you."

"He learned a lot from many different people."

"I know it's only been a few hours since the *Infinity's* last check-in, but that can't be a coincidence," Oriana said.

"Their last check-in had them going to the planet. All the reports show that there hasn't been any sign of an advanced civilization there. Sean and Noah wouldn't fly into a trap."

"But the fact of two ships suffering a malfunction with the subspace comms system in the exact same region of the star system can't be coincidental."

Connor nodded. "You're right. You know, Noah thought he could increase the speed that the I-Drive was capable of."

"Yes, he did, but it's dependent upon the capabilities of our sensor arrays and the computing core."

"The *Phantom* is a heavy cruiser with computing power to spare. Perhaps we can make up the lost time on the actual journey," Connor said.

"It's possible, but without testing the drive, we don't know how the system will react."

Connor nodded. "So, we increase the I-Drive's output incrementally and observe. Do the same thing that Noah and the rest of the crew did but at a faster pace."

"We can try, Connor. I don't want to make promises that simply can't be delivered," Oriana replied and paused for a moment. "As much as I'd like to keep speculating about what's possible, I'm eager to get back to it. Otherwise, we'll never get there."

"Go. I'll follow up with you later."

13

As Noah sat in his ready room thinking about how quickly they'd put together a plan to investigate the whereabouts of the two away teams that left the *Ark II* more than six months ago, the door opened and Kara walked in, quirking an eyebrow at him.

"You're in my seat," she quipped.

Noah grinned. "Actually, your seat is the commander's chair on the bridge, but you can use my office here while I'm gone."

Kara pursed her full lips and moved with liquid grace, as if she were surveying his office. Her eyes twinkled. "I think I might make a few changes in here while you're gone. The place could use a woman's touch."

Noah chuckled and stood. "'A woman's touch.' Well, for you that means turning this place into an engineering lab. I've always wanted a workbench right over there," he said, gesturing toward the wall next to him.

Kara smiled. "I'll see what I can do," she said and then kissed him.

He regarded her for a moment. "I can't think of how to override the security lockdown on the *Ark II*."

"I'll figure something out."

"You could fly the ship away from the planet. Figure out where the subspace comms interference ends and get some help from COMCENT," he said.

Kara shook her head. "Can't take the risk. What if you run into trouble down there and need extraction? I don't want to be in the outer system talking to COMCENT and have you guys waiting for us to get back and pull your asses out of the fire."

Noah tilted his head to the side a little. "Assuming we're going to find nothing but trouble on the planet, are you?"

"It's a safe assumption. If everything was hunky-dory on that planet, we wouldn't have to investigate where the *Ark II*'s away teams went because we'd be talking to them right now."

"Good point, but I'd rather think positive. Maybe they've been stuck down there for some reason. They'd have brought enough survival equipment to live this long," he said. She gave him a long look. "Okay, I won't mention it again, except for this. We go down there and find where they're camped. We'll check in with you, and if everything is fine, *then* you'll consider flying the ship to the edge of the star system and reporting back to COMCENT."

"Maybe."

Noah sighed. "I could make it an order."

Kara chuckled. "This isn't the military, Noah. If it was, I'd outrank you and make *you* stay here."

Noah frowned. "You don't think I'd have been promoted by now if I'd remained in the CDF?"

Kara raised her eyebrows.

"Maybe not a colonel, but surely I'd be a major by now… You know what—"

"Forget I said it, Noah. I'll think about it, but I'm going to wait for you to check in more than once before I'll even consider leaving the area. Besides, there are other ways to gain access to the *Ark II*," Kara said.

Noah shot her a warning look. "I thought we talked about taking unnecessary risks."

Kara shrugged. "No reason not to plan something in case today's unnecessary risks become tomorrow's necessities."

Noah smiled in amusement. "Very good, love. I'll have to remember that one. I'll keep it up here," he said, gently tapping the side of his head with his index finger.

Kara rolled her eyes and palmed the door controls.

"Too bad we didn't bring any comms drones with us. Could have used some right about now."

Kara stepped into the corridor. "I'll monitor you from here. Stay safe, love."

"You, too," he replied and walked away from her.

When he glanced behind, he saw Kara watching him go. She'd crossed her arms in front of her chest. The lighting above her cast small shadows over her face as the distance between them increased. There was something in the way she stood that made him slow down, drawing the moment out as long as he could. She looked vulnerable and determined at the same time. She was worried about him and intent on watching him leave. She wouldn't look away, but worrying about him also wouldn't keep her from doing what needed to be done. He threw her one last wave, and she did the same. Turning down the corridor, he lost sight of her and headed for the elevators.

The elevator stopped a couple of decks below and Carter Lachlan, Ezra Coffman, and Kyle Regan entered.

Noah smiled at the science team. They were all carrying their gear except Lachlan. "Are you going to join us, Dr. Lachlan?"

"I was planning to, but the data collected by the observer satellites show a number of anomalies that I think are worth investigating from here," Lachlan replied.

The planetary scientist had been determined to join them on the away team. Whatever he'd found in the sensor logs must have been significant for him to change his mind.

"I figured I could catch up to you later. Besides, Kyle and Ezra wouldn't miss the opportunity to go down to the planet," Lachlan continued.

Noah nodded. "There'll be plenty for us to do. First priority is to find the *Ark II* away team, but I'll make sure there's time for both of you to complete your respective assessments of the area."

Kyle Regan's specialization was in biology, while Ezra Coffman was a geologist.

"Where's Gibbs? Despite there being no evidence of advanced life here, I'd still like to have his linguistic talents available should we need him."

Kyle hitched his shoulder up, adjusting the strap of the bag he carried. "He's already heading down to the hangar. Couldn't wait to go."

Noah nodded. They were all eager to visit the planet. As with most scientists Noah had met, nothing beat working in the field.

The elevator stopped on H-Deck where the hangar was located. Lachlan and Kyle Regan were out first and stepped over to the side, talking.

After a short corridor, the doors to the hangar bay were open. Noah noticed Ezra Coffman frowning in thought.

"Are you all right?" Noah asked.

Ezra blinked as if he'd startled her but then smiled a little. "I'm fine, I guess."

They stepped off the elevator.

"If you have concerns, I'd like to know what they are."

Ezra inhaled and sighed. "I'm... it's the soldiers, Captain. Usually, authority during off-world missions rests squarely with them."

Off-world usually meant traveling to another universe, but even though what they were doing was different, he thought he understood her hesitation.

"They're here to keep us safe. I'm still the mission commander."

Ezra nodded. "I'm glad to hear you say that, meaning no offense to any of the soldiers who are coming with us. I just want to be sure that Kyle and I really will be able to study the area while we're down there."

Noah had retired from the military quite a long time ago, but he was comfortable around soldiers, more so than specialists who had never been part of the CDF.

Ezra moved to stand with Kyle and Lachlan.

As Noah walked into the hangar bay, he saw two Pathfinder shuttles being loaded on the far side. He also noticed CDF soldiers gathered on the other side of the shuttles. He heard shouting coming from there as well.

"Donlon, you secure that crap right now or I'll do it for you!"

"Sergeant Staggart, what's going on here?" Noah heard Sean ask.

"Colonel, Private Donlon thought the other soldiers were interested in his opinion, so I reminded him that opinions aren't part of standard-issue equipment, sir," Sergeant Staggart replied.

Noah's wrist computer buzzed an alert and he checked it.

"What's the problem, Private Donlon?" Sean asked.

The message contained the most recent data dumps from the observer satellites. He started reading while listening to the soldiers at the same time.

"Colonel, me and some of the other soldiers were wondering why you're not in command of the mission," Private Donlon said.

Noah frowned and looked up from his personal holoscreen. The soldiers were on the other side of the shuttle, so he could only see their legs.

"Captain Barker is the mission commander. We're guests aboard this ship," Sean replied.

"Understood, Colonel," Private Donlon said.

There were a few moments of silence and then Noah heard Sean ask, "Show of hands, how many of you are wondering about this?"

"Permission to speak, Colonel," Sergeant Staggart said.

"Go ahead," Sean replied.

"This is no slight against Captain Barker, Colonel, but this is an away mission that will be danger-close. This type of mission should come under the auspice of the CDF, sir," Sergeant Staggart said.

"Oh, I see what the problem is here," Sean said. "Those of you who agree with Private Donlon and Sergeant Staggart here believe that Noah Barker isn't capable of commanding our mission to the planet's surface."

No one answered him.

"Normally, I wouldn't stand here and take the time to explain this to you. You're here to do a job and follow orders. However, since we've got a few minutes and we're all in the opinion-giving mood, I think I'll share a few things with you. I'll say this here and now—none of you have done even a fraction of what Noah Barker has done for this colony. You probably think that since he doesn't wear the same uniform he's not that dangerous. It's been a while since he was in the CDF, so he's not dangerous. Am I right?"

Sean paused for a few moments.

"Am I right!" he asked again with an edge in his tone.

Several soldiers voiced their agreement.

"It's all right. You can say it. He's not here."

More soldiers voiced their agreement. Noah frowned, wondering where Sean was going with this.

I'm right here.

He was listening in on their conversation but knew better than to go barging over there now. Better to let Sean sort this out.

"Is everything all right, Captain?"

Noah twisted his neck, startled. Lieutenant Jesse Rhoades was approaching him from behind. He must have just come from the elevators.

He grimaced. "Yes, I was just listening to Colonel Quinn give the soldiers a pep talk."

Rhoades smiled and nodded. "He does have a way with them."

Noah nodded and they both stood there, waiting for Sean to continue.

"Noah Barker is among the most dangerous people in the colony. Certainly more so than anyone on this ship, including me," Sean said. "Did you know that the current iteration of the Nexstar combat suit we brought with us was only possible because of the work Captain Barker has done? The HADES V missile—you know, the one that saved us from the Vemus and helped us defeat the Krake? Yeah, that was him as well. Most weapons development for both our fleet ships, down to the AR-74 you've been trained with, has been directly influenced or improved upon by his work. Imagine, if you will, what our lives would have been if he'd never done those things. And those are just a few of the things he's done. You're standing in the latest thing that's come from him. We've traveled three lightyears in the span of a couple of months. But you want to question his leadership because he doesn't appear to be dangerous? That he'll balk at making tough decisions?"

Sean paused again. Lieutenant Rhoades glanced at Noah and shifted uncomfortably.

"He might. It happens to the best of us, and I'll be there for him if it does. What I won't be doing is spending my time questioning whether he's the right man for the job. He is, unequivocally. I'd follow him to hell and back if that's what it took. He'd do the same for me. You're lucky that he's here. And if the shit hits the airlock down on that planet, you can be sure Noah Barker will be the last person cowering to the side like a sniveling wreck, wondering what to do next. Is that clear!"

"Yes, Colonel!" a chorus of voices replied.

Noah glanced behind him and saw that Kyle Regan and Ezra Coffman were also standing there. Not knowing what to say to any of them, Noah walked toward the shuttle.

Sean came around the loading ramp and spotted him.

Noah walked over to Sean and leaned in. "Good speech."

Sean's eyes widened a little and then he tipped his head to the side. "Meant every word."

Noah grinned nervously and winced. "And now I've just shattered this whole hero persona you worked so hard to build."

Sean looked at him with a solemn expression. "Years to build, annihilated in seconds. We're doomed before we even start."

He nodded. "I'm going to go cower on the shuttle over here."

Sean grinned and gestured for Noah to lead the way.

They checked the shuttles' systems. Pilots Gil Parnell and Sima Bruhanski went through their pre-flight checks.

The Pathfinder shuttles were capable of carrying heavy loads, so they were able to bring a lot of equipment with them. The CDF soldiers wore their Nexstar combat suits, while Noah and others wore civilian Pathfinder suits. They shared some foundational design principles of the Nexstar combat suits but without the armament and armor. They'd be able to keep up with the CDF soldiers, which was enough for Noah. The Pathfinder suits were designed for exploration in almost any terrain they would come across. The suit computers supported scientific instruments to assist in the assessment of their surroundings, and they could be customized to the individual wearer's capabilities and specializations. They just lacked things like heavy weapons, but that's why the soldiers were here.

Dwight Gibbs climbed aboard the shuttle and looked at Noah. "Any chance I could get one of those?" he asked, gesturing toward the AR-74 Noah carried.

Gibbs was a brilliant young man who was adept at linguistics and psychology, with a specialization in alien first contact.

"Unless you've been in the CDF or received specialized training for it, you'll have to stick with the sidearm that comes with your suit," Noah replied.

Gibbs nodded, looking disappointed. "If I'd known that, I would have tried to get qualified on the way here."

Noah shook his head. "Wouldn't have worked. Certification requires actually using the weapon for a designated amount of time to build up proficiency. None of these guys are going to give you their weapons, and it's not like you'd be allowed to fire a weapon on the ship."

Gibbs shrugged. "Oh well, can't blame a guy for trying."

Kyle grinned, and Gibbs looked at him with a frown.

"What?" Gibbs asked.

"I was just wondering if you've had a lot of practice saying that recently." Gibbs frowned and Kyle grinned. "You know, after a woman refuses your advances?"

Noah chuckled.

Gibbs rolled his eyes and smiled. "Law of percentages, gents. The more shots you take, the better your chances are going to be."

"Keep telling yourself that," Kyle said. "I prefer to pick more amenable recipients."

Ezra looked over at them. "We're women, not targets, amenable recipients, or anything else you can think of. You overcome that hurdle and you'll go a long way toward getting a yes from us."

Kyle and Gibbs laughed.

"That reminds me, Ezra," Gibbs began.

"Don't even think about it," she warned.

Gibbs shrugged. Then he stepped into his Pathfinder suit and it closed around him, securing him inside.

Noah walked toward the front of the shuttle, and Sean met him up there.

"We're ready to go," Sean said.

Noah nodded. "All right, Gil. Take us out of here."

14

The *Infinity's* hangar bay could be sealed into multiple sections to accommodate the two shuttles, as well as the smaller drones that were used for hull repairs and maintenance.

"Hangar section is cleared, and we're authorized to leave, Captain," Gil Parnell said.

"Take us out," Noah replied.

Gil nodded. "*Infinity*, this is *Pathfinder 1*. We're departing. Don't go far away now."

"Acknowledged, *Pathfinder 1*. We'll stay in the neighborhood. Safe travels," Jessica Yu replied over comlink with a hint of amusement in her voice.

The atmospheric shield became active, and after the hangar bay doors opened, the shuttle engaged its engines and Gil flew them away from the *Infinity*. A few minutes later, the HUD showed that *Pathfinder 2* had cleared the ship as well. Maneuvering thrusters swung the shuttle's nose over sixty degrees, and a distant view of Zeta-Alpha-5 appeared on the main holoscreen. Large areas of the planet's atmosphere were a reddish-violet color, while other areas seemed to gleam with greens and blues. Noah's gaze slid toward several bright areas that pierced the clouds on the dark side of the planet, as if someone were shining an intense light from the surface. As he was trying to think of a reason for those brighter areas, he heard Kyle mention it being some kind of massive bioluminescence.

"Quite the view," Gil said in appreciation.

"Yes, it is," Noah agreed.

He brought up subspace comms and tried to reach the *Infinity*. They'd only traveled a short distance, but the subspace transceiver couldn't establish a connection.

He looked at Sean. "I didn't think it would work but wanted to try it anyway."

Sean nodded. "Don't know what it could be that's interfering with it."

"Me either. There won't be much of a lag in comms once we reach the planet's surface, so it shouldn't cause too much of a problem for us," Noah said.

"If there's interference, we can use the satellites in orbit to communicate with the *Infinity*," Sean replied.

The two Pathfinder shuttles flew toward the alien planet. It was exotic in so many ways, but life had definitely evolved on the planet.

Kyle Regan joined Noah near the front of the shuttle.

"It doesn't look smaller than New Earth. The cloud cover is estimated to be at sixty-five point… let's call it sixty-six percent. That's not bad, considering, I guess. I wonder how the shuttles will perform in the atmosphere?" Kyle said.

"What do you mean?" Sean asked.

"The atmosphere is dense in comparison to back home."

Sean nodded. "It'll be fine. These shuttles can handle the extra load, so there shouldn't be a problem with it at all."

"It's us that'll need to adjust," Noah said.

Kyle frowned. "Us? Why would we need to adjust? I figured with the lower gravity it would be easier for us to get around."

"It's going to be different," Noah replied. "The suits will help us get around, but with a denser atmosphere, it's going to feel like we're experiencing resistance every step of the way, at least until the suit computers figure out how to compensate for it."

Kyle nodded in understanding. "At least we won't be walking around without them."

"What is it about the atmosphere that makes it so different?" Gil asked.

Kyle looked at Noah with raised eyebrows, and Noah nodded for him to answer.

Kyle looked at Gil. "It's the Xenon gas in the atmosphere. It's heavier, but it's pretty much nonreactive and odorless, too. And there's enough of it that we're going to feel it once we get there. Also, the high concentrations of carbon dioxide will make things feel different."

Gil looked at Noah. "In the unlikely event that one of our helmets breaks, is it instant death, or can we survive for a few minutes?"

"It's not instant death," Noah replied and frowned a little. "Were you at the briefing for this?"

"I was replacing one of the control panels on the shuttle, so I missed part of it."

"The atmosphere has high amounts of carbon dioxide, which makes it poisonous for us. Without a helmet, you'd start feeling the effects of hypoxia in under a minute and probably lose consciousness around then as well. Between the seven-to-ten-minute mark, you'd be dead. On the other hand, you'd have a better chance of surviving on the planet than you would if you lost your helmet out there," Noah said, lifting his chin toward the main holoscreen.

"Understood. Thank you, Captain," Gil replied.

Noah looked at Sean. "I wonder if there's a way to make a filter that we could use to breathe the atmosphere. Something in case of an emergency in a habitat unit or something like that."

Sean considered it for a moment. "Without an envirosuit?"

Noah nodded.

"We should be able to, once we get actual atmospheric samples to gauge the equipment."

A CDF soldier walked toward them from the back of the shuttle.

"Captain Barker, Colonel Quinn, I have a data connection to the observer satellite network," Specialist Denny said.

He was tall, well over two meters, with enough muscle to warrant increased protein packs for meal consumption. What surprised Noah was that he was the platoon's technical specialist. By all appearances, Noah expected him to serve in the heavy infantry division, but he was wrong. It would seem that tech specialists came in all shapes and sizes.

Specialist Denny had his personal holoscreen active. They moved away from the cockpit and Denny expanded it so they could all see.

"I was able to extract the timestamps for when the two *Ark II* shuttles last accessed the satellite network. It looks like they were focusing their reconnaissance grid between three thousand and four thousand kilometers north of the equatorial line on these two continents," Specialist Denny said.

The planet, while smaller than New Earth, was home to over nine continents spread among vast oceans. New Earth had one supercontinent centered on the equator and was surrounded by an immense ocean. Noah remembered the seven major continents of Old Earth and wondered whether they would break apart after millions of years, similar to what he was seeing on the holoscreen. Ezra would know, but she was sitting near the back of the shuttle. He'd ask her about it later.

"Milder climate in those areas, but not by much," Kyle said.

Noah nodded and looked at Specialist Denny. "Can we narrow it down further than that?"

"I'm sorry, sir, I can't. They just queried the satellites for specific regional data that fit certain criteria. The check-in that confirms where they were going would most likely have been sent to the *Ark II*," Specialist Denny replied.

Noah looked at the highlighted regions on the holoscreen. "That's assuming they actually had an established flight plan, which I'm not convinced they had."

Sean frowned. "They should have filed one."

"And there should have been a small crew awake on the *Ark II*, but there wasn't anyone. This was just supposed to be a scouting mission. Maybe they were going to build a base camp to scout different areas. They must have known that subspace had stopped working, but they could have sent mission updates to the *Ark II* in other ways."

Sean nodded with lips pressed together. "You make a compelling argument."

Noah twitched his eyebrows in acknowledgement. "I keep getting the feeling that they weren't sure if they were going to start a colony here. For some reason, Saul Ashworth only took a small team down to the planet's surface to see what the viability was. The lockdown keeps throwing me off. I can't figure out why."

"Could be his reaction to loss of subspace comms. He didn't know what he was dealing with, so he took what he thought was the appropriate action," Sean replied.

"You're probably right. Lars or Xander Ludwig, head of security, could have advised him to enable the lockdown."

Sean nodded.

Lars Mallory was Xander Ludwig's second-in-command for the *Ark II*'s security forces. Noah supposed he could imagine Lars recommending the lockdown, especially if there was no one waiting for them to return. But it wouldn't have been much of a burden to wake three more people on the *Ark II* so someone was at least monitoring for them.

Kyle exhaled and shook his head. "I can't imagine they'd come all this way and not stay here."

Sean considered it for a moment. "They did have contingency plans if the planet wasn't habitable, but I wouldn't necessarily classify this planet as uninhabitable. Challenging to build a colony, but hardly something that required them bypassing the star system entirely."

Noah nodded. "Breathable atmosphere aside, it has a lot going for it. We haven't even gotten there, but just by the sight of the planet any number of scientists would be falling over themselves to study it."

"They'd never be able to go outside without an envirosuit on," Specialist Denny said.

"Not at first," Kyle replied. "We don't know the soil composition either, so we can't rule out whether it would support plants that are edible for us. You know, we all need our veggies."

Denny looked unconvinced and shrugged a muscular shoulder. "I'm just the tech specialist, but I'm pretty sure I heard someone say that terraforming the planet would be unethical."

"Oh, I didn't mean terraforming the entire planet. I was thinking of just a small area. Basically, build our own bubble. A dome. See if there's a way to coexist. That sort of thing," Kyle replied.

Denny glanced at Noah and Sean for a second. "I'd take living on New Earth over living here anytime. At least there we've got fresh air to breathe and an ecosystem more compatible with humans."

Kyle shrugged and looked at the main holoscreen. "Not every star system is going to have a veritable garden-world like New Earth. I'm still amazed that the astronomers of Old Earth managed to find it at all."

Noah tilted his head. "There must have been some new breakthroughs after the *Ark* left Earth, or they managed to analyze more star systems. There was a twenty-year span before the *Ark's* mission parameters were overridden."

"While they were fighting the Vemus," Sean said. "Finding the star system with New Earth was a secret they'd hoped to keep, so there was a certain amount of desperation at work."

Speculation on the twenty years of lost history when the original *Ark* left the Sol system had been discussed and debated at length by members of the colony. They had fragments of data. There were plenty of theories, but they'd never really know until the probes they'd sent reported back or they sent an expedition to the Sol system to see if anyone had survived.

Sean arched an eyebrow toward him.

Noah shrugged. "I was just thinking that there's a good possibility we could send someone back to find out what really happened."

Kyle's eyes widened. "You mean back to Earth."

Noah nodded.

The young scientist blinked several times and then exhaled slowly.

"One thing at a time," Sean said, and Kyle nodded. "Let's figure out what happened here first, then make it back home. After that, we can decide where we go."

"You'd have to bring more than one ship on an expedition like that. If there are any Vemus still around…" Kyle said and paused. He shook his head. "Never mind, I'll just focus on this planet now."

Noah smiled and then looked at Sean for a moment. "Gil, set us up for at least one orbital pass over those two continents. Let's see if we can detect any distress beacons."

"Course entered, Captain," Gil Parnell replied.

Noah turned toward Specialist Denny. "Would you mind monitoring the sensors? Do a sweep as we fly over the targets?"

"Yes, sir, I can do that," Specialist Denny said.

The big CDF soldier sat in the copilot's seat and brought up his own holoscreen. His lack of hesitation at accepting Noah's request meant that Sean must have ordered the soldiers to cooperate with the civilian crew. As long as the request being made was reasonable, cooperation would be given.

The Pathfinder shuttles flew toward the planet and altered their trajectory so they could settle into lower orbit. The two continents they were interested in were practically neighbors, but it still took them some time to pass over them both. No signals were detected.

They orbited the planet, allowing their sensors to scan it. The data that came in confirmed what the observer satellites had already detected.

"Let's try holding our position above that first continent there," Noah said.

The shape of the continents appeared as if there were a planet-sized belt that only managed to break through the ocean's surface through somewhat mountainous terrain. From what they could observe through the cloud cover, the terrain varied from mountains to plains and everything between. It would take much longer for them to scan the entire planet, but at least they had a high-level view of what the surface was like. Many of the continents had an abundance of forests and jungles that spanned the entire landmass in some areas.

They'd completed their first pass around the planet, and Gil instructed the shuttle's engines to match the speed of the planet's rotation, putting them in a geostationary orbit. *Pathfinder 2* went into geostationary orbit over the second target continent.

They waited while telemetry data continued to update on the shuttle's systems. Periodic data bursts were sent to the *Infinity*.

At the forty-minute mark, Kyle Regan could stand it no longer. "How long are we going to wait here? What are we waiting for anyway?"

Noah shared a look with Sean. "Should be within the next ten to fifteen minutes or so, wouldn't you think?"

Sean nodded. "That sounds about right."

Kyle frowned at both of them. "What sounds about right?"

"Patience," Noah chided.

Kyle chuckled and raised his hands in front of his chest. "I have plenty of patience," he said and leaned forward a little. "I can be the beacon of patience, but will someone answer my question? Please?"

Noah arched an eyebrow toward Sean. "I don't think he's that patient."

Sean nodded. "He doesn't sound that patient to me. What is it about these guys? I bet Ezra has patience. See her way back there, working away, probably making good use of her time, too."

The three of them looked down the length of the shuttle. Ezra Coffman had two holoscreens open and was focused on the data windows.

"She's just working away," Sean said.

"That's because she hates flying… Maybe *hate* is too strong a word. She doesn't like it, so she's just making herself busy," Kyle said defensively.

Noah pursed his lips. "I think she's preparing herself by reviewing the most current data. Maybe she's even going over the analysis she plans to do once we get down there."

Kyle's mouth hung open halfway between a smile and surprise. "I'm prepared…Wait a second, when did I become the target here?"

"Since you started asking too many questions," Sean replied with the hint of a whiny nasally tone.

"Are we there yet?" Noah asked.

A laugh bubbled out of Sean, and Noah joined him. Gil and Denny did as well.

Kyle rolled his eyes and bowed. "Thank you. No, thank you, sir! I'll be your inflight entertainment. Please remember to return for our evening performance."

Noah smiled and tossed the young scientist a nod. He'd been on the receiving end of Connor's humor enough times to appreciate how it could ease the tension.

An alert appeared on Specialist Denny's workstation. "I think we've got something. It's a weak signal. It's fragmented, but it does match colonial communications protocols."

Noah peered at the alert. "Good, can you get a lock on it?"

Specialist Denny entered a few commands and a waypoint flashed on a region of the continent.

"Send that over to *Pathfinder 2*. Tell Bruhanski to hold her position for another hour. If no other signals are detected, then she's to follow us here," Noah said.

"Yes, Captain," Specialist Denny replied.

"Gil, send another data burst to the *Infinity* with this information," Noah said.

He wasn't going to take anything for granted. He'd keep Kara and the *Infinity* as up to date with the current situation as he could.

Kyle eyed him for a moment, and Noah grinned.

"Want to know how we suspected there would be a distress beacon?" Noah asked.

Kyle leaned back against the bulkhead and nodded. "Yes, please, thank you."

"It's likely an automated signal. Can't be sure until we get close enough to get a clear signal. The beacon is probably from one of the *Ark II*'s shuttles, but since it's been here for months, it only transmits intermittently to conserve power."

Kyle considered it for a few moments. "How do you know it's automated?"

"Because," Sean said, "if it wasn't, there would have been a comlink after. The power for the transmitter must be almost gone if the signal is that weak."

"Couldn't it just be some other kind of interference?" Kyle asked.

Sean shook his head. "Doubtful. Also, the team down there is more concerned about surviving than making someone responsible to manually send a distress beacon."

Kyle nodded. "I hope they're still there for us to find."

"It's time we find out. Gil, take us in," Noah said.

15

The *Pathfinder 1* entered Zeta-Alpha-5's atmosphere, and the nav computer helped Gil compensate for the thicker air. The region they flew toward had an extensive cloud cover that was extremely high in the atmosphere, much higher than Noah would've expected.

They'd sat down and strapped themselves in before making the drop. Noah and Sean sat behind Gil and Denny.

Noah watched the active holoscreen displaying multiple windows online with live external video feeds. Soon after the shuttle breached the troposphere, they were engulfed in dense, pinkish clouds.

"This reminds me of something," Kyle said and pressed his lips together. "I just read about this the other day. Some kind of pink... cotton candy! That's what it looks like." He sighed explosively. "I'm glad I could remember what it was. Otherwise, it would have been nagging me all day."

Sean eyed him for a moment. "The struggle is real," he said dryly.

Noah chuckled. "The coloring might resemble that, but the layers of clouds have more of a gradient effect."

He thought Dr. Lachlan could explain why there were layers and made a mental note to ask him about it.

The shuttle emerged from a thick layer of clouds, but it didn't descend long before they were at the next level. Before they'd fully submerged, Noah thought he saw a dark shape flying nearby, slightly disrupting the blanket of clouds.

He leaned toward the holoscreen and blinked several times.

"What is it?" Sean asked.

"I thought I saw something just before we entered this next level of clouds."

Sean considered it for a moment. "Specialist Denny, do an aerial sensor sweep, see if anything shows up on our scanners."

"At once, Colonel," Denny replied.

Noah brought the sensor feed onto the holoscreen. Several returns came back almost immediately.

"What is that?" Kyle asked.

Noah shook his head. "I don't know," he replied and waited for data to populate the scan-return data.

"They're showing up as biomasses," Sean said.

Kyle's eyes widened. "Biological! But with scans that big they'd have to be…"

"My God!" Noah said.

An enormous creature flew by the shuttle with a languid grace, making them seem tiny and inconsequential in comparison. The white underlay of its wings flashed with each flap. The creature had four sets of leathery wings that it angled as it soared through the air. It had a white underbelly with a reddish top layer that had swirls of lighter colors, allowing it to blend in. It dipped its large, wedge-shaped head downward and flapped its front wings while the rear wings angled to help the massive creature turn. It had a long, dark tail with curling ridges that angled upward.

Kyle gasped. "Look at the size of that thing. It could swallow us whole if it wanted to."

Noah's eyes widened as he saw more creatures appear on the holoscreen. There were so many that he quickly lost count of them all. Their craggy top half looked more like the side of a mountain that had broken away and taken flight. The only time he'd seen creatures this big was in the ocean. The graceful way they flew reminded him of the large creatures that resided deep in the ocean.

"It's got to be the denser atmosphere and lower gravity. It could never fly like this back home," Noah said.

"Their bone composition could be different as well. What should we call them?" Kyle asked.

"Keep it simple," Sean replied. "Flying whales. It's straight to the point and easy to remember. Are we getting a recording of this?"

Noah nodded. "Absolutely. Look at how many of them there are. Are they all together as part of the same group, or is this something else?"

Several flying whales seemed to notice them and angled toward them as if coming for a closer look.

"A convention of flying whales… Shit, they're coming right for us," Kyle said.

Noah watched the video feed for a few moments.

"What do you want me to do, Captain?" Gil asked.

"Nothing. They're just curious. Keep us on our current trajectory. Maintain speed and heading. Let's not spook them."

One of the creatures' enormous head lifted, revealing a grouping of large eyes under a thick cranial brow line. Its mouth was shut, so there was no way for them to tell if it had any teeth.

"See the short spikes on its back but none on the bottom? Whatever hunts these things attacks from above," Sean said.

Noah considered this for a few moments. "Ambush predators."

"Yup. They likely use the cloud cover to attack," Sean replied.

"Why not attack them from underneath?" Gil asked. His voice sounded a little strained.

Noah didn't want them to get any closer than necessary, but he knew running at this point might cause them to chase instinctively. It would be much better if they could appear as innocuous as possible.

"That's easy," Kyle said. "Attacking a creature that size could make it fall on you, or you could become trapped. Attack from above and you have a way to escape."

Gil turned and looked at Kyle for a moment, unsure whether he should believe him.

Noah nodded.

"Huh," Gil said. "I wonder what they eat."

"Probably not anything like us," Sean said.

"How do you know?" Gil asked.

"Everything about it is designed for defense."

Kyle nodded. "That's right. It must feed off something found in these clouds. Maybe elsewhere too. I wish I could get a sample." He looked at Noah hopefully.

"We can send a drone out later to collect samples. Right now, let's just focus on reaching the ground and finding that shuttle."

"Understood," Kyle replied.

Noah enabled the audio feed, which had filters in place to all but eliminate the wind noise. After a few moments they heard deep, low rumblings that seemed to move all around them. It didn't quite sound like thunder. Despite the cloud cover, they weren't flying through a storm system.

Several high-pitched squeals came from farther away. They sounded high in tone and then dropped, as if whatever was making the noise had plunged away.

"They don't like that," Kyle said and gestured toward one of the video feeds.

The flying whales clustered in tighter formations, and Noah couldn't help but be impressed. He was a fair pilot himself, but flying in defensive formations was something only combat pilots were adept at doing. Seeing these massive creatures do it was awe inspiring.

Noah cycled through the video feeds until he had a view from beneath the shuttle. Forty meters below was the craggy, roughened hide of a flying whale.

"Gil," Noah said, trying not to alarm the pilot. "We're not in the best location here. Ease us forward. We don't want to spook them any more than they already are."

"Oh, okay, I see it. Okay, I've got it now," Gil replied.

The shuttle's velocity increased, and they began to distance themselves from the behemoth underneath them.

Kyle exhaled with a soft whistle. "You know I'd hate to be caught under these things when they cut loose."

"What do you mean cut loose?" Specialist Denny asked.

Kyle's lips lifted. "Biological excrement. I bet it's quite a sight when it happens."

"Eww, that's disgusting," Specialist Denny said, shaking his head and shivering at the thought. "Man, now I can't get that image out of my head."

"What image? We haven't seen them even so much as—"

"That's about enough of that," Noah cut in. He didn't want to imagine it himself.

Something white sped by in a blur, and highly pitched screeches seemed to sound from all around them. Another white thing streaked by the shuttle and banked around, rolling through the air. It had a dome-shaped head, with a heavily muscled neck and body. Two large, leathery wings stretched over its thick bones and the length of the body except for a long tail. The creature was sleek and powerfully built. It folded its wings in and rammed one of the flying whales' bodies with its thick skull. Dozens more did the same, pelting the massive creatures. Noah winced at the force of impact, imagining the sound of a powerful smack as the two creatures collided. The predators used their talons to grip the flying whale's hide and tear into it with powerful teeth. Sounds of screeches surrounded them, and the sky filled with the white predators.

Noah's mouth hung open as he watched the attack. The white predators screeched as they dive-bombed the flying whales, their battle cries cutting off the moment they made contact. The dome-like shape of their heads was designed for ramming their prey. There were so many of them that it seemed as if the attack would never end.

The nearest flying whales bellowed a call that was taken up by the others. They flapped their powerful wings, causing them to thrust higher in seconds. More answering calls sounded from nearby.

Sean seized the video feed controls so they could see above them. Another flying whale flew above and steadied itself. Then the whale being attacked flapped its giant wings even harder, and its body rose in an almost elegant, fleshy wave as it slammed into the other whale.

"They're crashing into each other!" Kyle said.

Noah watched as the entire spectacle repeated itself among the other whales. Some of them rolled onto their backs and sank down onto another one. Then they'd break apart and do it again.

"They're defending themselves! They're rubbing each other to get rid of the predators."

The white predators fell limply off the whales, their faces covered with dark blood. Some of them tried to fly with broken wings and smashed bodies, but they quickly faded from view. Not all of them fell. Others held on, somehow missing the onslaught of smashing bodies.

More of the flying whales slammed into each other, and Gil swung the shuttle out of the way, narrowly avoiding being crushed.

"Gil, get us out of here!" Noah said.

"You don't have to tell me twice!" Gil said and shoved the accelerator all the way up.

The shuttle's engines burst full of energy and their velocity increased.

"Don't just go forward. Take us down. It's the only way out of this mess," Sean said.

The shuttle angled downward, but Gil didn't take them full on vertical. They were still in the clouds and there was no way for them to see what was beyond. The scanners detected more flying whales, all of which seemed to be in some kind of defensive frenzy.

One of the flying whales' thick wingtips grazed the back of the shuttle, nearly putting them into a spin, but the stabilizing thrusters kept them from flipping over.

"These are definitely not so friendly skies!" Kyle said.

The Pathfinder shuttle had nowhere near the agility of a CDF combat shuttle. It was meant for transport of equipment and personnel, but Gil squeezed out every bit of agility the shuttle could give and then some.

The shuttle sank into an angular dive, and Noah held onto his seat. There wasn't anything for him to do but watch, hope, and pray. Proximity alarms sounded mere moments before another group of flying whales were seen being harried by the white predators.

The shuttle banked hard, stressing the inertia dampeners for a few moments, and then Gil leveled them off. The cloud layer lessened, and they could see a vast forest below.

Noah blew out a breath and looked at Sean. "Next time we should bring a few Talon V Stingers to fly escort."

Sean grinned, gesturing toward the roof. "Or put some point-defense cannons on this thing. Although I doubt those things would hardly notice."

"That's it," Kyle said. "Those white predator things. I'm calling them howlers."

"They screeched," Sean replied.

"Screechers then."

"It only sounded like a howl because they dove in from above. Pretty high above actually," Noah said.

The skies cleared, but Noah could still see the fight going on in the distance. "I wonder how long that will go on."

Kyle frowned at the holoscreen. "I've never seen pack hunters attack quite on this scale before."

"Did you forget about the ryklars?" Noah asked.

Kyle nodded slowly. "No, but they were genetically modified and conditioned to respond to signals that caused them to attack."

"They also hunted. If these… screechers are anything like the ryklars, they'll keep attacking until they get a meal out of it," Noah replied.

Kyle scratched the side of his head. "I wonder how often they actually kill one of them. Those whales are large enough to survive the attack. I bet once I review the recordings, I'll find evidence of previous attacks. Scars and whatnot."

Noah looked at Sean. "We should create a scanning profile to detect those creatures so we can avoid them in the future."

Sean nodded and looked at Denny.

"I think I can do that, sir," Specialist Denny said.

"Add it to the list, Specialist. We're below the clouds now, so let's focus on trying to find the *Ark II's* away team," Sean said.

"Understood, Colonel."

They flew over a dense forest canopy that ranged in color from greens and blues to areas that were a blend of reds to violets. Noah tried to catch a view of the ground but couldn't. Smaller creatures flew among the treetops. They were too far away to see well, but if he had to guess, these creatures had leathery-type wings akin to certain species of Old Earth dinosaurs. He hadn't spent much time learning about them. Most of that knowledge was secondary to the abundant lifeforms they'd found on New Earth. However, now that they were here on a new world teeming with life, the study of a whole new ecosystem would be required.

They'd been broadcasting a comlink since they first entered the atmosphere but hadn't gotten a reply. Noah brought up a countdown timer he'd set up based on when they'd detected the weakened signal of a distress beacon. He had to estimate the check-in interval that was being used.

They flew for another forty minutes, and at the speed they were traveling, they'd only covered a small portion of the continent.

"Should be any time now," Sean said.

Noah nodded.

Specialist Denny looked over at them. "I've increased the sensitivity of our sensors and created a filter that should reduce the chance of false positives."

"Good. Do you mind if I take a quick look at it?" Noah asked.

Denny made a passing motion from his holoscreen, and a new data window appeared in front of Noah.

He reviewed the data filter the CDF tech specialist had created. When they'd sent an update to the *Pathfinder 2*, they'd discovered that their comlink was distorted but couldn't pinpoint the exact reason. They were flying over a heavily forested area, but that alone couldn't account for comms interference. The data filter Denny had applied to the shuttle's computer systems attempted to remove things they'd determined to be interference while amplifying colonial broadcast comms sensitivity.

Noah gave Denny an approving nod. "This looks great. Good work. If you ever want—"

Sean cleared his throat, and Noah gave him a guilty look.

Specialist Denny frowned. "Did I miss something, sirs?"

Noah gave Sean a pointed look and arched an eyebrow. Sean shrugged.

"I was just going to say that if you ever think about what you'd like to do outside of the CDF, let me know," Noah said.

Denny blinked and his eyes darted toward Sean.

Sean smiled a little. "It's all right. Coming from him, that's a very high compliment."

Denny smiled and looked at Noah. "Thank you."

Sean leveled his gaze at Noah. "Now stop trying to poach my soldiers."

Noah grinned. "Never. What can I say? I've developed an eye for talent. Besides, isn't that what you high-brass types do, steal each other's talented personnel?"

Sean smirked and shook his head. "All's fair, I guess. Just remember—what goes around comes around."

A few minutes went by, and they received another distress signal that was much stronger.

Specialist Denny shook his head. "I'm unable to establish a comlink, but I was able to triangulate the source. Sending coordinates now."

Noah looked at the data. The source was over three hundred kilometers away. "Gil, head to those coordinates. Best speed."

"On our way, Captain," Gil replied.

Kyle cleared his throat and looked at Denny. "How'd you figure out where the source was? You said you weren't able to establish a comlink with the beacon."

"It's no big mystery. Traced the source of the signal from this shuttle, and then I checked it against the closest observer satellites. That gives us an approximate area of around a kilometer."

Kyle nodded. "Not a mystery to you, but I find that stuff fascinating. My brother works at Field Ops out of Delphi. He's probably familiar with what you did."

"Field Ops, huh? How'd you end up as a field biologist?" Denny asked.

"Fell into it, actually," Kyle replied.

Noah stood and walked to the back of the shuttle. Ezra Coffman looked up at him.

"I'm hoping there's something you can help me with," Noah said.

Ezra closed her holoscreen. "Of course. What can I do to help?"

Sean joined them.

"We're trying to figure out why we're having comms interference," Noah said.

"I thought the signal was weak because of power depletion," Ezra replied.

"That's part of it, but we've noticed it between the two Pathfinders. It could be atmospheric, but I want to rule everything out. When we land, can you prioritize your test kit for metals and anything else you can think of that could be the cause of the interference?"

"Of course," she said.

Noah left her to it and headed back toward the front of the shuttle.

"Kyle's a talker, isn't he?" Sean said.

Noah grinned. "Yeah. He works hard and can focus when he has to, but yes, he thinks out loud."

"Yeah, I know the type," Sean said.

Noah stopped and looked back at his friend. Then he rolled his eyes. "That's right, he's a kindred speaker. We're all talkers here. It's a huge problem for people prone to sullen silences."

Sean chuckled and shook his head. "Sullen silences. Sometimes the rest of us like to think through problems in silence."

It was an old joke they shared. After knowing each other more than twenty years, it had become one of those things. Noah talked while he worked, even when there was no one else around. It was just something he'd always done.

"You know I could start singing while I work. I know a few songs I think you'll really like."

Sean regarded him for a moment. "I should have gone on the other shuttle."

Noah gave him a solemn look. "That hurts my feelings," he said and started walking again. "You've really crossed the line, Colonel Quinn!"

He heard Sean chuckle as he followed.

It didn't take them long to reach the area Denny had tracked the signal to. They flew a search grid and soon found the lost shuttle.

Noah looked at the video feed and frowned. They'd located what remained of a camp and one of the *Ark II* shuttles.

"The shuttle looks intact," Noah said.

A hundred meters around the entire camp was blackened landscape where nothing grew.

"Kind of hard to miss it," Sean said.

Noah looked at him. "Could the shuttle's engines have done this?"

Sean considered it for a few moments. "It's possible, but I can't figure out why."

"How'd they do it?" Kyle asked.

"They used the shuttle's engines to scorch the area to make a sort of landing pad," Sean said.

"A hundred meters is a bit extreme," Noah said. "Doesn't look like anyone has been here for a while."

"Agreed," Sean replied.

"Gil, set us down close enough that we can transfer power from our shuttle to theirs if we need to," Noah said.

They went to their own individual life support systems. Once Gil set the shuttle down, the CDF soldiers were first off the loading ramp. They performed a quick survey of the area and then the rest of them disembarked. Kyle and Ezra carried their test kits and moved off to the side.

Noah stepped off the loading ramp onto the blackened ground. He felt an odd feeling of lightness, as if his head were full, as well as a peculiar looseness in his chest and stomach. He took a few moments to get used to the low gravity. For some reason, the away team had sanitized the entire area, but since they were using their own life support, they were safe from foreign contaminates. The alien forest was much sparser in the area beyond the blackened ground.

"Kyle, when you start getting your samples, can you find out how deep this goes?" Noah said.

"Will do," Kyle replied. He retrieved a small shovel from his kit and began digging.

Noah walked toward the shuttle. He looked up at the alien sky, trying to take in the sight, and had trouble getting his footing right. He felt his envirosuit try to compensate for the new environment. Without his suit, he and others probably would have tripped by now. Between the lower gravity and denser atmosphere, it would no doubt feel as if the wind were pushing against them. The ground was mainly smooth, and it felt as if his feet could slide out from under him relatively easily. He saw a few of the soldiers try to elongate their steps, but quickly stopped.

Within a few minutes, his suit computer began helping him balance so he could walk better. It would continue to fine-tune the process the longer they were there, but it would take some time getting used to it.

They reached the shuttle. Specialist Denny was already trying to access the rear hatch.

The CDF soldier looked at him and sighed. "They've locked it down."

Noah knew trying his own colonial credentials wouldn't work any better than what Denny had tried.

"This is getting annoying," Sean said.

"Yeah," Noah agreed.

"We can cut our way inside," Sean offered.

Noah sighed. "Let's not. At least not yet. I'm sure there's a way to bypass it, but it's going to take a little time."

Sean nodded. "It's your call. We'll scout the area in the

meantime," he said and walked over to the CDF soldiers.

Specialist Denny watched Noah.

"I guess it's up to us to get past the lockdown," Noah said.

"If you say so. I would've suggested cutting through the hatch as well. It would save us the most time," Specialist Denny said.

"Maybe, but I'd rather not damage anything."

"We can repair it once we're inside."

"I know that, but with a lockdown there could be other kinds of problems if we try to force our way inside."

Specialist Denny regarded the shuttle for a few seconds and shook his head. "If you say so, sir."

"You don't know my friend Lars. If he thought there was some kind of threat, he'd probably leave a few surprises inside if we don't do this the right way."

"Some kind of self-destruct?"

Noah shook his head. "I doubt it. But he could have the data core purge itself in the event that the shuttle was breeched."

Denny snorted appreciatively. "I hadn't thought of that. I figured they'd just locked the shuttle because they intended to come back."

"Lars is as clever as they come. He knows his way around a secure system. Given what we've found on the *Ark II* and here, I think it's safe to say that they weren't taking any chances," Noah said.

He brought up a couple of holoscreens and began probing the shuttle's security systems.

"Okay, we'll go at this logically. The security on the shuttle can't be that extensive. We just need to figure out which door to open," Noah said.

Specialist Denny brought up his own holoscreen, and they both started searching for a way to bypass the security systems.

16

Kara had moved the *Infinity* to a location halfway between the alpha moon and Zeta-Alpha-5. Since they couldn't use subspace comms, she needed a location to maximize the comlink window with both the Pathfinder shuttles and the *Ark II*.

She'd never liked sitting for long stretches of time, so she stood in front of the commander's chair on the bridge. She had three holoscreens active, with one of them blank in case she needed it. Noah had left a few hours ago and the last update they'd received confirmed their arrival on the planet. Dr. Carter Lachlan, who was working at one of the auxiliary workstations on the other side of the bridge, was very excited by the data and video recordings they'd already sent back. He couldn't wait to go down there.

Chief Markovich stood up from his workstation nearby and peered at the data on Kara's screen.

"What do you think, Jeremy?" she asked.

He pressed his lips together and shook his head. "It doesn't work."

Kara smiled a little and rolled her eyes. One of the data windows showed her most recent attempt to bypass the *Ark II*'s security systems. "That's a huge help. I guess we'll just leave it at that."

Jeremy grinned. "I didn't say that, but you're much better at secure systems than I am. I'm good at this ship, making sure she's maintained and ready to fly. Bypassing security systems isn't a skillset I currently possess."

"I should kick you off my bridge," she replied and grinned. "I appreciate your honesty, as always."

He smiled. "I really wish there was something I could do. All the ships I've worked on could communicate with each other. If it weren't for that point-defense system, I'd say we should send someone over there. There must be a manual override for a hatch somewhere."

"There is, but as you've said, we can't get to it."

The door to the bridge opened and Peter Blood walked in. Blood was trained in salvage and repair operations. He was a bit on the shorter side but had an athletic build. Kara waved him over.

He joined them and looked at the holoscreen. "Still can't get the *Ark II*'s computer system to play nice?"

She shook her head. "No, I think we've hit a dead end trying to access the ship systems remotely."

Blood crossed his muscular arms and rubbed his chin in thought. "Then we're going to have to go there. Is there any way we can beat the point-defense system? Use some drones for decoys and sneak past it?"

Kara shook her head. She'd had a long career in the CDF designing weapons, ships, outposts, and space stations. "Not with anything we have aboard. There's no way we can make a frontal assault and hope for the best. Your family would never forgive me if you died on my watch. Whatever we sent would get picked off no matter how small it was."

Blood nodded. "They'd miss me terribly. Regardless, I didn't like the thought of holding onto a comms drone while it ferried me onto the *Ark II*'s hull."

"Neither did I," she said. The two men simply stared at her. "Yeah, I know. Light duty only," she said. She needed to follow up with Dr. Hathaway about that. Her hips and back hardly ached anymore, and she was getting stronger every day. The time to coddle her was coming to an end. She felt her teeth clench a little in frustration. The envirosuits helped the wearer with their movements, so it wasn't as if she'd strain herself.

Kara sighed and regarded the two men. "So, we can agree that the only way we're going to access that ship is by going over there."

"I would have to agree," Chief Markovich replied.

"Same here, but how can we get there safely? I'm pretty confident I could remote-pilot a repair drone to the hull, but after that, who knows if they have security measures active inside the ship?" Blood said.

Kara shook her head. "It's not a warship. There aren't any automated defensive measures inside. It's just getting there that's the problem. I tried spoofing the IDs of one of the *Ark II*'s resource drones, but that only lets me send a status report and nothing else. The lockdown must enforce more secure communications as well."

Jeremy Markovich frowned in thought. "If it let you send a report, couldn't you attach a special program that would allow you to bypass the security lockout?"

"No, you're talking about remote code execution, and it won't work here. The ship's computer systems accept the report and files it away. There's nothing to execute. Even if I used something more sophisticated, the access it would have would be limited. There are security measures in place on all computer systems we use that prevent that kind of tampering. Programs aren't allowed to run from an array designated for data storage," Kara replied.

"Then we're back to square one with trying to get past the point-defense system."

Kara regarded them for a few moments. She'd been considering an idea, but it came with its own set of issues. "I do have an idea about that. It's risky though."

Blood blinked a few times and the edges of his lips lifted. "Does it have me flying through space on the wing of a prayer?"

"A little bit," she admitted.

Blood glanced at Markovich for a second and leaned forward. "What do you have in mind?"

"Nothing we have on this ship will get us past the point-defense systems. So, we need to capture a couple of the resource-gathering drones that the *Ark II* has deployed."

"Okay, we find some drones, but then what?" Markovich asked.

"I'm not sure what we gain. It's not like you can use the drone's interface to initiate a remote override of the lockdown," Blood said.

"You're right; that wouldn't work. However, we could initiate a repair cycle. Make it so that the drone has to return to the *Ark II* for maintenance," Kara said.

Blood pursed his lips and looked toward the main holoscreen for a moment. "We'd have to try this twice."

"Why twice?" Markovich asked.

"Once to be sure it works and the drone *does* return to the *Ark II* without issues. The second time is for me and a few members of my team to catch a ride if this works," Blood said.

Kara smiled. "That's the plan."

Blood regarded her for a moment. "Will you be able to walk me through disabling the lockdown?"

Markovich looked at her, his eyebrows raised in concern.

They expected her to want to go, and they weren't wrong. It would be easier if she went with him, but in spite of her frustration with the amount of time her recovery was taking, she didn't need to take unnecessary risks. She did appreciate their concern.

"I should be able to. We'll attach one of our own comlinks to the first drone and see if we can get a link established. If that works, I should be able to walk you through it," Kara said.

Blood nodded. "Sounds good to me. Now all we need to do is find a couple of drones to capture."

Markovich nodded. "Sounds like a good plan."

"I'm glad you both approve. Their drones won't have any security measures, so capturing them shouldn't be that much of a challenge," Kara said, and they began putting together a plan to capture the drones.

She would have preferred to have found a way to bypass the security remotely, but that wasn't possible with the resources they had available. Once they were aboard the ship and ended the lockdown, hopefully they could learn what had happened to Saul Ashworth and his crew. Then, they could also confirm the status of the five thousand colonists aboard the *Ark II*.

17

THE SHUTTLE WAS empty and only had a small percentage of emergency power left. Once Noah and Specialist Denny had bypassed the security lock, they had to run a hardwired connection to *Pathfinder 1's* power core. Noah heard the whine of the shuttle's engines outside.

He opened a comlink to Gil. "Stand by to cut the power. I think we've charged it enough."

"Copy that," Gil replied.

Specialist Denny stood nearby and had one of the consoles open. "Initiating startup sequence."

A few moments later, the shuttle's interior lights flickered on, and holoscreens became active.

"We're at twenty percent power, Captain," Specialist Denny said.

That was enough for the shuttle to make it back to the *Ark II* to refuel. "That's more than enough to retrieve the logs," Noah said and activated his comlink to Gil. "Cut the power."

"Power tap has been disabled, Captain," Gil said.

"Thanks. Retract the power tap and put the shuttle in standby," Noah said.

Someone began walking up the loading ramp, and Noah turned to see Sean striding toward them. He glanced at the open hatch for a moment. Noah had taken apart the panel with the door controls, exposing what was inside.

"I see the bypass worked. What did you do?" Sean asked.

"Just tricked the sensor into thinking it was open when it should be closed."

Sean nodded appreciatively. "I guess they never expected someone to reverse the sensor feeds, so they were reversed."

Noah smiled. "It wasn't that easy. I forced the locking mechanism to reset because of a small power surge. That allowed me to tamper with the sensor."

"Practical *and* devious. Nice job," Sean said.

Specialist Denny stood up. "I'll go put the panel back together and reset the sensor back to normal."

Sean closed the distance to where Noah sat. "How'd he do?"

"He's good. He's just not used to trying to bypass a perfectly good security system."

Sean nodded. "We'll have to add that to the tech specialists' training regimen."

"See, process improvement across the board," Noah said. He turned back toward the holoscreen. "How's the scouting going outside?"

"It's a jungle out there. According to Mr. Regan, the scorched earth goes down about thirty centimeters. They wanted to make sure nothing grew near the shuttle."

"Seems like overkill to me, but maybe there's something here that will shed light on why they did it," Noah said.

They spent the next hour reviewing the logs. Saul Ashworth, Xander Ludwig, and Lars Malory all had log entries stored on the shuttle's computer system. The earlier entries were mainly about scouting the area, looking for possible settlement sites.

"Lars didn't like that there was no one monitoring for them on the *Ark II*," Noah said.

Sean nodded. "I saw that as well. The way these entries read it was as if they'd only expected to be down here for about a week. This wasn't the first site they scouted either."

"Yeah, but this is the last place they were before they disappeared. They were going on a deep scouting mission using the rovers to set up a base camp and never came back."

Specialist Denny cleared his throat. "Have you ever heard of something called an Uvai?"

Noah shook his head.

"Me either. What does it say?" Sean asked.

"It's in the later entries from one of the other sites. They encountered more of the local fauna, herbivores mostly, but their scouting teams have been reporting strange sounds. There's a video of it here," Specialist Denny said.

He started playing the recording. They heard forest sounds—from chirps and knocks to something that sounded more like a hawk.

"Did you hear that?" someone on the recording asked. They were standing off to the side.

The drone that was recording hovered in the air and turned toward Lars. "I didn't hear anything. Is your head still hurting?" he asked.

The camera swung toward another person. The name Gervais Schaeffer appeared. "Yeah, but—"

The voice cut out when countless wings flapped, as if a horde of creatures had suddenly taken flight.

Noah wished he could control the video feed. He peered at

the background, trying to get a look at whatever was making that noise.

The camera swung around, and in the distance they saw a large group of brown flying creatures taking off from one of the thick trees nearby. A swarm of them suddenly leaped into the air, which was followed by another group.

"I wonder what spooked them this time," Gervais Schaeffer said.

Several loud knocks sounded in the distance. The knocks were repeated and soon were echoing all around them. The recon drone tried to identify the source, but with so many sources, the sensors became overwhelmed. The knocks reached a crescendo, and then came a deep, roaring, vibrato sound with various modulations. The vibrato intensified and the sounds drowned out what the colonists were saying. They shouted, but Noah couldn't understand what they were saying.

Noah watched Lars gesture toward the others, calling them back. The last image before the recording stopped was of Lars and the others running away.

"I couldn't see what was making that sound. Could any of you?" Noah asked.

"I don't think the drone was able to see what it was," Sean said.

"Whatever it was, it sounds creepy. I guess you could say it made a sound like an elongated *Uvai*," Specialist Denny said.

"It's strange," Noah said. "I'm going to copy that recording. See if there are any other videos in the logs. We can analyze them later."

"Data storage on the shuttle's computer systems is limited. They probably uploaded most of it to the *Ark II*," Specialist Denny said.

Sean looked at Noah. "Can we access the *Ark II* now that power has been restored?"

Noah shook his head. "I tried, but we're out of range. I can still access the satellites, but when I tried to initiate a connection to the *Ark II*, it wanted me to provide the credentials of someone from the mission."

"That damn security lockdown again. It's becoming a real thorn in my side."

Noah arched an eyebrow. "It's great until it's inconvenient. Is that what you're saying?"

Sean sighed explosively. "Can't you copy the credentials from the shuttle's computer systems?"

Noah shook his head. "Only if they'd left an open session, but it's been so long since anyone has been here that all sessions have been closed. Still not having any luck with that, but I've heard from Kara that they have a plan in the works that will gain us access to the *Ark II*."

"That's something at least. You know what this means, right?"

"We're going to have to go out there and retrace their steps. It's the only way we're going to find them," Noah replied.

Sean nodded. "They took the rovers, which we should be able to track. Even though it's been months there should still be some indication in the terrain that they came through there." He arched an eyebrow. "Aren't you glad I came along?"

"Never regretted it for a second," Noah replied and paused for a moment. "I don't know how many hours of daylight we have left."

"It shouldn't be much of a problem," Specialist Denny replied.

"How come?" Sean asked.

"Bioluminescence at night. I saw that mentioned, too. It

doesn't really get that dark here all that often, sir," Specialist Denny replied.

Kyle Regan walked toward them. "Did I hear someone mention bioluminescence?"

"Yeah, it's in the logs we found," Noah replied.

"That makes sense," Kyle said. "I was able to get a closer look at some of the animals here. Many of them have multiple sets of eyes. We've seen similar developments back on New Earth. They basically have two sets of eyes. One set is more attuned to seeing during the day, while the other is more sensitive to seeing at night. It's like their own night vision but without implants or helmets." He looked at Denny. "Can you show me the logs that mention…"

Sean looked at Noah. "When do you want to head out?"

"Soon, but we should probably give people a chance to eat first. We can use the shuttles to scout the area, but with a forest canopy like what we saw in the video, I don't know how much help it'll be for us on the ground."

Sean nodded. "Every little bit helps. Let's take a look at the last entries and figure out where they went."

Noah regarded his friend for a moment. "They were worried about whatever was making that noise. This Uvai. I'm going to run a few queries to see if I can speed up these log reviews."

"Good idea. I'll help you with the filter," Sean said.

He frowned. "What makes you think I need help with it?"

"Nothing, but what if you've gotten sloppy with this sort of grunt work? I mean, I *am* talking to half of the brilliant team that created the I-Drive," Sean said.

Noah chuckled. "It's not quite a compliment sandwich, but it's pretty close. All right, I'll let you look over my shoulder, but don't touch anything."

"You have my word."

18

Noah scrounged up every bit of data that was available on the *Ark II's* shuttle computer system and copied it to his own data storage device. He'd tasked a few subroutines and an analysis AI to mine the data, searching for patterns of information that could be useful to them. He'd have to review it later, but it did free him up so they could leave.

Kyle Regan walked up the loading ramp. The holoscreen above his wrist computer had just disappeared. "Thanks for giving me access to that data. I'll take a look at it while we're on the move."

"Did you get a chance to review some of the videos we found?" Noah asked.

They walked back down the loading ramp. Noah stopped at the console and put the shuttle's power systems on standby. He'd disabled the distress beacon and recorded his own message in case anyone from the *Ark II*'s away team happened to come back. He refused to believe that Lars or any of the others were dead, and he wouldn't change his mind unless they found them that way. He'd reviewed the supply manifest, and while they'd only planned on a short scouting mission, they'd brought enough provisions with them to last for six months. The shuttles had been stocked for a scouting mission that involved about a hundred people, but since only a dozen had come, they had plenty of provisions to spare.

"Yes, I just watched it a few times on my way here," Kyle said.

They paused at the bottom of the ramp. Noah closed it and the ramp lifted to seal off the shuttle.

"It's strange. The Uvai noise thing is peculiar to say the least. The other creatures in the area seemed to react to it. The only thing I noticed when I zoomed into a particular area was some kind of reddish glow. It was subtle, but definitely happened around the same time as that knocking sound."

Noah arched an eyebrow. "Strange and peculiar are the same thing. The glow might not be anything. Is that really all you got out of it?"

"No," Kyle said, shaking his head. "I have a tendency to get too technical sometimes. I'd say that this Uvai thing was reacting to the colonial presence, as if the colonials were in its territory and this was its way of telling them to leave. That's surface-level analysis based only on the evidence in that short video. It's not enough for us to be conclusive about anything other than to avoid it if we can."

Noah snorted. "We don't even know what it looks like."

"Yeah, I know. It's frustrating. The others ran away from whatever it was, so if we encounter it, then maybe we should do the same—you know, run away until we better understand what we're dealing with."

Noah regarded the young field biologist for a few moments. He'd spent over two decades exploring New Earth, and he knew perfectly well that there were times when keeping your distance from something dangerous just wasn't an option.

Kyle frowned. "If you don't mind me asking, what's that look for, sir?"

Noah chuckled and wished he could remove his helmet to scratch his neck. Sometimes it itched from dry skin. The only thing he could do for it was a half shrug and a roll of his shoulder a little bit. That almost got the right spot, but like Kyle's sage advice, it just wasn't enough.

"It's nothing. What you said does make sense to me, but things seldom compartmentalize the way we want them to," Noah replied.

Kyle smiled in understanding. "That's life in the field, right? We're pioneers on the edge of everything. Pushing the boundaries."

Noah smiled and nodded. The young man's enthusiasm was a little infectious. "I'm glad nothing has dampened your spirits."

Kyle shook his head. "You must be joking. I live for this." He glanced toward the jungle line nearby for a few seconds. "I just hope the others are okay."

"Me, too," Noah agreed.

"I'll do whatever I can to help unravel the mysteries of this place. I mean it."

No one could ever say that Kyle Regan wasn't eager about being there. Noah could still remember being that young and motivated to have an impact, to make his mark. He supposed he'd never outgrown that drive in himself.

"Believe me, Kyle, I appreciate it. You're doing fine. Okay? Just remember to stay focused and keep your wits about you. If you see something you want to investigate, catalog it with the reconnaissance drone, but if you think it could help lead us to the away team, then let me know immediately."

"Will do. Of course. Absolutely, I will," Kyle replied.

They walked back toward their own Pathfinder shuttle where CDF soldiers were offloading two rovers. The vehicles' chrome-colored armored plating had copper accents, and they were sleek at the nose, with three doors on either side. A large storage cabin and mobile lab were located behind the passenger compartment of each six-wheeled vehicle. The mobile lab wasn't anything as extensive as what they had on the ship, but it would have to do. Noah had hoped that when they found the away team's home base or camp, they'd have a more extensive lab setup.

Ezra Coffman came to join them. "Oh good, they're offloading the mobile lab. I've gathered some samples I'd like to analyze."

"What have you found so far?" Noah asked.

"I wasn't allowed to venture that far, but I think there's a new mineral here that we haven't encountered before. I was only able to find trace amounts with my field kit. I'm hoping to collect some samples on the way and maybe even find a deposit of it somewhere to use for further testing."

"Any potential applications?" Kyle asked.

Ezra shook her head. "Too soon to tell at this point. Trace amounts, like I said, but it's definitely not something we've encountered before."

Kyle smiled and lowered his chin once.

"You might not be able to run those samples just yet. I doubt the road we're taking is going to be smooth. However, you could take what you've got and ride on one of the Pathfinders while they scout overhead. There's a mobile lab setup on them as well."

Ezra considered it for a moment and then shook her head. "That's fine. I can wait and collect more samples on the way."

"That seems to be the name of the game for now," Kyle said.

Ezra looked at Noah. "Something to be aware of is that this

planet likely experiences more tectonic activity than we do on New Earth."

"Why is that?" Noah asked.

"I think it's because of the proximity of the two moons. They exert more stress on the planetary crust itself. This likely accounts for the higher amounts of carbon dioxide and hydrogen sulfide in the atmosphere."

"I thought this place smelled funny," Kyle replied and twitched his eyebrows. "Sorry, I couldn't resist. It makes sense. Even with all this flora here, the plants cannot produce enough oxygen to have a noticeable effect on the amount of volcanic activity on the planet."

"I know we've only been here a few hours, but are there any indications of volcanic activity nearby?" Noah asked.

Ezra shook her head. "I took a seismic reading and left the sensor in place for as long as we've been down here. Nothing alarming or what I'd consider to be out of the ordinary has been recorded. I also checked with the observer satellites and it's relatively stable here. Atmospheric data doesn't show any signs of recent volcanic activity. It's probably one of the reasons they were scouting this area in the first place."

"All right," Noah replied, content that they didn't need to worry about any calderas forming while they were in the area.

"There's one more thing. There seems to be high amounts of magnetism in the area. If we had an old-style compass, it would be spinning wildly. Anyway, it could just be the area we're in, or it could be something more widespread... as in globally. It's too soon for me to make a determination one way or the other."

Noah considered it for a few moments. "I remember Lars asking one of the other people about headaches. Are the fields strong enough to trigger them or other symptoms?"

Ezra pressed her lips together in thought. "Sensitivity to

magnetic fields can vary from person to person. I can let the medics know about it so they're aware."

"Thanks for that," Noah replied.

Sean called everyone over to the rovers.

"In a few minutes we're going to leave the area to track the missing away team. The log entries we've found on the shuttle do indicate that some of the creatures will be hostile toward us. All scouting missions will be in pairs. No one goes anywhere alone," Sean said and looked at Kyle and Ezra. "I know Noah probably already told you this, but if you see something you think we need to take a closer look at, let one of my people know and we'll try to accommodate you as quickly as possible."

Kyle and Ezra both gave him a firm nod.

"Our first priority is the safety of our mission. I don't want to lose anyone because of some foolish mistake. We need to watch each other's backs out here. I've explored dozens of worlds. Lieutenant Rhoades has also been on scouting missions through the spacegates. The best piece of advice I can give you is that you cannot afford to take anything you see here at face value. We don't know this world at all. This place is alien to us, and we don't belong here. What might seem familiar to you could be something quite different from what we've encountered before. Remember that, and we'll get through this just fine."

Noah came over to stand next to Sean. "Log data showed that the previous away team encountered different species of creatures here. One commonality among them is their size. Due to the low gravity of this world, the creatures evolved to be much taller than we're used to. I've extracted high-level summaries for the creatures encountered so far and have sent them to all of your wrist computers. Take a quick look to familiarize yourself because there's a good chance we'll encounter them in there," he said, gesturing toward the thick jungle nearby.

"All right, do as the man says," Sean said.

The soldiers began reviewing the data Noah had sent them. He gestured for Gil Parnell and Sima Bruhanski to come over to them. "I'm going to need both of you to scout the area ahead of us while making a sweep to search for the away team. This needs to be a coordinated effort, as if you were doing a search and rescue mission."

Gil glanced at Sima for a second and then looked a Noah. "If this is to be a SAR mission, one of us must stay relatively close to you the whole time. What's the minimum safe distance you want from us?"

Noah considered it for a moment and then looked at Sean. A long time ago he'd been part of the first SAR team for Field Ops. "What do you think? Would ten kilometers do it?"

Sean nodded. "That should be fine. If things get too hot, we should be able to hold out for you to come get us."

"Well, there you have it. I don't want either of you flying alone, so both of you will have a member of the CDF with you," Noah said.

Sean brought up his wrist computer and tapped one of the buttons on the holo-interface. Two soldiers trotted over to them. Noah recognized one as Private Donlon. The other soldier was a man named Rich Suh.

Donlon didn't so much as glance in Noah's direction.

Sean spoke to the soldiers. "Both of you are on escort duty with Mr. Parnell and Ms. Bruhanski."

Gil cleared his throat. "Colonel Quinn, if you don't mind, I'd like Donlon to ride with me."

Sean didn't even look at Donlon. "You've got him."

Noah looked at Gil, but his expression didn't give anything away. The two CDF soldiers and pilots went to their respective shuttles.

"What's that about?" Sean asked.

Noah shook his head. "I have no idea." He frowned for a moment and snorted. "It might have to do with Donlon's opinion of my leadership capabilities."

"Donlon is young. He'll learn," Sean replied.

Noah nodded. "Yeah, I think Gil might help with some of that teaching he needs."

Sean winced. "I said he's young. I didn't say he wasn't dangerous."

"I'm sure they'll play nice."

"Speaking of which, we haven't talked about it, but I'd like you to stay by me."

"Sure. You're not riding in one of the rovers?" Noah asked.

"Not at first. I prefer to walk. Get the lay of the land. Lieutenant Rhoades is going to monitor the recon drones."

Noah regarded his friend for a moment and then took in their surroundings. "Do you miss it? This type of field mission, I mean."

"You mean marching through a jungle or dense rain forest where the local fauna wants to take a piece out of me? Oh yeah, I can't wait," Sean replied dryly.

Noah snorted. "I can't imagine you get much opportunity for it during fleet operations."

"I don't. See, this is my vacation, and I chose to spend it with you, way out here. Don't ever say I don't do anything for you," Sean replied.

Although it had been months, and the jungle had done its best to regrow over the path taken by the away team's rover, not all the signs had been erased. Sergeant John Staggart was quite the tracker. The CDF soldier took the lead with his squad of soldiers. Using the reconnaissance drones, they were able to identify the path taken by the *Ark II's* rovers and blaze their own path through the jungle. To avoid surprising the local creatures, they didn't try to hide their presence as they trekked through the dense overgrowth. The rovers were equipped with short-range plasma cutters that easily sliced through thick foliage growing over the path.

Noah opened a comlink to Kyle. "Do you think there's something to this new growth over the path? Even if it's been months since the others went through here, would it really grow back this much?"

Kyle didn't reply right away. "It's not impossible. Sometimes when plants are pruned, it triggers them to grow back twice as big as before. Given the amount of rain and nutrients in the soil, there isn't a good reason for it not to regrow so fast."

Noah wasn't a botanist, so his expertise in plant ecology was somewhat lacking. He looked around at the area, and the remnant of the path that had been cut through just seemed artificial in its regrowth, as if something were trying to erase that the path had ever existed.

The terrain was hardly ever level and was often covered with a root system, as if all the tall trees and even the low-lying shrubs were a single entity. There were also paths of open ground that large creatures must use regularly to keep the jungle from encroaching upon them. The *Ark II's* away team hadn't followed one of the established paths, preferring for some reason to make their own, and Noah couldn't figure out why.

The Nexstar combat suits and the civilian environmental suits assisted the wearers over the rough terrain. They'd even had to use the rover's winch attachment to climb a twenty-meter cliff face. Sergeant Staggart climbed up the cliff with his squad and then placed temporary handholds and safety ropes so the rest of them could follow.

As the hours went by, they began to gather an audience.

Different kinds of creatures seemed to gather to watch them pass. There were things clustered above them that made their home among the countless tree branches above. Noah heard so many different types of creatures that he couldn't keep track of them all. He'd traveled all over the supercontinent of New Earth, from wide-open plains, dense forests, and even a few jungles. There was always a familiar rhythm to how the animals interacted that was easy for him to get a feel for, but Zeta-Alpha-5 was different. The cadence and rhythms were off-kilter, at least to him, and this seemed to increase the team's anxiety with what they were doing. It manifested in subtle ways, like the fact that they spoke to each other in almost hushed tones, as if they had an unspoken agreement not to draw attention to themselves. Noah tried to dismiss those behaviors in himself, but they kept coming back little by little.

Not all of them were anxious. Kyle Regan had lost none of his excitement at the chance to explore a new world. He said that many of the sounds they were hearing probably had to do with gathering food, claiming or protecting a territory, or attracting a mate. Most sounds in any place out of touch with civilization could be whittled down to those three categories.

"Find or claim a safe place. Get food. Make babies. It's the never-ending cycle of nature," Kyle said.

"What are the odds of us finding an intelligent species here?" Noah asked.

"If you mean like us or the Ovarrow, or even the Krake, I'd say the odds are pretty low. None of the observer satellites found anything remotely resembling a city. Maybe we've just come at the wrong time," Kyle said.

"Millions of years too early or millions of years too late?"

"High intelligence requires predator-prey cycles and mobility, which is here in abundance, so the possibility must also exist."

Noah looked around. "If you say so."

"I do say so. What would be really interesting to find would be a clumsy predator or even a scavenger—something that's highly adaptable but that can do well in multiple niches. However, it couldn't be a master of a particular niche because then it wouldn't be as adaptable."

"Why?" Noah asked.

Kyle regarded him for a long moment. "Do you think we evolved because we were the fastest runners or had the biggest claws and teeth? No. Quite the opposite, actually. We were clumsy in comparison to the other creatures back on Old Earth. To survive we had to be clever. Need is the fuel of invention, but it also sparked intelligence in our brains. We're great at problem-solving and making things. Controlling our environment."

Noah considered this for a beat. "We are, but we also create problems."

Kyle nodded. "Comes with the territory."

"Well, we haven't come up against anything we haven't been able to solve. We're here, lightyears away from anywhere."

Kyle was about to respond when something massive stomped on the ground, and it seemed to send shockwaves through the plants nearby. Everyone stopped moving, and CDF soldiers readied their weapons. Noah grabbed his AR-74. There was a blast of air that sounded like something huge was clearing its throat, except whatever it was had to be the size of a house. Several more stomps could be heard, and smaller creatures scurried away. Noah suspected that if he hadn't been wearing his envirosuit, he could've felt the ground shake.

Sean waved Noah and Kyle over.

Sean had a holoscreen opened above his wrist computer, and a drone video feed was active. Thirty meters away was a large group of blue-and-gray-skinned creatures with light brown legs.

They stood over six meters tall and were twice as long. They had wide heads, with a bone structure that made it appear as if they were wearing a headpiece made of tissue that had ossified to one solid piece. Several of the large males cocked their heads to the side, listening. Another snorted a blast of air from its mouth and stomped on the ground.

"Colonel Quinn, this is a territorial display. If we don't get out of here, they're going to charge, maybe even get all of them to attack," Kyle said in a low voice just above a whisper.

The recon drone swung around, and they could see hundreds of them scattered across the area they needed to go through.

Noah looked at Sean. "We might need to backtrack the way we…" He stopped speaking. More of these giant herbivores had somehow wandered over the area they'd just traveled, barely over a hundred meters away.

"Okay, extremely large herds. Check. But how'd they sneak up on us?" Kyle asked.

Throughout the area, several creatures raised their heads, and Noah thought he could hear a low rumbling sound. Others nearby continued to graze on the shrubbery, except for the closest group.

"Falling back to the rovers isn't going to help. They look like they out-mass the damn rover," Noah said.

They were surrounded, and it had happened so quickly that it left his head spinning. Sean had scouts and reconnaissance drones patrolling the area. They'd made plenty of noise that would have alarmed anything they'd come across. However, with these creatures it didn't matter. They appeared more than willing to follow up on their territorial display. Noah didn't think they were bluffing, which either meant it was a good bluff or those creatures were about to attack the entire group of explorers.

"I have an idea," Sean said.

"I'm glad *you* do, because all I want to do is get the hell out of here," Noah replied.

Sean opened a broadcast comlink to the entire group. "We're going to see if we can get these things to move along so the rest of us can get away. Non-military personnel, make your way to the rovers and climb aboard."

Kyle looked at Noah. "I guess that's our cue."

"Go ahead, I'll be right behind you," Noah replied.

Lieutenant Rhoades, Sergeant Staggart, and Sergeant Unwin hastened over to Sean and Noah.

"Where's Denny?" Sean asked.

A few seconds later, the big tech specialist joined them.

"Denny, I want you to take control of two recon drones and buzz that big male that's closest to us. Make sure you fly around and approach him from the rear. I want to see if he'll spin around and focus on them. If he chases the drones, then all the better," Sean said.

"Yes, Colonel. I'll get the drones into position and buzz the big guy when you give the order, sir," Specialist Denny replied.

"Sergeant Unwin, if the drones don't work, then you and your squad are up. Get them to follow you away from here and meet back up with us at this waypoint," Sean said and gestured toward a set of coordinates on his holoscreen.

"Yes, Colonel," Sergeant Unwin said and stepped away, calling for his squad of soldiers to join him.

"The rest of us will be backup in case Sergeant Unwin is unable to lure the creatures away. We'll have to fight our way out of this. They have overlapping body plates, but it looks like there are soft spots underneath. You can see it on the lighter-toned skin. The hide has to be tough, regardless. Don't hesitate to use your heaviest round configuration from your ammo packs," Sean said.

The loud snorts now came with a shrill growl, as if the alpha male was losing patience, working himself up into a fury that promised death and destruction.

Noah followed Sean to the rover in the front. Sean looked at him. "It would've been nice if we'd had an extra combat suit for you."

Noah nodded. "It would've, but that's why I'm going to stay behind you," he said and paused for a moment.

"What?" Sean asked.

Noah shook his head. "Later."

Sean opened a comlink to Specialist Denny. "Go ahead. Get his attention."

A loud screech sounded from the recon drones' speakers, and it became louder the closer they came.

The alpha male spun toward the drones, natural instinct causing him to face the most immediate threat than what was only a potential one. Six or seven of the others did the same. Their heads jerked toward the sounds, rather than following the drones' flight paths.

Denny flew the drones right toward the alpha male's face, which lowered its thick skull and charged. It bellowed as it ran toward the drone, and the other creatures followed on pure instinct.

Noah saw other creatures nearby raise their heads, listening. They seemed to be more adept at hearing than they were at seeing. He opened a comlink to Specialist Denny. "Send one of the drones toward that group in front of us. If we can get enough of them moving, they'll ignore us completely!"

One of the recon drones flew off ahead of them, squawking loudly as it closed in on the group of titan herbivores forty meters in front of them. The nearest males bellowed a roar and charged the drone. Denny had slowed it down to make it a more effective lure, and it was working.

"Good work," Sean said. "Let's start moving forward."

The rovers' electric motors weren't very loud to begin with so they shouldn't attract much attention, and they moved at a quick pace. Noah grabbed a handhold and climbed onto the back of one of the rovers. He reached the perch at the top, and Sean joined him. The rough terrain jostled them, but they had a better view than from the ground.

Noah heard stomping bellows from farther away and saw more creatures to his left. The jungle seemed to thin as they traveled, and they had a clear view of them.

"Sean!" Noah shouted and gestured.

Sean looked at him and his gaze darted toward a new group of creatures. "Sergeant Unwin, your team is up."

Unwin and six CDF soldiers kicked their combat suits into high gear and hauled ass away from the rovers. Nexstar combat suits were capable of moving at speeds that rivaled that of any rover on smooth terrain. In a jungle such as this, the suits had no equal, and the soldiers inside them were highly trained.

Sergeant Unwin ran straight toward the big bull, screaming as he went. The creature turned toward the new threat and stomped the ground. Unwin squeezed off a few shots as he ran, which clipped the broad head, startling the creature for half a second before it charged in a rage.

Unwin and the squad of soldiers angled their approach to guide them away from the rovers.

Sean banged his fist on top of the rover. "Go! Go! Go!"

The rover thrust forward, plasma cutters blazing a path in front of them. Thick shrubs fell to the ground, and the rover's powerful wheels pummeled what remained into the jungle floor.

Sean spun around looking for the closest threat, and then shook his head. "Is it me, or is the landscape changing?"

Noah's eyebrows raised. "I thought it was just me. I was going to mention it before all the fun began."

"I'm not sure, but I swear the way forward looks different than it did before."

"We can figure it out later. Let's get the hell out of here!" Noah said.

He looked to where Sergeant Unwin had run off, but he and the other soldiers were out of sight. He could still hear the creatures' bellows as they headed away from them.

A loud clang sounded, and the rover lurched forward violently. It went up on its two front wheels in bursts and didn't come down. Noah grabbed onto the rim of the perch and looked behind. One the creatures had plowed right into them, shoving the rover forward as if it didn't weigh anything. The back of the rover had crunched inward, accordion style. The creature didn't stop after it made contact, it just kept thrusting forward in a blind rage. Noah tried to raise his assault rifle, but the rover bucked beneath him, throwing him off-balance. Sean grabbed him and pulled him back to safety. Noah then managed to raise his rifle, firing it on full auto, and Sean joined in with his own weapon. Deadly, high-density darts turned the creature's armored skull into slag of torn flesh and bone. The creature howled in pain and jerked its massive head back. The back of the rover slammed to the ground.

Sean changed one of the settings on his AR-74, firing a glowing object into the creature's face, and then pulled Noah down below the perch wall. An explosion roared with heat and force, blocking out all other sounds. They stood and watched as the creature sank to the ground with half its face obliterated.

Then more came, and the fight really began.

19

Plasma cutters protected the front of the rover, but the overgrowth seemed to be thickening no matter what path they took. A few of the broadheads tried to attack the rovers from the front, but the drivers increased power to the plasma cutters, which proved effective at penetrating the creatures' armored heads. They soon changed tactics and began to come at the sides. CDF soldiers in Nexstar combat suits tried to defend against the titan herbivores, but nothing short of combat suit heavies could lay down enough fire to make them stop, and they only stopped for a short while.

Sean growled in disgust. "If they want us to leave, why do they keep chasing us?"

Noah provided covering fire from his side of the rover's perch. The vehicle lurched up and forward as it climbed over a set of boulders. A burst from the thrusters gave them the boost they needed to climb the rest of the way.

"They're in a frenzy," Noah said.

"I'll give them a fucking frenzy," Sean bellowed, firing his weapon at a broadhead's snout as it charged toward their flank.

With the creature's head lowered to charge, it was a hard shot to make. Noah hadn't been able to do it. But the creature squealed in pain and lost its footing, tumbling toward them. Noah brought his weapon up and fired in controlled bursts at the creature's underbelly, tearing the flesh. Brown viscous blood splattered from gushing wounds, and the broadhead howled a mournful wail.

They stopped firing their weapons. Dead broadheads laid along the path they'd taken, but this didn't seem to dissuade the creatures from attacking.

Sean scowled. "It's only a matter of time before the scavengers show up to feed on the dead bodies. Then the bigger predators will come."

Noah looked above them. The combat HUD of his suit flashed red and began highlighting hostile creatures. Clustered among the mass of tree branches and thick vines were some kind of ambush predators. Forward-facing, baleful eyes were locked in on Noah, looking as if they were seeking revenge with the utmost prejudice. The long, thick muscles of the creatures' arms rippled under brown skin as it pulled itself forward. It straddled the mass of vines from underneath, and Noah could only glimpse the dark talons on its long-fingered hands and feet. It had an extensive tail with thick barbs along the back. The creature's jowls opened wide, revealing long, pointy teeth. A screech came from the back of its throat, and a mid-dorsal crest of spines sprang up, rippling as it shook, sounding like dozens of rattles all shaking at the same time. The creature rocked back and launched itself toward Noah, outstretched claws racing toward him. A thin membrane of skin opened near the creature's armpits and legs, helping it to glide rather than just fall toward him.

"Sean! Death from above!" Noah screamed and fired his weapon.

He heard Sean fire next to him.

High-density darts sprayed into the predator's face, and the force of them knocked it off course. Sean screamed a warning to the others as more brown predators dive-bombed from above.

Noah looked toward the ground. One of the creatures regained its feet, but Specialist Denny planted an armored boot on its thick neck and blew its head off. There was movement behind him, and Denny tried to turn around, but another predator burst from cover. Standing on all fours, the creature was taller than even Denny in a combat suit. A clawed hand shot out and grabbed him, snatching him up like a rag doll and flinging him away from the rover.

Noah screamed and fired his weapon at the predator's back. The creature didn't slow down despite the darts tearing into its hide but continued to charge toward where it had thrown Denny.

The creature moved so fast that Noah had trouble tracking it. He had to check his fire, because there were CDF soldiers on the ground helping to defend the rovers. He used the pause to change the output of his ammo.

Specialist Denny staggered to his feet as the creature bounded toward him, but then its body seemed to slither as it crawled low to the ground.

Noah raised his weapon and fired a plasma bolt. The creature's crest of spines blew apart as the plasma bolt seared into its back. When the creature stumbled to the side, the soldiers on the ground finished it off.

Noah turned toward Sean. "We need to find some cover. We're sitting ducks out here."

Sean nodded. "You're right. We can't keep this up," he said, looking around.

"There's rock face up ahead about half a klick, Colonel," Lieutenant Rhoades said over comlink.

A waypoint highlighted on their HUD, and it took Noah a few seconds to figure out what Lieutenant Rhoades was pointing out.

"Got it," Sean replied. "Let's head over there."

A message was broadcast to the others, and both rovers began heading up a steep incline toward the rock face. The higher ground would help their defense, but Noah hoped it didn't also trap them.

Sean muttered a curse and Noah looked at him. "We're running low on ammunition. Can you get Gil to do a supply drop?"

Noah squatted down and opened a comlink to the shuttle. "Gil, we need a supply drop. Ammunition to the following location."

"Understood, Captain. I'm on my way," Gil replied.

"As fast as you can," Noah replied and closed the comlink. He looked at Sean. "He's on his way."

The broadheads still harried them but never appeared with the ambush predators.

"We're going to have to abandon the rovers," Sean said.

Noah's eyes widened. Their supplies were inside, along with Kyle and Ezra. Noah's combat skills were rusty, but at least he'd been trained. Kyle and Ezra didn't have any training.

Noah gave him a grim nod. "I'll warn them."

"Already done," Sean replied.

The rovers bounced over the rough terrain, and CDF soldiers in combat suits raced ahead toward the rock face. There was a shelf with a cave above. Amid the weapons fire, enormous creatures trying to kill them, and a jungle that seemed to want them trapped, the explorers pushed toward the waypoint.

The CDF soldiers formed a phalanx around the area near the rock face. Some of them switched to flame throwers for their ammo configuration, and smoke began to fill the air as they burned the jungle away.

Noah glanced above and saw the ambush predators trying to encircle them. The thin membrane of skin near the creature's armpits and legs that allowed them to glide in elongated leaps from distant branches folded like an accordion. They crawled around using thick branches as cover from CDF weapons. Either it hadn't taken them long to adapt, or they'd encountered weapons like theirs before.

Sergeant Staggart ordered two soldiers up the rock face and turned his attention back to a group of broadheads breaking through a tangle of vines.

The rovers came to an abrupt halt, nearly crashing into the sheer dark walls of the cliff. Noah and Sean leapt off the perch as the doors to the rovers opened and the occupants sprang out.

Noah looked up toward a ledge where the CDF soldiers had just been. One of them poked his head back into view and waved them up, giving them the all-clear.

"We're good to go," Noah said.

"Get up there. We're right behind you!" Sean said.

Kyle Regan and Ezra Coffman ran toward the cliff and began climbing. Noah hastened over and engaged his suit jets. He jumped and the jets propelled him upward in a powerful boost, allowing him to grab the ledge and pull himself the rest of the way. Scrambling out of the way so Kyle and Ezra could follow him, he moved farther along the ledge and began giving covering fire to the soldiers below.

The jungle seemed to spring to life as shockwaves among the

trees rippled toward them. Noah could hardly see the broadheads charging toward them, but there was no mistaking their bellows. They'd tear the whole jungle apart just to get to them.

Noah opened a broadcast comlink. "Get out of there, now! No time. No time!"

CDF soldiers began climbing up to the ledge using their own suit jets.

Kyle and Ezra stayed near the ledge to help them get the rest of the way.

Noah watched as Sean engaged his suit jets and leapt into the air. He was halfway up when one of the ambush predators swooped down and crashed into him. Sean hit the wall. He tried to grab onto something, but his armored hands kept slipping until one of them seized a thick vine. The predator held onto Sean's torso, dragging him down. Clawed feet flailed as the creature squirmed violently.

Noah couldn't get a clear shot. Neither could any of the CDF soldiers.

"Get back!" Sergeant Unwin shouted. He ran to the edge and jumped. A tether trailed behind him, and three soldiers braced themselves.

The tether became taut, and Unwin swung toward Sean. Feet raised, Unwin kicked the predator, taking it completely by surprise. The force of the blow caused the creature to release Sean, but then he began to fall. Unwin reached out with his hand and Sean barely managed to grab it.

"He's got him. Pull them up," Noah said.

The three soldiers began hauling on the tether.

Loud clangs sounded from below as the broadheads slammed into the rovers. The vehicles crashed into the cliff, and the force of the blow bent the reinforced alloyed frame. The broadheads stomped on them, ramming their armored skulls against the rovers over and over again.

Several soldiers lined up to begin shooting at the creatures, but Sean ordered them to stop.

"Conserve your ammo," Sean said.

Noah looked at Kyle and Ezra. They were walking toward the back of the ledge to the entrance of a nearby cave.

Noah walked to Sean. "Are you all right?"

"No," Sean said in a vicious, half-strangled growl. "I'm not okay."

The rovers were wrecked, and the only supplies they had were what they'd carried with them.

Noah glanced at the trees. They were only a short distance from the ledge. "We can't stay here. Those predators are coming," he said.

Sean nodded and glanced behind them with a sigh. "We don't know what could be in that cave either. Sergeant Staggart, get a recon drone in there. See if there's a way through," Sean said and looked back to Noah. "Wouldn't do us any good to get trapped in there."

Noah nodded and surveyed the area. "This almost looks like an attack."

Sean regarded him for a moment. "It *was* an attack. This was coordinated."

Noah blinked a few times, trying to wrap his mind around it. What could have coordinated the attack?

Specialist Denny came over to them. His combat suit was dented in several places, but it wasn't venting any atmosphere. "Sirs, the recon drone detected a faint distress beacon."

"Where?" Sean asked.

"While it was in the cave. It's not closed off, so the signal could be coming from outside."

Noah looked at Denny's holoscreen. "It's a suit beacon. It's Lars! That's his ID."

Loud knocks began from below and they immediately spread out. Noah peered into the jungle but couldn't see anything.

Thunder sounded from above, and a sudden downpour began to fall in sheets of fat rain, distorting his view.

Noah looked at Sean. He'd heard it too.

"We've got to go inside," Sean said.

Thunder crashed again from above, but Noah could still hear the knocking sound from the jungle floor. The smoke from the fires was all but gone.

The broadheads stopped pummeling the rovers. The knocking paused and a screech sounded. The broadheads gave an answering bellow before moving off to the side, heading out of sight.

"Let's go," Noah said.

They entered the cave and heard people shouting from farther inside.

"All I said was that the creatures of this world are fascinating," Kyle said.

A CDF soldier spun around and jabbed a finger toward the scientist. "Just shut up, Regan! If you think they're so bloody fascinating, then why don't you go back out there and have a nice chat with them. Maybe you'll even make some new friends."

"I don't know about that," Kyle replied. "I think *you* have a lot more in common with the broadheads."

"That's it! Your ass belongs to me."

"Come and get it!" Kyle shouted.

Noah saw a group of soldiers clustered, keeping the two men from tearing into one another.

"Apone, knock that shit off!" Sergeant Staggart said and shoved his burly frame in front of Apone.

Kyle held up his hands and backed away.

Apone spun toward Sergeant Staggart. "This is bullshit! Ferro, Wierzbowski, and Crowe are stuck out there, and that bloody idiot wants to talk about how enchanting this world is."

"Enchanting," Kyle shouted. "Did you almost break your brain coming up with that word?"

Noah stepped in front of Kyle. "That's not helping."

"What's going on here?" Sean asked.

Private Apone inhaled deeply. "Nothing, Colonel."

"It didn't sound like nothing. It sounded like two men were about to go at it and tear each other's heads off, none of which helps us in any way," Sean said. Kyle started to speak, but Sean didn't give him the chance. "I don't care who said what or whose prickly feelings are hurt."

Kyle clamped his mouth shut and looked away.

"Lieutenant Rhoades, who are we missing? I heard Apone mention three people already," Sean said.

"You heard Colonel Quinn. Sound off," Lieutenant Rhoades said.

As the soldiers checked in, Noah looked at Kyle.

"I'm sorry, but I'm not going to get pushed around by an ape with a gun," Kyle said.

Noah shook his head. "For a brilliant scientist, that's the dumbest thing you could've said. Are you scared, Kyle?"

Kyle's brows furrowed. "What?"

"Are you scared? I know I am, and so are they," Noah said and leaned toward him. "So are you."

Kyle looked away for a few moments, and then he sighed. "Maybe my curiosity got the better of me. It won't happen again."

"Good. We can't afford to be at each other's throats," Noah replied.

"Understood."

Noah walked to Sean. "How many people are missing?"

"Four," Sean replied. "Unwin is trying to reach them over comlink."

Noah's brows knitted into a tight frown. Four soldiers had gotten cut off from the rest of them. "Are they—"

"They're still alive. Their combat suits show that they're alive," Sean replied and watched Unwin.

Sergeant Unwin looked over at them. "I've got Crowe on comlink. He and the others are hiding about half a klick from our location."

"How'd they get so far away?" Noah asked.

"They were trying to lure some of the broadheads away like we did earlier, but another group arrived and cut them off from us," Sergeant Unwin replied.

"What's their status?" Sean asked.

"They're hiding. They're about a quarter of the way up one of the big trees, Colonel," Sergeant Unwin said.

Sean frowned. "That's not going to work for long."

"I can send Gil over with the shuttle to extract them," Noah said.

Sean considered it for a few moments. "Let's do that," he said and looked at Unwin. "They're going to need to climb higher. The shuttle has tethers that can be dropped to them, but they've got to get up more than halfway. Maybe even more."

"I'll tell them, Colonel," Sergeant Unwin replied.

Noah opened a comlink to the shuttle. "Gil, I'm sending you new coordinates. Four soldiers are cut off from us and need an evac."

"I've got the new location, Captain, but do you still want me to make a supply drop?" Gil asked.

Noah looked at Sean, who shook his head.

"We can wait for the supply drop. We're in a cave, so we've got some cover. I'll send you another location for the drop as soon as we figure out where these caves come out," Noah said.

"I have your location on the HUD. There are cave entrances on the other side. I can make a supply drop on my way to the evac site," Gil replied.

A set of coordinates appeared on Noah's HUD. "Okay, that's fine."

"Understood, Captain. *Pathfinder 1,* out."

The comlink closed and Noah looked at Sean.

"The recon drone is showing a couple of paths through, but it hasn't reached the end yet," Sean said.

"Really? That's quick," Noah replied.

"Yeah well, we need to move fast," Sean said, gesturing for Kyle Regan to join them.

"How can I help, Colonel?"

"Those predators—the ones in the trees. Do you think they'd come in these caves?" Sean asked.

Kyle considered it for a long moment, looking back at the cave entrance fifty meters away. "The opening is big enough for them to get in here, so I'd say that yes, there's a good chance they'd come in here after us."

Sean nodded. "I was afraid you'd say that."

Kyle shrugged, as if to say that's the way it was.

"We need to get moving," Noah said.

Lieutenant Rhoades joined them.

"We're moving out. Rhoades, I need a couple of soldiers watching our backs. Some of those creatures could follow us in here," Sean said.

"Understood, Colonel Quinn. I'll take point if that's all right with you?"

"It is," Sean said.

Lieutenant Rhoades walked over to Unwin and Staggart and began giving them orders.

Sean leaned toward Noah. "If the *Ark II* away team was attacked like that, they might not have made it."

Noah swallowed hard. "They could be holed up in a cave just like this."

Sean gave him a long look. "Noah, I know you don't want to hear this."

"Stop. Just stop. I'm not giving up on them."

"No one said anything about giving up, but we just got our asses handed to us. I'm just saying that they might have gotten more than they bargained for, and we need to be prepared for what that could mean."

Noah exhaled through his nose. "I understand, Sean. I'm not going to insist we keep going no matter the cost, but you have to admit that there's something strange going on with this planet. Something we haven't encountered before."

Sean considered it for a few moments and nodded. "Something strange is an understatement. What just happened is completely fu—" he paused and shook his head.

"We need to regroup. Let's get through this cave and see what's on the other side. Then we can figure out where that distress beacon is coming from. We're still not too far off the path the away team took," Noah said.

Sean blinked a few times and then chuckled. "Did you just set me on task?"

Noah smiled with half his mouth. "Yeah, I guess I did."

"Hunh," Sean said, with a slight nod. "Well, you *are* the mission commander. Lead on, then."

Noah regarded his friend for a moment. All of them had been shaken up by the attack and how it had escalated. They'd been reacting to an intensifying situation while continuing to push forward. Sean was right; they had to be careful that they didn't get in so deep that they couldn't get out. Perhaps the best thing they should do was regroup with the shuttle when they reached the other side of these caves.

They began walking through the cave, and the light from the entrance behind them faded from view.

"Those things really did a number on the rovers," Kyle said.

Noah was thinking the same thing.

"They really don't want us here. I've studied territorial displays before, but this is something else," Kyle continued.

"Noticed that, too," Noah said.

The cave was wide enough for three of them to walk side by side.

"Why are the walls here so smooth?" Sean asked.

"They're old lava tubes," Ezra answered. "Don't worry. It hasn't been active in a long time."

"How do you know they're lava tubes?" Kyle asked.

Ezra gestured above them. "Because of the tube-like structure and the basalt on the walls and the ground. It's got that new mineral as well."

Ezra squatted down and began scraping samples off the wall into a small container. She then pulled out a small probe and pressed the tip into the hole she'd made. A tiny arc of blue flashed. "Oh!" she said. The arc dissipated in a few seconds, but not before it had spread out from where she'd made contact with the probe.

"What was that?" Noah asked.

"It must be that new type of mineral. It's superconductive," Ezra replied, and looked at her personal holoscreen with a thoughtful frown. "Also highly magnetized."

"Uh, are we in danger?" Kyle asked.

Ezra shook her head. "So long as we don't run any serious

amounts of electricity in here, we should be fine. Not much of a chance of any static discharge happening with all this humidity. And that's not going to change no matter how deep this cave goes."

Noah nodded. "That's good to know."

They came across several smaller lava tubes both in the ceiling and angling up from the walls. This tube must have been one of the primary channels that other tubes used.

Noah was checking the progress of the two recon drones that were mapping out the tunnels ahead of them when a loud boom echoed from behind them.

Noah looked at Sean in alarm.

"We set a couple of traps near the entrance. It was only a matter of time before those predators decided to come in here after us," Sean said.

They quickened their pace in an unspoken agreement to put as much distance from the cave entrance as they could.

"I guess we'll see how stubborn they are," Noah said.

"The traps aren't near the entrance, but I'd rather not get caught in here," Sean said.

"I don't know how far those creatures would venture into the cave, no matter how good their night vision might be," Kyle replied.

"What do you mean?" Ezra asked.

"Two sets of eyes. I've seen it on a few species we've come across. That, combined with bioluminescence at night, might have made them evolve two sets of eyes, each set fulfilling a purpose," Kyle said.

Noah glanced at one of the smaller lava tubes in the wall. "What about creatures that live in caves?"

"If they live deep in caves, they might not have any skin pigment at all. Their eyesight is probably not that good either, but if the creatures follow the evolution of similar ones on other worlds, they're reliant on hearing and sensitivity to touch," Kyle replied.

Noah heard Sean mutter a curse.

"Listen up," Sean said. "Try to stay away from the lava tubes. We have no idea what could be living down here. Let's make it through as quickly as possible."

"Colonel, the creatures that dwell in caves are usually smaller. Shouldn't be much of a threat to us," Kyle said.

Sean regarded him for a second. "Do you really want to take that chance? Everything we've encountered on this planet is bigger than we're used to. It's safe to assume that goes for the cave critters as well."

Noah saw the soldiers walking ahead of them start to look around, searching for anything dangerous. The ends of their rifles strayed toward smaller tube openings. A little vigilance never hurt anyone.

Their helmets adjusted to the low light levels, allowing them to see quite well in the dark. There wasn't much for them to see other than dark volcanic rock and the occasional glitter of mineral deposits in the walls and floor.

The ground sloped downward, and at the bottom they reached an open area that was about twenty meters across. To their right was another tube that angled up and away from the chamber.

Sean glanced toward the other side of the chamber. "How long do you think it'll be before whatever lives down here comes to check us out?"

"Well, Kyle did say that things that lived in caves could hear better than most, so probably not that long. At least we're not finding the bones of other creatures that got caught down here," Noah replied.

"That's what I thought, too, but I saw something on the other side."

Noah peered in the direction Sean was looking but could only see more lava tubes.

"What did it look like?"

Sean gestured toward the others and they followed. "It looked like a damn spider. A big one, easily a meter across. I only saw it for a few seconds. It was white and had the legs to go with it."

Noah shuddered. He hated spiders or any creature that looked like one. He felt the same way about snakes or any reptiles, for that matter. "The sooner we get out of here the better," he said.

Sean grunted in agreement.

The tunnel curved up ahead and then sharply inclined. Lieutenant Rhoades sent two soldiers up it. Bright flashes from their suit jets lit the tunnel, and Noah thought he heard a hissing sound coming from behind them.

The two soldiers threw down a couple of ropes for the ones without suit jets.

Private Apone glanced behind them, peering into the gloom. "Colonel, I think there's something back here. I thought I heard something."

Sean turned around and looked. Noah couldn't see anything. The tunnel curved out of sight.

"I have a flare. Do you want me to shoot it back down there?" Kyle asked.

Apone regarded Kyle for a second. "Knock yourself out."

Kyle fired a flare back the way they'd come. A bright ball of light streaked down the tunnel and bounced off the wall, disappearing from view. A kind of loud gasp and hiss came from farther away.

Kyle flinched back at the sound. "Gah!"

"Get moving," Noah said and gave Kyle a little push toward the ropes.

"Colonel?" Apone asked.

"Hold your fire," Sean replied.

The others made their way up the sharp incline. Noah waited at the bottom for Kyle and Ezra to finish climbing up using the ropes and then engaged his suit jets, shooting toward the top.

Sean and Apone were the last ones up.

"Hey Regan, do you have any more of those flares?" Apone asked.

Kyle tossed one to the soldier.

Apone triggered the starter and tossed the flare back the way they'd come. "I figure if those things live in the dark, then they hate the light. That ought to buy us some time."

The tunnel had more curves than the others they'd taken. Noah glanced behind them, wondering if whatever had made those hissing noises was following them.

"Light up ahead!" Sergeant Unwin shouted.

They started jogging forward and the tunnel brightened as the ones in front reached the entrance. Their recon drones hovered a short distance outside the cave.

The soldiers paused a short distance away from the cave entrance and waited for the others to catch up. Several of them watched the jungle while some of the others kept an eye on the cave.

Noah heard the clawing patter of dozens of feet coming from behind him. "Don't stop!"

"Keep going," Sean said.

The others exited the cave and Noah ran toward the entrance, glancing behind him. There wasn't anything there, but he knew the cave dwellers were coming, and it felt like something was crawling up the backs of his legs inside his envirosuit. Nothing could have been, but it did make him run a little bit faster than he had been.

He emerged from the cave back into the jungle. They were on a short outcropping, and the jungle floor was only a few meters down. The ground sloped downward at a slight decline. He looked around, searching for more broadheads or those ambush predators they'd encountered before, but the jungle was quiet.

Dark shapes flew overhead, their large shadows blotting out what little sunlight pierced the jungle canopy—more of those flying whales they'd encountered on the way here.

"Come on. We don't want to stay near the cave entrance," Sean said.

Noah followed his friend.

"Colonel, there's a supply cache about a hundred meters to our right," Specialist Denny said.

Noah accessed the recon drones' communication systems. Lars's distress beacon was still active.

"First we resupply, then we investigate the beacon," Sean said.

They made their way to the supply cache that had dropped from the shuttle. It was a two-meter-wide metallic container.

Noah looked at Sean and saw him wince. "What is it?" he asked. He glanced back at the cave entrance and thought he saw something moving in the shadows, but nothing had ventured outside. There was no way they'd be camping anywhere near here.

Sean shook his head. "Just a headache. My head started throbbing back in that cave. I've taken something to help relieve the pain."

A comlink message appeared on Noah's HUD. "Gil reports

that the soldiers have been extracted. He's on his way back to us now," Noah said.

Sean grabbed a couple of the nano-robotic ammunition packs and passed one to Noah. After reloading, Sean spotted something red out of the corner of his eye. He turned toward it and saw a red fog billowing toward them.

A few others had started to notice it also and shouted a warning to the rest of them.

Noah looked around and noticed that the red fog seemed to rise from the ground on their left. Then the knocks sounded again, loud, with a deep, roaring vibrato.

"Run!" Sergeant Unwin shouted.

Noah spun toward him, but the fog had already caught up to them and it was getting difficult to see. The breath caught in his throat. He saw Sean running ahead of him and started to follow.

"Captain!" Ezra shouted. She sounded like she was ahead.

"I'm here. I'm coming toward you," Noah replied.

He spotted Kyle ahead and came up behind him. Together they reached Ezra. She grabbed Kyle's arm. "Stay by me," she said.

"Sean?" Noah called.

"Over here."

Noah turned and saw a flashing light coming from Sean's helmet.

"Turn on your helmet lights," Noah said.

Kyle and Ezra both did as he'd asked.

Private Apone was nearby and joined them.

"I can't find the others, Colonel," Apone said.

There were shouts from the others as they tried to find each other, but the loud knocks intensified. Then the modulated bellow of a broadhead was heard.

"Shit, it's those damn things again," Apone said.

"It sounds different," Kyle replied.

"Keep moving," Sean said.

Something thumped nearby and Noah spun toward it. His weapon lifted a little, and he kept it ready.

A screech from the ambush predator sounded from above. Noah jerked his weapon upward but could only see the red fog. He didn't fire.

Something pushed him from behind. Noah jumped and hastened forward. "Something just bumped into me."

"Move!" Sean said.

They started running.

Noah heard the others shouting for each other. Sean sent out a broadcast comlink to the others. "Head to this waypoint."

A path highlighted on Noah's HUD, and he started running, keeping pace with the others. None of them wanted to get lost in the fog. He heard the recon drones flying overhead. One of them flew above the fog and it registered at over twenty-five meters above the ground.

Something became tangled in Noah's feet, and he gasped, stumbled forward, and fell to the ground. He looked up and saw the fading light of the others' helmets as they ran. To his right was the knobbed head of a thick, red plant. It was the size of a rover's wheel. Spores shot out from the two-meter-wide top. Then something clunked from deep inside, and more spores were released.

Noah regained his feet and ran. The others had run ahead, and he couldn't see them anymore. He glanced to the side and saw more of those same plants all around, as if they'd all opened up at the same time.

He saw a large broadhead on its side and expected it to turn toward him, but the creature was dead. All around it, the red plants seemed to spring out of the ground. They looked to be absorbing the creature. Knocks sounded from inside the plants, and they increased as he got closer. The clunks seemed to reach a crescendo and then started again.

The deep vibrato sounded as if something were moaning a long guttural howl. "*Uuuuuuvvvvaaaiiiii.*"

It reminded Noah of chanting but way more menacing. He skirted around the fallen creature and quickened his pace to catch up with the others. The last thing he wanted to be in a place like this was alone.

20

Despite having a waypoint to follow, not as many managed to reach it. Noah caught up to Sean and some of the others, but the rest of them were nowhere to be found. The waypoint he'd been following was taking him to a different location than where he'd found Sean.

"The waypoint you sent doesn't match up with the nav on my suit computer. Mine had me going a hundred meters northwest of here," Noah said.

The fog looked as if it were beginning to lessen. Sean looked at Noah's waypoint and then at his own. "I don't know why it's incorrect. Has to be some kind of malfunction in the nav system in the suits," he said.

Apone was shouting for the others nearby. There were some answers, but Noah couldn't tell where they were.

Noah checked the recon drone and shook his head. "The fog goes on for kilometers all around us. We need to find some higher ground."

"I wouldn't recommend going back the way we came," Sean replied.

"Yeah, I saw something at the cave entrance, but I bet whatever they are don't come out until it's nighttime."

"Excuse me," Kyle said. "This is no ordinary fog. I mean, there's plenty of moisture in the air, but there's also some kind of spores. It's causing the red color."

Noah looked around at the plants nearby. They were covered with the crimson spores. "I saw the plant that was spewing the spores out. It's got a knobbed head like a mushroom. Broad body and large head, but the coloring is different. The sounds we've been hearing come from them. The Uvai are those plants. I saw them around the body of a broadhead on the way here."

Sean glanced around for a second. "Plants don't grow that fast. How big did you say these mushrooms were?"

"Some of them were tiny, but others were as big as we are," Noah replied, and frowned. "This is going to sound crazy, but it looked like they were absorbing the broadhead."

Sean's eyebrows arched. "Absorb?" he asked. Then said. "Do you mean like it was consuming it?"

Apone shook his head, muttering incoherently. "Meat-eating plants? What the hell kind of freak show is this place? Where's the shuttle? We need to get out of here now."

"Hold on. Wait a second. Don't jump to any conclusions," Kyle said. "We don't know how long the broadhead has been dead. Plants absorb the nutrients of dead animals all the time. This is no different."

Noah pressed his lips together. "I understand that, but this *is* different. There's something inside them."

"Okay, it's a new lifeform then. We should try studying it," Kyle said.

Apone sighed explosively. "Here we go again," he said and

jutted out his chin. "No, I get it. I know this is what you do, but shooting things is what I do… when ordered to, that is."

Noah looked at Sean and saw him peering away from them. "Sean, what are you looking at?"

Apone lifted his rifle a little and stared in the same direction.

Sean shook his head and blinked several times.

"Is it the headache?" Noah asked.

Sean nodded a little. "It comes and goes."

"I've been getting them too," Ezra said. "Anyone else?"

"I haven't felt right since we set foot on this damn planet," Apone said.

"I feel a little pressure near my forehead, but it's not bad," Kyle said.

Sean eyed Noah. "You?"

"Not really. The lower gravity still feels strange, but no headaches," Noah replied.

He'd had his share of headaches as a result of his head injuries, so his tolerance for them might be higher than the others.

Noah looked at Sean. "Is that all?"

Sean sighed. "I thought I saw something."

"What did you see?"

"Someone running right over there," Sean said, gesturing to where he'd been staring at a few moments before. "Except they didn't have an envirosuit on."

Noah frowned. "No suit."

Sean nodded. "I know. It sounds crazy."

"Did you get a good look at who it was?" Kyle asked.

Ezra shot him a look.

Noah waited for Sean to answer.

"No, I didn't," Sean grudgingly replied.

Noah wasn't sure whether he believed him. If Sean said he

saw something then he did, but for some reason he didn't want to share who he thought he saw.

"Maybe we should contact the *Infinity*. See what the doctors up there think about this," Ezra said.

Apone stared at her for a moment. "What are you saying? There's nothing wrong with Colonel Quinn."

"No, I'm not saying there's anything wrong with him, but could it hurt to get a second opinion? A medical one at that?"

The knocking sounds could still be heard in the distance, but they didn't sound like they were coming any closer.

"Once we get back on the shuttle, I'll check in with the doc," Sean said.

"All right, but tell me if the headaches get worse or…" Noah said and paused. How was he supposed to suggest that Sean tell him if he was hallucinating when he wasn't sure if that's what it was? "If you see something else that doesn't have an explanation."

Sean smiled wryly. "Or if I think I'm imagining it. It's fine, I'm not afraid to admit it, but the same goes for all of us."

Apone shook his head. "With so much weird shit here, I'm not sure if it's just part of the featured tour or something that's affecting my brain."

"I'll keep an eye out for you," Kyle said. "Seriously, you see something, then point it out to me, or anyone else really. If two people see it, it can't be an illusion."

Noah considered it for a few moments. "That's a good idea," he said and looked at Sean.

Something stomped toward them. Sean and Apone readied their weapons. Noah was only a second behind.

"Is someone there?" Noah asked.

"Captain Barker, is that you?" Specialist Denny said.

The big CDF tech soldier trotted toward them with a huge

smile on his face. "I'm so glad I found you guys. I've been roaming around here trying to find someone."

"Why didn't you use the comlink?" Noah asked.

"I tried. No one would respond. The waypoint location kept moving."

Something was definitely interfering with their comms. Noah tried to open a comlink to the shuttle, but there was no response. "I can't reach the shuttle."

"Neither can I," Sean said. He tried to reach the others, but there wasn't any response.

"How far away could they have gotten?" Kyle asked.

Noah checked his comlink to the recon drone overhead. It still worked. "I've still got a connection to the recon drone."

"Good, try and use its comms system as a relay," Sean said.

Noah brought up his holoscreen and accessed the control interface for the recon drone. He broadcast a comlink, and the shuttle answered almost immediately.

"Captain, is that you?" Gil asked, sounding relieved.

"Yes, it's me," Noah said and told him who else was with him. "Have you heard from any of the others?"

"You're the first, sir. I was on my way to you when this fog rolled in. Something is throwing off the navigation instruments," Gil said.

"Yeah, we've been seeing it here, too. Don't know why it's happening."

"Captain, I can try to make it to your location, but with this fog I don't think I can navigate below the tree line for a pickup," Gil said.

"We're fine for the moment. I want you to fly over this area and try to locate the others first. Extract them if you can. We'll be in touch," Noah said.

"Understood, Captain. We'll be back for you. Oh, and *Pathfinder 2* is on its way back here," Gil said.

The comlink disconnected. The second shuttle returning to the area should make finding the others much easier.

Sean looked at Noah, his eyes wide. "What are you doing?"

"Lars's signal. It's not that far away," Noah said.

"Noah," Sean said and paused. He shook his head. "I don't think they made it."

Noah set his jaw. "That's what we came here to find out," he replied.

Sean's eyes went skyward for a moment, and he pressed his lips together. "This isn't the way to do it. We need to regroup with the others."

"What do you suggest? Should we just start wandering around, shouting for them? Gil is searching for them right now with the shuttle. He can cover more ground than we can."

Sean frowned. "If we try to find Lars's distress beacon and get attacked again, we might not be able to hold them off."

Noah clenched his teeth for a few seconds. "I'm not giving up on them. Not until I know what happened."

"I think it's pretty obvious what happened," Sean replied.

The others had been quiet before, and now they hardly dared to move.

"You want to give up? Fine, I'm not."

"Well, I'm not going to let you throw your life away."

Noah glared at Sean for a few moments as the tension mounted. Noah looked away, inhaling through his nostrils, and sighed. Snapping at his friend wasn't going to help. He might not have a headache, but maybe he was experiencing the effects of the planet in other ways.

"When we were in the rovers, I thought I heard something imitating the sounds the broadheads made," Noah said.

Sean blinked a few times. "Imitating?"

Noah nodded. "Yeah, I thought maybe it was something else. As if the broadhead had been wounded, but it happened more than once."

Kyle cleared his throat. "Did it sound like this?" he asked.

The young scientist held up his wrist computer and a sound began to play. It sounded like a slightly modulated form of the broadheads' growls. There were others that had different intonations, but they all sounded a little bit different from the broadheads they'd heard.

"And there's this, also," Kyle said.

A growling, hissing noise began to play from his wrist computer.

"Those predators," Noah said with a nod.

Kyle inclined his chin once. "Yeah, I was recording almost the entire time we were running. It happened by accident. I only realized it when we were in the cave, so I isolated the sounds and cleaned it up a bit while we walked."

"That's great, but what does it mean?" Sean asked.

"I think it means that something was communicating with the broadheads and the predators. You said that the attacks were coordinated. Maybe this was it. This was what was giving them orders," Noah said.

"What was giving them orders? What was making that sound? What was mimicking their language?" Sean asked.

"I think it's the Uvai," Noah said. Sean's mouth hung open a little. "Seriously. The timing of those recordings coincided with the knocking sounds—the vibrato sounds as well. What if it's those... it seems too simplistic to call them plants. They're more than that, and what if they're controlling the environment somehow?"

Sean shook his head. "That's a hell of a stretch."

Noah nodded. "Yeah, well look where we are. It's the only explanation that makes any sense."

"So, you're saying intelligent plants are doing this?" Apone asked.

"Yeah, I am," Noah said.

Sean turned toward Kyle. "You're awfully quiet all of a sudden. What have you got to say about this?"

"Actually, it makes sense. Plants have intricate ways of communicating in complex ways, as do fungi, which might be more accurate since they resemble a mushroom. This seems a bit extreme, but it's not outside the realm of possibility. There are fungi that are part of complex systems and hierarchies on New Earth. I'm sure if I checked our records on the *Infinity*, I could confirm the same on Old Earth," Kyle replied.

"There, see? It's not so crazy after all," Noah said. "Who said that the only intelligent life out there has to walk and talk in ways we're familiar with?"

Sean chewed on his lower lip for a second. "I think the message they're sending is pretty clear."

"What do you mean?" Noah asked.

"If what you're saying is true, these Uvai are the things that have been orchestrating events. And their message is pretty clear. They want us to leave," Sean said.

"Maybe."

Sean's eyebrows raised. "Maybe?"

"Remember when we first started communicating with the Ovarrow? Remember how many miscommunications there were in the beginning? Maybe we've done something to agitate it."

Sean chuckled. "You want to try talking to it?"

Noah bobbed his head to the side a little. "Yeah. I mean we tried shooting them and that didn't work."

"We haven't shot at them. We defended ourselves against the creatures the Uvai set on us," Sean said.

"I doubt it views events in quite those terms. If it can mimic or actually communicate with multiple species here, maybe it can help us find the away team, or maybe we can reason with it," Noah said.

Sean's mouth hung open again and he blew out a breath. "Okay, how do you want to do this? For the record I think this is crazy, but it's not the craziest thing I've ever heard."

Noah looked away for a few seconds. "I'm going to need a few minutes."

21

THE RED FOG had lessened in the area, but Noah couldn't see very far into the distance. Pieces of the landscape were somewhat visible, but it was as if the jungle all around them was shrouded in mystery.

They'd started making their way toward Lars's distress beacon. They were traveling slower than they had been, and the jungle, despite the red fog, had settled into a somewhat familiar rhythm.

Sean and Apone shouted for the other soldiers.

"I don't even know if it's safe to approach one of them," Kyle said.

Noah nodded. "I know. It definitely seemed to react when I got closer. I more or less stumbled on it."

"We could try using one of the recon drones to take a closer look. Do you think they'll let us use one?" Kyle asked.

"It's not us and them, Kyle. We're all on the same team."

Kyle glanced at Ezra, and the two of them seemed to share some unspoken bit of knowledge between them.

"You said I should be honest with you," Kyle said. "It *is* us and them. It's their equipment."

There would always be lines drawn between military personnel and civilians when they worked together for a common goal. Noah was the mission commander, but if Sean decided that their lives were in danger or the risk was too much, it was his responsibility to ensure their safety, which included overruling whatever Noah wanted to do. The shared responsibility had worked fine, with only a few hiccups along the way, but Noah knew that Kyle had made up his mind about how things were going to work, and he didn't think he could change it. To be fair, Kyle wasn't entirely wrong, but he and Sean had been close friends for a long time. Friendship still counted for something in Noah's mind.

Noah walked over to Sean. Apone shouted for the others a short distance away.

"I need to use the recon drone to take a closer look at the Uvai," Noah said.

Sean nodded. "There's never quite enough of them to go around."

Noah chuckled. "I had more in the rovers."

Sean snorted, and then made a passing motion to Noah.

Noah's holoscreen became active with the control interface for the drone. Kyle and Ezra stood on either side of him.

Answering shouts came in the distance.

"Colonel Quinn, I think I hear Sergeant Staggart, sir," Apone said.

Noah heard the crackly sound of a comlink coming from Sean's wrist computer.

He turned his attention back to the drone and flew it closer to the ground. Specialist Denny came to join them.

Noah glanced at the big soldier. "I should've asked you to do this."

"I can take over if you want, sir," Specialist Denny offered.

"Only if I get into trouble," Noah replied.

He'd been flying drones that served all manner of functions since before the others had been born. He almost winced at the thought. He'd just had an "old man" thought… well, an older man's thought, anyway.

Noah activated the option that tracked the signal range. It was based on a ping-back through the communication protocol used with the drones.

"I didn't know you could do that," Kyle said. "The signal range thing."

"They all function within an estimated range, which can be extended via the satellites or with subspace," Specialist Denny replied. "But I haven't seen one self-adjust like this before."

The edges of Noah's lips lifted a little. "I looped the ping-back protocol and added a subroutine to estimate the range based on the signal strength. You can always get more out of the tools you have on hand."

Specialist Denny smiled. "That's great. I'm going to have to remember that."

He flew the drone closer to the ground, settling at two meters above it, and had the drone run the video feed through multiple visual spectrums. After a few minutes of searching, they found a cluster of Uvai near the trunk of a massive tree.

"That's interesting," Kyle said, gesturing toward the screen. "They have their own root system. See the ground around it?"

"I thought those were vines," Noah said, peering at the image. "But they're connected. Look at that. They're all connected."

"Have the drone circle around to the other side," Kyle said.

Noah flew the drone around the cluster of Uvai. Their root system was intertwined with the nearby tree.

"There!" Kyle said. "This is amazing. It connects with the root system of the tree. It's just intertwined. They're joined. I bet it's joined with the other plants nearby, which means we're walking in a highly sophisticated network of fungi."

Ezra cleared her throat. "Why don't the other plants reject it?"

"I wish I knew," Kyle replied.

"Not even a guess?" Specialist Denny asked.

Kyle shook his head. "It wouldn't be a good guess. This isn't something that can be answered with simple observation, not in the amount of time we have left. I'd need physical samples of the tree and the Uvai to determine how integrated they are. And they'd need to be compared with other regions that don't have Uvai. That statement has a lot of assumptions associated with it, but you get my meaning."

Noah looked around. The fog still carried the reddish tinge of the spores that had come from the Uvai. If they functioned like other plants and fungi, the spores were how it reproduced, but that didn't explain the rapid growth they'd suspected was happening. "This is more complicated than we previously thought, even just a few minutes ago," Noah said.

"Why?" Specialist Denny asked.

"If they're interconnected across species, we're dealing with an emerging consciousness… or maybe a fully emerged consciousness, as in an intelligent lifeform," Noah said.

Kyle's eyes widened with excitement. "You might be right. Its behavior is reactionary to us being here, and it also coordinated the attack earlier. It's the only explanation that makes sense. It used the other creatures and even the jungle itself to… I don't know what it wanted to do."

"It tried to kill us," Specialist Denny said, as if it couldn't be more obvious.

"Yeah," Kyle said, sounding only partially convinced. "No doubt, but it was also trying to trap us. It was herding us in a particular direction."

Noah nodded. "Problem solving. It was reacting to us, like we were reacting to it. On this kind of scale, it's beyond anything we've ever encountered."

Sean walked over to them. "Found something?"

Sergeant Staggart followed him over, while the other CDF soldiers kept watch nearby.

"Yeah," Noah said, looking at Sergeant Staggart and the other soldiers. "Are you guys all right?"

Staggart gave him a firm nod. "Right as rain, sir."

"Good," Noah replied and proceeded to bring Sean up to speed about what they'd been discussing.

Sean regarded them for a few moments before he spoke. "A smart fungus."

Sergeant Staggart grinned, and Noah did as well.

"That's an oversimplification of what we just told you."

Sean smiled.

Noah thought he looked calmer. The medicine must be helping with the pain.

"Okay, how do we know how complex they are?" Sean asked.

Noah considered it for a few seconds, and Kyle waited for him to respond. "That's difficult to figure out. Kyle, I think you can explain it better than I can."

"I'll try my best," Kyle said. He gestured to an image on his holoscreen. "See how the Uvai has multiple connections to the tree nearby, but it also has connections going to other Uvai. There are even connections into the ground that might go beyond this area completely."

Sean nodded.

Kyle compressed his lips for a second before he continued. "The structure of a vine has multiple folds or layers inside. It makes them incredibly strong in some cases. See the thickness of connections here? There are bumps that occur every thirty centimeters or so. I think that if I were to cut one of them open, it would reveal a complex organ, almost akin to the nerve endings in us. The connection to the brain. Our brain is among the most complex biological systems we've ever come across. However, we're not alone in that. There are some animals that have similarly complex structures, like the dolphins of Old Earth, or even the Ovarrow of New Earth."

Sean frowned. "I understand that you think these connections among the Uvai are very complex and that there are biological implications that come with it."

"It's more than that," Noah said. "The Uvai might all be part of the same being. The same consciousness. These are merely extensions of it."

Sean blinked several times with a thoughtful frown. "Noah, these things are spread out over kilometers. They could be all over this continent and maybe even the entire planet. Are you saying they could all be connected to each other?"

"Maybe, Sean, maybe. But what we've seen here is that they *are* connected. And not only that, but they are also more than aware of the other creatures of this world," Noah replied.

"What do you mean by more than aware?"

"I'm willing to bet that they can exert a certain amount of mastery over most of the creatures here. They're the top of the food chain," Noah said.

"Top of the food chain," Kyle said and smiled. "That's a perfect way to put this."

"Just how intelligent is this thing?" Sean asked.

"I'm not exactly sure," Kyle said. "Just because it's big and complex doesn't mean it thinks or processes information any faster than we do."

"But there's no way to know for sure," Sean replied.

Kyle shook his head.

Noah regarded Sean for a few moments. He could guess what his friend was thinking. "The Vemus?"

Sean nodded.

The Vemus were a bacteria-viral hybrid that targeted mammalian life on Old Earth. It eventually spread to humanity, causing dormant genes in human DNA to express themselves to extremes.

"The Vemus were commanded by an alpha—a centralized intelligence," Sean said.

Kyle nodded. "I can see where you'd think there are similarities, but this is quite different. The Vemus took over the host and made them into a drone to serve a hive mind. That's not happening here."

"Maybe not yet, but it's a possibility."

"Based on what? The fact that a connection exists between multiple lifeforms? We can't assume the connection is a nefarious one," Kyle replied.

Sean looked at Noah. "It made those creatures attack us."

"They could be allies. It probably thinks we're some kind of invader," Noah said.

"We *are* invaders," Sean said.

"Fair enough. So, we just need to figure out how to reason with it. If it's intelligent enough to communicate with all these creatures, then why wouldn't it talk to us somehow?"

Sean's eyebrow flicked up. "Assuming it wants to talk to us."

"There's only one way to find out," Noah said.

Sean looked away from him for a moment. "Kara is going to kill me."

Kyle frowned. "Why would she kill you?"

"Because our fearless leader intends to strike up a conversation with the Uvai," Sean replied.

Noah smiled a little. "Just tell her I made you let me do it."

Sean was among the most experienced men Noah knew. Not only did Sean have a long career in the CDF, but he'd been part of special operations for the CDF. Dangerous missions came with the territory. Sean was formidable as a fleet commander, but he'd had almost as much experience with all manner of warfare. If Sean wanted to, he could stop Noah from doing anything if he thought it would protect him. Not that he would. Sean was a lot of things, but he wasn't a bully.

"Okay, we'll do it, but not without some rules," Sean replied.

"Such as?" Noah asked.

"If I think the Uvai are going to attack you, I'm going to send them a very aggressive message, starting with the one that's closest to you when you try," Sean said.

"Wait a second," Kyle said. "We're going to try to communicate with the Uvai, but you're also going to have a weapon pointed at it?"

Sean smiled grimly. "More than one of them, and if I can reach the shuttle, I might get a few attack drones deployed."

Noah had forgotten about the attack drones they'd brought with them. They'd been reverse engineered from Krake technology. The attack drones could puncture the armored hulls of CDF warships, and Noah doubted there was anything on this planet that could stop them once they were activated. He knew there was no argument he could make that would change Sean's mind. And if he was being honest with himself, he didn't want to change his friend's mind. However, he didn't want to unleash devastating destruction on this world either.

Noah tilted his head toward Kyle. "They weren't around the first time Connor accidentally brought an Ovarrow out of stasis."

Sean gave him a knowing smile. "I'm glad we see eye to eye on this."

"Just don't miss," Noah replied.

Sean grinned. "I don't. Not often, anyway."

"Sir, I'd like to come with you," Kyle said.

Noah considered it for a heartbeat, then nodded. "All right. You're with me."

Kyle's eyes widened. "Really?"

"Yeah. You might see something I miss," Noah replied.

"Do you want to backtrack the way we came?" Sean asked.

Noah shook his head. "No, Lars's beacon is coming from that way. Plus, I think we should stay as far away from those caves as possible."

Sean nodded. "All right. Specialist Denny, take back control of the recon drone and have it scout ahead of us. Sergeant Staggart, you're with me. Two soldiers in front and two behind."

Noah passed control of the recon drone back to Specialist Denny.

Ezra sighed. She wasn't looking at anyone.

"Are you all right?" Noah asked.

She turned green eyes toward him. "I'm fine. I'm just ready to take this suit off. We've been drinking recycled water and liquid rations for almost two days. Also, I could really use a shower. A long soak in some hot water would be nice too."

Noah smiled. "I know what you mean. Soon enough."

The shuttles didn't have much in the way of showers, but they could remove their envirosuits for a bit. They could clean up and eat a meal rather than drink one. He tended to lose track of bodily necessities like that when he was focused on a problem.

"I never thought I'd say I missed Roy Green's cooking, but here I am," Kyle said.

"You act as if we've been here for a week. It's only been about forty hours. Talk to me when you've been trapped in a lifepod for days," Noah said.

"When were you trapped in a lifepod?" Kyle asked.

"During the Vemus War."

Kyle pursed his lips. "I didn't know you were trapped for that long."

"I wasn't alone. Kara was with me."

Kyle's eyes twinkled. "Oh, so it was like a vacation then. Just the two of you on a cozy little lifepod out in the great expanse."

Ezra laughed. "I'm sure it wasn't as romantic as you make it sound."

Noah smiled. "Well, when we finally realized we weren't going to die from the Vemus, let's just say we did our fair share of celebrating."

Kyle grinned, his eyes gleaming. "I just bet you did."

Noah shrugged.

Kyle looked at Ezra. "You know, if you feel like celebrating later…"

Ezra regarded him evenly. "Mr. Regan, I don't know if my heart can take it."

Kyle grinned but was wise enough not to reply.

They'd walked for a short distance when Specialist Denny spotted a cluster of Uvai. They were only about a meter and a half tall, but there were more than a few of them.

Noah looked at Sean. "All right, I'm going to walk up to it with Kyle."

"We've got your back, but try to keep your distance from it," Sean replied.

Noah glanced at the cluster of Uvai. It was about fifty meters away and barely discernible through the fog. Suddenly, a bunch of questions invaded his mind, and he tried to cast them aside one by one.

Noah inhaled deeply and began walking toward the cluster. He kept his pace even and unrushed, collapsing his rifle and securing it to the side carrier of his suit. He still had a sidearm that was readily accessible if he needed it.

He heard Kyle following him, but they both remained quiet.

Noah came to a stop within ten meters of the cluster. The lights of his helmet penetrated the thinning fog, and he engaged the speakers of his envirosuit.

"Hello," Noah said. He raised his hands to the side, hoping to convey that he didn't want to threaten it. He stepped closer to it. "Hello, are you able to hear me?"

The cluster of Uvai were a glossy red color and remained quiet.

Noah glanced at Kyle. "Any ideas?"

"Normally, I'd suggest offering it some food, but that's not going to work."

Noah frowned in thought. "If you can hear me, please respond."

The Uvai remained quiet.

Noah brought up one of the recordings he had of the knocking sound and played it over his speakers for five seconds.

A few more seconds went by, and then he heard a soft knocking sound from the cluster.

"I think that's working," Kyle whispered.

"Yeah, but we don't know what it means. "

Noah stepped closer and played the sound again. This time

he let the sound play longer. He added its mimicking of the broadhead. "We heard you make these noises."

The soft thumping sound became louder, and something slithered on the ground. Noah looked down, trying to see what it was. He squatted down to get a better look, and his right hand drifted toward his sidearm.

"Colonel Quinn!" Sergeant Staggart shouted and then repeated himself. "Where'd he go? Colonel Quinn!"

A loud thump came from within the cluster of Uvai.

"Sir, I don't know where he went. He was just here," Apone replied.

"Spread out. Find him," Sergeant Staggart said.

Noah stood up and backed away from the Uvai. He opened a comlink to Sergeant Staggart.

"Sir, I need you to come back here. Colonel Quinn has disappeared."

"What do you mean he disappeared? He was right next to you," Noah replied.

Another thump sounded from inside the cluster of Uvai.

"I know, sir. His combat suit isn't even registering as being nearby."

Noah continued to back away, and Kyle grabbed his arm.

"Look," Kyle said.

Noah turned back toward the Uvai. A bunch of dark red spores swirled in the air for a second, rising up from the cluster of Uvai, and began to form a humanoid pattern. Noah's mouth hung open. The pattern became more detailed, forming a representation of a Pathfinder suit. On the chest was a sphere with a ring around it, and to the side, as if it were in the background, was a grouping of spheres orbiting a central one.

"Oh my God," Kyle said.

"It's the *Ark II* mission logo," Noah said.

22

Kara faced the smooth ivory wall of the examination room in the medical center.

"Okay, now squat down," Dr. Claire Hathaway said.

Kara tightened her core muscles and sank down.

"Good. Now hold it at the bottom," Hathaway said.

Kara held the pose while keeping her breathing even and controlled. She resisted the urge to glance at the clock. Watching the seconds tick by would only play tricks with her mind, and it was better if she stayed focused on her breathing. Her physical therapy routine had been designed to build back her strength.

"Okay, that's time," Hathaway said. Kara stood and turned around. "How did that feel?"

"It felt fine. I feel stiff in my hips and back by the end of the day, but when I exercise, it loosens me up."

Hathaway nodded and some of her brown curls bounced lazily with the movement of her head. "How about the sauna baths?"

Kara looked away for half a second. "There hasn't been time.

I know… I know it helps. I never thought I'd like a dry sauna until you made me use the ones here."

She did enjoy how she felt after she'd spent thirty minutes in the sauna and sweated a good bit. Her muscles relaxed and she just felt calmer overall. But she hadn't had thirty minutes to spare over the past few days.

Dr. Hathaway regarded her with compassionate but stern brown eyes. "The proof of its effectiveness is in the reports from your biochip. All I can advise is that you make every effort to block out time for your recovery. The exercises and stretches certainly help, but you want to recover as quickly as possible. This requires that you do all the activities that have been prescribed. That's all. It's in your hands, Kara."

She nodded. When she was tired, the aches in her lower back and hips made her limp a little. The muscles were tight, which required rest and stretches to work them out. She eyed Hathaway. "So, the elephant in the room."

Hathaway smiled. "I see no reason that you should remain on restricted duty, as long as you follow up with me and maintain the regimen we've put together for you."

"Thank you."

"I'll be checking your biochip over the next month to ensure your recovery stays on track."

Kara would stick to the regimen. If anything, it helped alleviate her aches and pains, which Hathaway assured her would continue to fade over time. Hathaway was also within her rights to check Kara's biochip while they were on the *Infinity*.

A comlink chimed from the small speaker by the door, and a monotone AI voice relayed a message requesting Kara come to the bridge.

"Duty calls," Kara said.

"Will you be joining us later?" Hathaway asked.

Hathaway's spin classes with the exercise bikes had become quite popular with the crew. She followed the classes with a yoga session. Both were part of Kara's exercise regimen.

"I plan on it," Kara replied as she headed for the door.

"Good, I'll see you later then," Hathaway said, following her out.

Kara took several steps and turned back. "Thank you, Claire. I appreciate everything you've done to get me this far."

Claire Hathaway's lips lifted. "You're welcome, but you did all the work," she replied with a twitch of her eyebrows.

Kara left the medical center and headed for the bridge. Blood and his team had captured a few of the *Ark II*'s automated resource acquisition drones, and they'd been brought near the *Infinity*'s hangar. They were as long as the Pathfinder shuttles but were meant to haul material for use by the *Ark II*'s onboard autofactory.

She walked onto the bridge and could feel the tension in the air. She headed straight toward Markovich.

"Ma'am," Markovich said. "The *Ark II*'s orbit is deteriorating."

He gestured toward the main holoscreen, which showed how the *Ark II* was steadily moving closer to the alpha moon.

"When did this start happening?" Kara asked.

Delta Mattison joined them. "Our sensors picked up activity from their maneuvering thrusters, which isn't odd. It has to maintain that orbit. But we started to notice that orbital degradation was becoming more prominent instead of less."

Kara studied the data on the main holoscreen and looked at Markovich.

"They must be having an issue with navigation."

"More than an issue if the *Ark II*'s own engines are pushing the ship toward that moon. Did you detect any automated landing gear deployed for the habitat sections of the ship?" Kara asked.

The *Ark II* was designed to be separated into sections that would be used to help establish the colony.

"Negative, ma'am," Mattison replied.

Kara looked at Markovich. "Is our navigation system affected?"

"There has been an increase in magnetism from the planet, which is being echoed from the alpha moon, but that shouldn't have an effect on the *Ark II*'s navigation system."

"Something has to be affecting it because it's flying into the moon. What's the impact trajectory?"

Markovich frowned and then quickly calculated it. "Catastrophic."

Kara opened a holoscreen from a nearby workstation, and the main holoscreen updated with a predictive orbital path for the *Ark II*. "We have sixteen hours to fix this before a crash can't be avoided."

She looked over at Jessica Yu. "Get me the hangar bay. I need Blood, now!"

Jessica opened a comlink to the hangar. A few minutes later a video comlink appeared at the workstation in front of Kara.

Peter Blood looked into the camera.

"How fast can you reach the *Ark II* with those drones you captured?" Kara asked.

"About six hours."

Kara gritted her teeth and shook her head. "Can you shave that down?"

"I can certainly try, but we might trigger the point-defense systems. What's going on?" Blood asked.

Kara gave him a quick rundown of the situation.

"Okay, I think I could get it down to four hours. I can't be positive until we're en route."

Kara exhaled forcefully. "At best, that gives us twelve hours to fix whatever's broken over there. I don't know if that's enough time."

"Why wouldn't it be enough time? Twelve hours sounds like plenty of time to me," Blood said.

"We don't know how much fuel is available for the course correction. The automated systems should've kept power reserves going, but I don't want to make any assumptions."

"What about firing up the main engines?" Blood asked.

Markovich shook his head.

"That's not going to work. They've been offline for months. Assuming everything was working, it would still take too much time to bring them up. No, we need to use the maneuvering thrusters to save the ship," Kara said.

She regarded Blood for a few seconds. "How many people were you planning to bring with you?"

"Six."

Kara glanced at Markovich for a moment. He looked as if he'd swallowed something sour.

"Knock that number down to five. I'm coming with you," Kara said.

Blood blinked a couple of times.

"I'm not asking you. I'm telling you."

Blood recovered quickly. "Yes, ma'am. I'll get my team ready to leave ASAP."

The comlink closed.

Markovich looked at Delta for a second. "Would you give us a moment, please?"

Delta Mattison nodded and went back to her workstation.

"Ma'am, send me instead. I know how to operate the maneuvering thrusters. Blood and his team can get me inside."

"Can you bypass the lockdown?"

Markovich stared at her for a long moment. "You can walk me through it."

Kara smiled a little and shook her head. "Not this time. Remote access won't be available until we can stop the lockdown. It's more complicated than disabling one particular system."

Markovich grimaced. "I know. I just wish I could help more."

"If we fail, there's the backup plan. We're not going to use the other drone Blood captured," Kara said.

If they failed to reach the *Ark II*, they'd use the second drone to take out the point-defense systems. The *Infinity* might have enough time to dock and nudge the ship to safety.

Markovich nodded. "I hope it doesn't come to that."

"So do I," Kara said. Too many things could go wrong with that plan. "I better get down there."

Kara left the bridge and took the elevator down to the hangar deck. Peter Blood met her by the doors.

"We're setting up over here," Blood said, and they headed toward a mobile staging area with EVA suits.

Kara walked over to the rack and removed her jacket so that all she wore was her blue jumpsuit. The EVA suit was attached to a charging station. She grabbed the handholds, hoisted herself up to a small platform, turned, and sat down into the suit. She raised her arms on either side of her and the chassis closed, sealing her inside. Her helmet lowered and the HUD came online as the EVA suit went through a systems check.

Kara saw someone running toward the staging area.

Dr. Hathaway hastened over to them. Blood intercepted her and the two of them spoke. Both of them glanced in her direction. Her system check was still processing, so she couldn't hear what they were saying, but they quickly finished.

Kara took control of the mechanized EVA suit and walked over to them. "What's going on?"

"I need to come with you," Hathaway said.

Kara's eyebrows raised and she pursed her lips. She'd expected Hathaway would try to stop her from going, and instead, she was insisting that she join them. "Why?"

"You don't know the status of any of the colonists aboard. What if they need medical attention? What if something is wrong with the stasis pods? None of you are qualified for this," Hathaway said.

Kara glanced at Blood. He was grim-faced but determined.

"Claire, we're not taking a shuttle over to the *Ark II*. We're hitching a ride using one of their automated drones. When was the last time you even trained with an EVA suit?" Kara asked.

Hathaway grimaced as she looked at the drone hovering just beyond the shield. "All I have to do is hold on," she said.

"Absolutely not!" Blood said. "This is a dangerous mission. You could become separated from the drone. Then we'd have to retrieve you, putting our lives at risk."

"Then tether me to it, or better yet, tether me to one of you. All I'm saying is that you need someone with medical training to go with you. All the medics are currently down on the planet. I'm not going to volunteer someone from my staff, so it looks like you're stuck with me," Hathaway said.

Kara considered it for a few moments. "She's right, Peter. Take whatever precautions you think are necessary, but she's coming with us."

Peter Blood looked as if he were going to protest again but then gave a curt nod. "Okay," he said and gestured toward one of the EVA suits. "Collins, you're sitting this one out."

Collins had just climbed into the EVA suit but hadn't closed it yet. He blinked a few times and stared at Blood for a second. "Me, sir?" he asked.

Blood nodded. "Next time. Come on down from there."

Collins sighed and shut down the holo-interface used to control the suit. He climbed down and looked at Hathaway for a second. "She's all ready to go. Once you login with your ID, if your personal profile has preferences for this model EVA suit, they should be applied. Otherwise, you'll be using the standard configuration."

"Understood," Hathaway said and climbed up.

Kara watched as Hathaway got settled in and looked at the suit controls with a frown.

Peter swung a mobile staircase over to Hathaway's suit. He climbed up and spoke quietly to her.

"Ah, I see. That makes sense. Thank you," Hathaway said.

The EVA suit closed, and Hathaway gave her the thumbs-up signal, which was universal for 'ready to go.'

Blood climbed into his own EVA suit. The gray exterior looked as if it had been battered a few times but was still serviceable. Kara watched as he did a quick check and gestured for them to follow him.

"Ladies," Blood said to both of them, "I believe you know Rex Linn, Sam Swoop, and Jessie Butler. Rex, you'll be riding with a tether to Dr. Hathaway."

Rex glanced at Hathaway for a second and then looked at Blood. "All right, got it, boss. Okay, Dr. Hathaway, if you'll come stand by me, I'll get you sorted out."

Blood gave Kara a sidelong glance. He started to speak, but Kara cut him off. "I'll take a tether too, Peter."

Blood blew out a breath and smiled. A tether attachment extended from the back of his suit and connected to hers. Kara had been trained in the use of EVA suits, but it had been a while, and it seemed foolish to her not to rely on someone who had more recent experience than she had.

"And here I thought I was going to have to convince you," Blood said.

They lined up at the edge of the hangar bay and stood on a maintenance platform. Railings rose from the floor and stopped at just over a meter in height. Blood used the controls to extend the platform out of the hangar toward the drone outside.

The drone was mostly a large rectangular storage container that had a set of thrusters, along with a booster at the back. Blood and his team had attached harnesses to the outside of the drone earlier.

The maintenance platform got them most of the way to the gray outer hull of the drone. Blood lowered the forward railing.

"Okay, Swoop. You and Jessie go first," Blood said.

Swoop and Jessie walked to the edge of the platform and pushed off, using their suit thrusters to cross the distance to the drone. Once they secured themselves to the safety harness, Blood told Rex and Hathaway to go next.

Kara watched as Rex stood behind Hathaway and guided her to the drone.

Blood looked at Kara.

"Ready," Kara said.

Blood moved to stand next to her.

"Let's go," Blood said.

Together they crossed over to the drone, angling their route so they went straight toward the remaining harnesses.

Kara had the ability to hyper-focus on almost anything she set her mind to. When she pushed off from the maintenance platform, she focused all her attention on reaching the harness, ignoring everything else around her until she reached her objective. Noah often told her she worked as if she had tunnel vision, which was a bit like the pot calling the kettle black. He was the same way. She hoped he was okay down there on that planet.

Once she was in the harness, she looked around and saw the maintenance platform retract back to the *Infinity*. She then took a deep breath and admired the view of the stars, looking at Zeta-Alpha-5 for a long moment. The bright planet was stunning to look at, but she felt a pang of concern for Noah and the others. She whispered a prayer for their safety and turned her attention toward the *Ark II*. A four-hour journey seemed like a long time, but it really wasn't.

23

A REMINDER APPEARED on Kara's HUD, and she snorted. "Hey, Claire, I'm going to miss your exercise class."

She grinned. "You get a pass for today."

The drone flew steadily closer to the *Ark II*. The ship was the size of about two CDF heavy cruisers but had none of the armored dignity of a warship. There were five thousand colonists aboard, and she wasn't going to allow a lockdown or system malfunction to end those lives.

She maintained a comlink to the *Infinity*'s computer systems. The sensors hadn't shown any reaction from the *Ark II*'s Guardian point-defense systems.

They'd spent the first couple of hours going over the plan once they reached the ship but then slipped into a determined silence that tended to happen on missions like this. Sometimes she missed serving in the CDF. The camaraderie was different outside of the military. She'd never give up what she and Noah had built together, but there were times when she enjoyed remembering being part of the CDF.

Blood opened a comlink to her. "I really had to resist the urge to make the drone travel faster, but this is the average speed the drones seem to use."

Kara nodded. "Better safe than sorry. The plan is working so far."

They were approaching the four-hour mark of their journey, so that left them twelve hours to fix the *Ark II*. Kara checked her suit computer to be sure it had all the different security tools she'd chosen to bring with her. Each of them had a purpose for which it was designed, but sometimes she felt as if she'd overlooked something. Noah did that sometimes. He called it his "gut check." She'd learned to trust his instincts a long time ago back on Titan Space Station.

The drone approached the *Ark II,* nearing the outer hull of the ship.

Blood laughed. "We made it past the point-defense system."

"Excellent," Kara said. "Now all we need to do is get inside."

Blood used the drone's thrusters to slow them down and match speed with the *Ark II*. Once they were within six meters of the hull, they crossed over to it in pairs. Swoop and Butler went first. Then Kara and Blood crossed, followed by Rex and Claire.

Blood released control of the drone, and it flew toward the maintenance dock near the stern of the ship. They activated their mag boots and walked along the outer hull of the ship.

"There's an airlock right over there," Kara said, gesturing ahead of them.

Blood stayed behind her as she started walking, grabbing the handrail and pulling herself toward the airlock doors. It was a maintenance airlock located midship. She tapped the control interface for the airlock doors. An authentication prompt appeared. She reached below the panel and opened a small hatch.

Then she yanked on the manual override. The outer airlock doors opened.

Kara climbed inside, and the lights from her helmet lit up the area. The others followed her inside, and the outer airlock doors closed. She had to use the manual override again to open the inner doors.

Blood sighed in relief. "I thought the lockdown might've prevented the manual override from working."

Kara shook her head. "It's a civilian ship. No matter what the lockdown does, there are safety protocols that are hardwired into the system. That prompt was just irritating."

They entered a darkened maintenance corridor. The overhead lighting came on and the life support systems became active. Heated air began to fill the corridor.

They started walking and by the time they were halfway to the door that would take them to the interior of the ship, they could remove their helmets.

Kara retracted her helmet and inhaled the cool air. The others did the same.

She palmed the door controls and they opened to an interior corridor. Amber lighting activated and the white walls were almost gleaming.

"That's a good sign," Kara said, gesturing toward the pristine walls.

"Why is that?" Hathaway asked.

"If the atmospheric scrubbers had stopped working, these walls would be pretty grimy. Slimy to the touch. But they're not, which means the scrubbers are working."

"They didn't maintain an atmosphere inside the ship for the entire ten-year journey, did they?" Blood asked.

"No, not the entire journey. There's a hydroponic section that would have been activated during the last thirty months of the journey. That way, when the colonists were brought out of stasis, they had a stockpile of food, along with mature plants to get started with," Kara replied.

"Why are the life support systems working now?" Blood asked.

"They would have come online for the early risers. I guess no one turned them off when they went to the planet. They wouldn't need to. The life support system can operate for years as long as proper maintenance is followed."

Blood sniffed. "It would smell bad in here if it hadn't. It's good to know the automated systems are working."

Kara followed the signs on the walls to the computing core several decks below the main bridge. With the lockdown in place, she couldn't access the bridge, but common systems worked just fine. They took the elevator to the computing core, but the doors to it were locked.

"Okay, Blood. Time to make use of those cutting tools you brought," Kara said.

The salvage team brought out their plasma cutters and began making a hole for them. The doors weren't armored or reinforced, so it only took Blood and the others about ten minutes to cut a hole big enough for them to climb through.

Once inside, Kara walked over to one of the consoles. She brought up the control interface and felt a glimmer of hope as a list of menu items appeared. However, when she tried to access the security system, she was thwarted by the security prompt.

Kara gritted her teeth and let out a frustrated sigh.

"Are you going to be able to bypass the security system?" Blood asked.

Kara nodded slowly. "Yes, I'm pretty sure I can, but it's going to take some time."

"How much time?"

Kara glanced at the large open expanse that was the computing core of the ship. Rows of towers for processing and storage arrays stretched out beyond. "I need to find the right physical access point. Then it should be simple."

Blood snorted. "Simple doesn't mean easy."

"No, it doesn't," Kara agreed.

"I have an idea," Hathaway said.

Kara regarded her for a moment. "It's fine. We should be able to find it in time."

Hathaway nodded. "Of course. I don't doubt it for a second, but I think there's an easier way."

Kara pursed her lips and then smiled. "Okay, what is it?"

"This security lockout is so that only someone from the *Ark II* can access the ship's systems, right?"

Kara nodded.

"Then why don't we bring one of the crew out of stasis and get them to end the lockdown," Hathaway said.

Kara exhaled forcefully and her eyes flicked upward for half a second.

Hathaway smiled sweetly. "Wouldn't that be easier?"

"We'd have to find them among the five thousand passengers aboard," Blood said.

Hathaway frowned. She hadn't considered that.

"Actually," Kara said, "senior officers would have their own section near the bridge."

Hathaway smiled and looked at Blood.

"How long will the revival protocol take?" Kara asked.

Hathaway bit her lip and then opened her personal holoscreen. "The minimum time is six hours to come out of a long-term stasis. I'm sorry I can't make it go any faster."

Kara checked how much time remained, and they had just over eleven hours.

"Okay, let's try the two-pronged approach to this. I'll stay here and work on bypassing the security systems. Blood, you take Dr. Hathaway and bring the most senior officer out of stasis," Kara said.

"I'll stay and give you a hand," Blood said and turned toward his team. "You guys help Dr. Hathaway get access to the crew's stasis pods near the bridge." He looked at Kara. "If that's all right with you?"

"It's fine," Kara replied.

The others left and Blood came to stand next to her.

"If you can't access critical systems, how are you going to find where you need to go to bypass them?"

"There are layers to security. It's not an all-or-nothing control like most people think. There are a few things I can try from here. One of them is getting us added to the *Ark II* crew manifest."

"Wouldn't the lockdown prevent that?"

"It might, but I won't know until I try it. The lockdown seems designed to prevent getting access to the ship, and the ship's system is more like a secondary side effect to it, and not the design."

Blood nodded. "Right, but wouldn't access control, like those tied to crew manifests, be part of a secure system?"

Kara nodded. "That's why I'm going to go through the backup systems and trigger a recovery. It should override the current manifest records."

"Heh. That's pretty clever. You really have a knack for this."

Kara smiled. "You should see what Noah can do."

"I hope they're okay," Blood said.

"I do, too," Kara replied.

A comlink registered on her wrist computer. It was from the *Infinity*.

"Kara, thank God I was able to reach you," Markovich said.

"I'm getting you loud and clear. What's happening?" she asked.

"The orbital degradation is speeding up. Current estimate for minimum time to course correction is four and a half hours," Markovich said.

Kara's eyes widened and her thoughts flatlined for a few seconds. "Copy that. Four and a half hours."

They didn't have enough time. What she was going to try could take hours to get done.

"Are you able to access the ship's systems yet?" Markovich asked.

"We're working on it. Hathaway is bringing one of the senior crew out of stasis, but the minimum time for that is six hours."

"You could slow it down by disabling the maneuvering thrusters," Markovich said.

"Won't that prevent us from doing a course correction?" Blood asked.

Kara shook her head. "No, we wouldn't disable all of them. Just enough in key locations. Jeremy, send me the ship's current trajectory."

"Done."

Kara brought up her personal holoscreen and then activated a secondary screen. She opened a schematic for the *Ark II* and then ran through a few calculations to determine how many thrusters they'd have to disable to make a difference.

"Too bad we can't have the thrusters change direction for us," Blood said.

Kara blinked several times, Blood's comment sending a jolt of an idea into her brain. "That's it!"

Blood's eyes widened. "What's it? We can't control the ship's systems."

"No, we can't. Okay, this is what we're going to do. After the others get Hathaway access to the crew stasis pods, you and they are going to manually disable a list of thrusters I'm going to give you. It's going to take time because they're spread out in groups."

Blood nodded, following along with what she said. "Okay, what are you going to do?"

Kara closed her holoscreen and started walking toward the door. "I'm going to find the sensor arrays used by the nav system."

Blood kept pace with her. "Why?"

"Because the nav system wouldn't force the ship to crash into the moon. Something must be wrong with the data from the sensor array that's making this happen. If I can fix it, then I can get the maneuvering thrusters to stop working against us."

"Okay. Hopefully, that will buy us enough time to end the lockdown," Blood said.

It had to, otherwise five thousand sleeping colonists were going to die.

24

Noah stared at the Uvai's depiction of a humanoid specter in front of him. He could see through the speckled dusting of dark red spores, but they were definitely holding a pattern, a clearly discernible pattern. Especially in the chest area.

Thump. Thump.

The sound came from the Uvai, reminiscent of a human heartbeat.

Thump. Thump.

It seemed to be coming from deep amid the crimson folds at the base of the Uvai, where countless roots had plunged to the ground.

"Captain Barker!" Sergeant Staggart shouted.

Noah stopped moving back and gestured toward the spores. "Where are they?"

The humanoid pattern maintained by the spores seemed to loosen formation and drift apart, as if whatever force was holding them together was gone.

Kyle groaned and raised his hands to his helmet. His fingers went toward the release mechanism so he could remove it from his head.

Noah lunged toward him, grabbing his hands and pulling them down. "What are you doing!"

Kyle's eyes were squeezed shut.

"Stop trying to take your helmet off," Noah said.

Kyle didn't try to raise his hands again, and Noah guided him back away from the cluster of Uvai. He wasn't sure if this was something they were orchestrating, but he couldn't rule it out either. How could they be causing this to happen?

He glanced over at the cluster of Uvai. The spores had disappeared, and the thumping sounds had stopped.

Kyle exhaled forcefully as he looked at Noah. "I don't know what happened. All of a sudden, I had this terrible headache. I just wanted to get this helmet off so I could massage my temples. The pressure was unbearable."

They continued to back away from the cluster of Uvai and didn't turn around until they couldn't see it anymore. He couldn't decide if it was foolish or not, but it felt like the right thing to do.

"Do you still feel it now?" Noah asked.

Kyle shook his head. "No, the pressure's gone. It's gone. No pain meds were administered by the suit. It's just gone."

Noah frowned, making a thoughtful sound.

Sergeant Staggart shouted for them again, and they both started running back to the others.

Staggart waved them over. "Come on. He disappeared this way." The soldier turned on his heel and led them away.

"What happened?" Noah asked. He had to jog to keep up with the CDF soldier.

"I don't know. Apone said Colonel Quinn was muttering

something and then just took off into the jungle. I can't reach him through suit comms. None of us can."

Staggart had sent the others ahead to find Sean while he waited for Noah and Kyle to return.

The CDF soldiers marked the path with flares they'd dropped along the way. Smoke rose from the flares on the ground.

Kyle ran up beside him. "Do you think they attacked me?"

"They might have, but I don't know why it was you and not me. I was closer and actually trying to interact with them," Noah said.

"It doesn't make sense. Why would they target some of us and not the others? It seems random. There has to be more to it than that."

"I don't think it's random," Noah replied.

It couldn't be coincidence that the Uvai were somehow affecting Sean. Had they targeted him because he commanded the soldiers, or was it really a coincidence? Were the Uvai probing them to see how they'd react? The sound they'd made before had to have been a human heartbeat, but what were they trying to tell them? What did it mean?

Sergeant Staggart slowed his pace and looked back at him. "I need to know what we're dealing with here."

"Sergeant, I barely know what we're dealing with. I'm as much in the dark about this as you are," Noah said.

Staggart gritted his teeth and muttered a curse. "You have to know more than the rest of us. I can see the wheels turning. What aren't you saying?"

Noah ran faster. He didn't want to fill Staggart's head with suspicions and hunches that might not help. They needed to focus on getting to Sean first.

"How'd Colonel Quinn get so far ahead of us?" Kyle asked.

"Our combat suits," Staggart replied. "You've only seen a

little of what they can do. In a jungle like this, we can run circles around those rovers we had."

An alert appeared on Noah's HUD. It was another emergency beacon broadcast from Lars's Pathfinder suit but stronger than it had been before. Noah looked ahead and saw another flare on the ground ahead of them.

"He's heading toward the emergency beacon. I've just received another broadcast," Noah said.

Staggart lifted his arm and checked his own holoscreen. "Would you look at that?"

"Sergeant, tell Apone and the others to have their weapons ready."

"Why?" Staggart asked.

"Because this could be a trap," Noah said.

Sergeant Staggart narrowed his gaze and then opened a comlink to his squad. "Keep a sharp lookout. Attack could be imminent. Make sure you check your fire. These Uvai are likely toying with us."

Kyle looked at Noah. "A trap? Why would it lure us into a trap? We were already by a cluster of them."

Noah retrieved his rifle from the side compartment of his suit and brought it out of standby. "Your guess is as good as mine."

Kyle shook his head. "Not quite."

"It showed us… it mimicked a Pathfinder suit with the *Ark II* mission logo. Then Colonel Quinn goes running off, chasing who knows what. The two have to be related."

Noah used his implants to initiate a comlink to Sean's combat suit. There was no reply, and he frowned as he ran. Sean wasn't acknowledging the request, but that didn't mean he wasn't receiving it. The request was timing out from lack of acknowledgement.

"They might be," Noah said. He leaped over a fallen tree and kept going.

Staggart followed him.

"Sir, can we engage the Uvai?" Apone asked.

Without Sean here Staggart was next in command of the CDF soldiers, but he was asking for guidance from Noah. It was a gray area at best, but Noah had been an officer in the CDF.

"It's better if we avoid them," Noah said, and Staggart scowled. "I know that's not what you wanted to hear, Sergeant, but we could make things worse. We hardly understand what's happening as it is. The only thing we haven't done is engage the Uvai directly. If they attack us directly, then that's one thing, but they haven't."

Staggart grumbled something incoherently. "Negative, Apone. Do not engage the Uvai unless they attack us directly."

The fog lifted completely. One moment they'd been running through a thinning fog and then they'd crossed some invisible barrier. Noah glanced behind them. According to his suit sensors, the temperature in the area was rising.

Noah opened a data comlink to Sean's combat suit. The connection didn't require an acknowledgement from Sean, and it went through almost immediately. He accessed the microphone from inside Sean's suit.

"Stop running!" Sean growled.

His breaths came in gasps.

"It's not her. It's not her. It's not her," Sean panted.

He'd stopped, and all Noah could hear was Sean breathing heavily.

"You're not here," Sean said. "You know I couldn't let him go by himself. You told me you understood. No, I'm not being selfish. You're the one—grrr get out of my head!"

Noah activated Sean's comms systems and opened a channel.

"Sean, it's me, Noah. We're on our way to you."

"Noah!" Sean said. "No, it's not. You're not going to get me to listen. You hear me?"

Noah heard Sean firing his rifle.

"Weapons fire!" Staggart shouted. "Converge on that location."

Staggart ran ahead of them, and Noah couldn't keep up, not while he was accessing Sean's combat suit.

"Sean, it really is me. I opened a data connection to your suit and forced the comlink to connect."

Sean blew out a breath. "Noah, it's making me see Oriana. I can see her right in front of me. Look!"

Noah accessed Sean's helmet feeds. There was nothing but jungle in front of him. Then the helmet began to bob up and down as Sean started running again.

"No, Sean, stop! It's manipulating you. Just stop. Let the others catch up to you."

Sean cried out. "I can't. I can't stop! Why can't I stop?"

Noah stopped running and brought up several holoscreens from his wrist computer. The recon drone had already done an initial flyover of the area, and he sent a waypoint to Staggart and the others. On one holoscreen he had Sean's helmet feed, and on another he brought up the Nexstar combat suit controls.

"Noah," Kyle said. "He's heading… There's a drop off. Shit, it's a cliff!"

Noah brought up the control interface for the combat suit and locked motor controls. Sean tumbled to the ground and screamed in frustration.

Noah closed the holoscreens. "Come on. I don't know how long that will slow him down."

Kyle ran beside him. "Didn't you just lock his suit?"

"Only temporarily. He can get around it. All I did was buy

us some time," Noah replied.

Noah increased his pace, and his own Pathfinder suit assisted his movements, allowing him to run at speeds he had no hope of reaching without it.

They caught up with the CDF soldiers. Several of them were lying on the ground while the others stood over them.

Sergeant Staggart looked up from Apone. Noah looked down at the fallen soldier. His eyes were closed.

"He's unconscious," Staggart said. "The others are as well."

Noah looked at the other CDF soldiers. Their combat suits weren't damaged. They had just collapsed.

Kyle brought up his wrist computer and began navigating the holo-interface. "We need to move them away from here."

"Why?" Noah asked.

"There's a large deposit of that new mineral Ezra found. The magnetic field is off the chart. We need to move them and get away from here quickly," Kyle said. "We've been running along a big deposit of the stuff. A vein of it, I think it's called."

Staggart surged to his feet and began issuing orders.

Specialist Denny squatted down and lifted one of the soldiers. "Which way?"

Kyle walked to their left and then angled away. "This way. It's weaker over here."

Noah helped Staggart lift another soldier. "How do we get them to wake up?"

Kyle shook his head. "I don't know but moving them away has to help. Don't your suit computers have a medical interface? Something to use before a medic can check them out?"

"He's right," Noah said.

Staggart grunted. "It'll have to do."

None of the CDF medics were with them.

An alarm flashed on Noah's HUD.

"What is it?" Staggart asked.

"It's Sean. I locked his combat suit, but he's regaining control."

Staggart jerked his head to the side. "Go, we'll catch up to you."

Noah let go of the soldier's legs and Staggart continued to drag him toward Kyle.

As Noah ran for Sean's waypoint only a few hundred meters from where the others had been, he was thinking of how he really could have used the sensor protocol that would allow Kyle to detect the new mineral. He was running blind, and that pretty much summed up how this entire mission was going.

Gritting his teeth, Noah sped toward Sean. Pressure began to build in his head.

Sean had severed all comms, so Noah couldn't access his suit. He ran by several clusters of Uvai but didn't slow down. He had no idea if the crimson fungi even reacted to his passing.

He saw Sean crawling on the ground, heading toward the edge of a steep cliff. His movements were jerky, as if he was fighting himself.

Noah dove on top of Sean's legs. "No, you don't. I've got you!"

Sean cried out in frustration and struggled to get away.

Noah felt himself being pulled forward.

"Stop!" he shouted.

"I can't!" Sean cried.

Noah regained his feet and grabbed one of Sean's legs, pulling his friend to the side away from the cliff.

"She's down there. I saw her go down there," Sean pleaded, his hands outstretched toward the cliff.

"She's not here, Sean. Oriana's not here," Noah said.

Noah heard Sean repeat this several times and then stopped

struggling. Noah continued to pull him to the side as the pressure in his own head began to ease.

"That's better," Sean said.

Noah let go of Sean's leg, gasping for a few seconds. "Come on. Stand up. We need to keep moving, and I don't know if I can keep dragging your ass across this damn jungle."

Sean groaned as he stood up. Even with the combat suit assisting his movements, he seemed unsteady on his feet.

Together, they moved away to the side. Noah hoped it was enough.

"What the hell happened?" Noah asked.

Sean shook his head, his expression somewhat less haggard than it had been. "I saw her. I saw Oriana here. She was standing in front of me. She spoke. I know it was impossible, but I had to go after her even though I knew she wasn't real." Sean shuddered and swallowed hard. "What is this thing doing to us? I know what I saw wasn't real, but dammit, Noah. I saw it. I saw her. I swear to God, it was her. It was so real."

"I believe you. You're not crazy."

"Then what the..." Sean began and stopped. He brought up his wrist computer. "My biochip is reporting decreased blood pressure. My head is pounding."

"Okay, just wait a second," Noah said. He blinked several times while he looked around the area. "You saw Oriana, and you didn't just see her."

"I could smell her. It was like we were hugging, and I had my nose near her head. I could smell the shampoo she likes to use," Sean said.

Noah looked away, frowning in thought. "Maybe it triggered a memory somehow. A strong memory."

"A memory? How the hell would it do that?"

Noah shook his head. "I don't know. I don't even know if *it* knows what it's doing. It's not like it can read our minds."

"Are you sure about that?" Sean asked.

Noah nodded. "Yes. I prefer a simpler explanation."

"Well, I'm all ears."

"We know that physically manipulating the brain can cause all kinds of things to happen—smell things, see things, even say things. What if, somehow, the pressure that was applied happened to be in an area of your brain where your strongest memories are. You love your wife. It makes sense that she's on your mind, especially in times of stress. I know I've been thinking about Kara."

Sean considered it for a few moments, and Noah watched the wheels turning in his mind. He shook his head and looked at Noah. "Are you saying this is an accident?"

"Maybe. I don't know. It could just be a byproduct of something else."

"What the hell does that even mean?"

"It means that…" Noah paused, trying to think of the best way to explain it, "two independent forces are affecting one another, but both are ignorant of how or why the effects are happening."

Sean sighed. "It just feels so damn personal."

Noah nodded. He couldn't be exactly sure what was happening, and sometimes he thought it was a combination of all the things they'd been talking about. "Part of it could be intentional, but also part of it was not—"

He stopped speaking. Lars's distress beacon sent out another broadcast, and this time it was followed by another.

"Did you get the second one?" Sean asked.

Noah nodded. "It's from Saul Ashworth's Pathfinder suit," he said, gesturing toward the cliff. "They're down there, Sean. They're down there."

25

The *Ark II* was a big ship. Even with elevators, it took time to navigate through the entire space, but at least the ship's operations were somewhat consolidated in the middle. Kara made her way to one of the sensor arrays in the maintenance corridor. Blood and his team were running along the maintenance corridors on the other side of the ship, disabling maneuvering thrusters as they went. They had to cut the power to the thrusters by using the safety override in the area. This required that they race to power relays that supplied the thrusters. In some cases, they just had to access the power relay, but more often than not they had to visit the area where the thrusters were located. Too many other systems were tied into the power relays for them to take a chance on causing a cascade of failures. Kara was willing to bet that their current scenario had never been considered by any of the ship's designers, either on New Earth or even back on Old Earth.

She stopped in the middle of the corridor, opened one of the supply rooms nearby, and began retrieving the equipment she needed, making a pile in the corridor. The door on the far end opened and someone started walking toward her.

"Claire, what are you doing here?"

Dr. Claire Hathaway jogged toward her. "There isn't much I can do to make the end stasis protocol go any faster, so I thought I'd lend you a hand."

She looked down at the pile of equipment in the corridor and then at Kara.

"They're receivers. Come on, help me get some more," Kara said.

The receivers, square modular devices, were used for communications, and the sensor arrays were compatible with this model of receiver. Both women raided the stocked shelves of the supply room, piling the receivers into a storage container in the corridor.

Kara got on one side of the container and Claire on the other. They began to push and pull, respectively, and the weighty container began to slide down the corridor. Once they built up some momentum, it became easier to maintain it.

They reached the end of the corridor and Kara opened the interior airlock doors.

"What are you going to do with all of these?" Claire asked, gesturing toward the receivers.

"Hopefully fix the sensor arrays."

"How?"

"Let's get them outside and I'll show you," Kara replied.

Together, they shoved the storage container into the airlock. Kara secured the top so they wouldn't lose any receivers once they entered low gravity. The hull of the ship wasn't zero gravity, but they would be at the edge of the artificial gravity field, so it was much lower than on the ship.

An update flashed on her wrist computer. They'd managed to

increase the time to impact by thirty minutes. Kara knew that Blood and his team were working as fast as they could, but it wasn't going to be enough.

Kara initiated the airlock door sequence and warning alarms flashed. The atmosphere vented into space as the outer airlock doors opened. Kara attached a tether to the storage container, and two more snaked out of a side compartment to attach to the backs of their EVA suits. Once they got the storage container outside the airlock, it became significantly easier to move.

They headed toward the small towers and dishes of the *Ark II*'s sensor array. Kara guided the container toward the access panel of the first tower. She opened it and turned back to Claire.

"Come over here and watch what I'm doing," Kara said.

She opened the storage container and removed one of the receivers. "Take this and attach one of the patch cables to it. Then, we connect it to the auxiliary port on the side. Once that's done, we can activate the receiver."

Claire nodded. "I've got it. Seems simple enough."

"It is. Just make sure you attach the patch cable to the port marked 'Aux.' Otherwise, this won't work," Kara said.

"Okay, then what do we do?" Claire asked.

"We try to fool the sensor array with the help of the *Infinity*'s computing core," Kara replied.

They both set off, attaching receivers to the sensor towers that made up the array. It took them the better part of an hour to get them all. In that time, Blood and his team had managed to disable more maneuvering thrusters, but they hadn't gained more time like they thought they would because the ship's nav computer compensated by increasing thruster output from the ones still online.

Kara's solution with the receivers was their last-ditch effort to save the ship.

"We have one receiver left. Did we miss one of the towers?" Claire asked.

Kara shook her head. "No, this one is for me," she said. She connected a patch cable to the receiver and then to the data port on her wrist computer.

Kara opened a comlink to the *Infinity*.

"*Infinity* actual," Markovich said.

"I'm activating the receiver. Give it a minute to sync up with the others," Kara said.

Kara brought up the holo-interface and powered on the receiver. One by one the other receivers began to register a connection to Kara's EVA suit computer.

"Okay, *Infinity*, add the data connection and begin the upload," Kara said.

"Upload starting," Markovich said.

The alpha moon loomed beneath them. They were thousands of kilometers from the lunar surface, but being this close made her stomach sink to her feet.

"How will we know if this works?" Claire asked.

"What's happening now is that we're uploading new sensor data from the *Infinity*'s sensors. They're providing the *Ark II*'s nav computer with the actual coordinates of the ship."

Claire frowned. "This will override the data from these sensors here?"

Kara nodded. "In a way, yes. To the nav computer, it will appear that the sensors are picking up competing navigational data. The onboard AI operates with a set of rules to help the ship avoid collisions. The AI will have no choice but to prioritize the data that shows the ship is in the most danger."

Claire considered this for a few moments. "I hope this works."

Kara swallowed hard. She hadn't expected to do anything like this when she'd first come aboard the ship, but it was the best plan she'd been able to come up with. Her EVA suit computer was acting like a bridge between the two ships' navigation systems.

"*Infinity*, what's the status?" Kara asked.

"No change," Markovich replied.

Kara watched the upload. They were sending as much navigational data as they could over the limited bandwidth available on the EVA suit comms. Maybe she should have created something that had more data processing capabilities. This was a workaround and bypass to the current system that avoided her having to authenticate with the ship's computer system.

There was nothing they could do but wait, hope, and pray. Minutes went by so quickly that before she knew it, a half hour had passed. Blood and his team stopped disabling maneuvering thrusters.

"Kara," Markovich said.

"I'm here, Jeremy."

"The degradation appears to have stalled. I think it's working... Yes, it's working! You guys did it!" Markovich said.

Kara blew out a breath in a long sigh. It felt as if she'd been holding her breath almost the entire time she'd been out there.

Claire opened a comlink to Blood and gave him the update. Then she looked at Kara. "We did it. We can go back inside now. I should really check on Raif Hoenig."

Raif Hoenig was the First Officer of ship operations on the *Ark II*. He'd have the authority they needed to end the lockdown and grant them access to the ship's computer systems.

"You go ahead. I need to stay out here," Kara said.

Claire frowned. "Why?"

"The comlink to the *Infinity* is maintained through my suit comms. I don't want to take a chance of having the connection disrupted by going inside. The nav computer would just restart what it was doing before."

Claire pressed her lips together. "I don't have to go right this second. I should wait with you then. I don't want to leave you out here alone."

Kara smiled. "It's fine. Just get Raif Hoenig out of stasis so we can end this lockdown. Then we can untangle this mess."

Hathaway hesitated.

"Go on, Claire. I'll be fine," Kara said and sat down with her back against one of the towers.

Claire headed back to the airlock.

But Kara hadn't been alone for long when she looked up to see Peter Blood heading toward her.

"I figured you could use some company," he said.

"It does help the time pass. I could drink a whole bottle of wine right now."

Blood grinned and sat down next to her. "I could sleep for a few days."

"Yeah, me too," Kara said.

Blood regarded her for a few seconds. "I couldn't have pulled this off. I'd never have come up with half the things you did."

"At least one of the things we came up with actually worked," Kara replied.

Blood nodded. "These people owe you their lives."

"They get to live. That's payment enough for me," she said.

Blood leaned his head back and looked at the bright lunar surface. "Noah is a lucky man. I'm going to tell him the next time I see him."

Kara smiled a little and closed her eyes.

"Do you have a sister or a cousin?" Blood asked.

Kara snorted a little. "Shut up, Peter," she said sleepily.

He grinned softly, sounding sleepy himself. "Can't blame a guy for asking."

Soon, they were both asleep.

26

Noah watched the drone video feed. "Not just a cliff. It's a damn crater."

"More than forty kilometers across," Sean said.

The others watched the video feed in silence. The CDF soldiers had regained consciousness soon after they were moved away from the mineral deposit.

Noah looked at his friend. He'd been shaken up by what'd happened, hesitating as if he didn't trust himself yet.

"Are you sure about these settings?" Specialist Denny asked Kyle.

"It's the best I've got to detect that mineral. Without stopping to take samples every few feet, we need to rely on increases in the magnetic field," Kyle said.

Specialist Denny shook his head and looked at Noah. "Sir, based on the readings I'm getting from the recon drone, the magnetic fields are changing as if something is triggering them. Off the top of my head, you need an electrical charge to trigger a field like that, but these must be more powerful in order to affect us the way they did."

"Ezra did say that the new mineral is superconductive. That doesn't explain why it changes so often, but if we can avoid the worst of it, we should be fine," Noah replied.

Sergeant Staggart cleared his throat. "Do you have something to add, Specialist?"

Denny glanced at Noah and Sean for a second. "Negative, Sergeant. I was just pointing out that there's a risk if we go down into the caldera."

Staggart turned toward Sean. "Colonel, Denny is being too polite. If we go in there, there's a good chance this whole thing turns into yet another shit show."

Sean nodded and looked at Noah. "We can wait for the shuttle. By now Gil and Bruhanski should be extracting the others."

"Sean, I think the Uvai are trying to communicate with us. Look at this," Noah said. He activated his personal holoscreen and showed them the recording of his encounter. "The spores are being controlled. They made the *Ark II* mission logo. The only way it could have done that is if it's seen the away team."

Sean stared at the image for a few seconds. "It's remarkable. I'll give you that."

"You're still not convinced. I bet it was trying to get you to go down there."

"Yeah, by playing with my brain, Noah."

Noah pressed his lips together. "They don't have much time. The emergency beacon had suit telemetry data. They're running out of power, and they haven't been able to recharge them. Damn it, I didn't come all this way to watch them die. I won't do it."

He stomped toward the edge of the crater.

"Wait a second," Sean said.

Noah spun around. "None of you have to come, but I'm going down there. You can wait for the shuttle if you want."

He stepped toward the edge and jumped over the side, the others' screams trailing in his wake. Noah engaged the suit jets to slow his descent. He had plenty of reserves left because this was a lower-gravity world. Leaping off the top of a cliff didn't gain him nearly as much momentum as if he'd done the same on New Earth.

Noah landed on an outcropping and marched toward the edge. The trees were taller here and his view of the rest of the caldera was blocked. The waypoint to the *Ark II* away team was still active on his HUD.

A comlink registered on his suit.

"Wait, Noah," Sean said.

Noah turned around and looked up. Piercing the tree canopy, he saw the others coming down, using their suit jets to slow their descents.

Sean walked toward him, and Noah backed toward the edge. He wouldn't put it past Sean to take matters into his own hands to keep him safe, and he wasn't going to let that happen. If they got on that shuttle, there was very little chance of them returning, and even then it would be too late.

Sean rolled his eyes, irritated. "I'm not going to stop you from going down there. I'm going with you."

"We can still save them," Noah said.

Sean came to a stop a short distance away. The others were walking toward them.

Kyle waved. "There's no way I'm sitting this one out."

Sergeant Staggart and several of the other soldiers looked as if they'd rather be anywhere else, but they also had a stubborn gleam in their eyes. They followed Sean. Noah knew it. Sean was a legend in the CDF, and his achievements rivaled Connor's.

Sean stepped closer to the edge of the outcropping and peered down. Then he speared a look at Noah. "If you thought I was going to let you go down there by yourself, then allow me to educate you, my brilliant friend. If we're going to do this, then we do it the best way we can. We do it together, as a team. You understand? No one is going to cowboy this mission by themselves."

Noah regarded his friend for a few seconds and sighed. "Good, because I really didn't want to go down there by myself. I mean, I would have, but I really didn't want to."

Sean grinned tiredly. "I figured."

Noah smiled a little. "Thanks," he said quietly.

Sean nodded and looked at him intently. "I know you'd do the same if it was me down there. You have good reasons for questioning the things we've seen here. I don't know if I agree with all of them, but I can't make a good counter argument. If I'm going to take a leap of any kind, I'll always put my faith in you."

Noah felt his throat thicken for a second. "Damn," he said in a raspy voice. "I better not be wrong about this then."

"If you are, I'll never let you forget it," Sean replied.

Noah knew he wasn't lying about that, assuming they made it off this planet alive… *When* they made it off this planet alive.

Sean opened a comlink to the shuttle. After cycling through several attempts, the connection went through and the comlink finally established.

"Colonel Quinn," Gil said.

"Is Lieutenant Rhoades with you?" Sean asked.

"No, Colonel, we're almost to the evac site for him and the others," Gil replied.

"Okay, how about Private Donlon?"

"Yeah, he's right here."

"This is Donlon, Colonel."

"Donlon, I'm going to send you a set of coordinates. It's where the current emergency broadcast signals are coming from for the *Ark II* away team. We're heading there right now. I need you to relay this to Lieutenant Rhoades after he boards," Sean said.

"Yes, Colonel."

"Next, there's a locked storage container on the shuttle with the combat drones we brought with us," Sean said.

"Colonel, I'm not qualified to operate those drones," Donlon said.

"I know that, Private. Lieutenant Rhoades is. He is to prepare the drones for a strike on my command. Is that understood?" Sean said.

"Yes, Colonel Quinn. I'll tell Lieutenant Rhoades when he comes aboard," Donlon said.

"I'll be in touch," Sean said and closed the comlink.

Sean looked at Noah. "If they attack us again, I'm going to lay waste to the entire area."

Noah inhaled deeply and nodded. If the attack drones were as powerful as what was recorded in the mission reports from the Krake War, then Sean could do just that. The attack drones weren't a WMD in the way a bomb was, but they were almost unstoppable when armed. They'd pierced the battle-steel armor of CDF warships, and the best defense against them was gravity emitters.

"Sean," Noah said, "the drones need a reliable control signal to be effective."

He let the rest go unsaid, but Sean knew what he was implying.

"Yeah, I know. They'll have to be close to us in order to use them," Sean said.

The attack drones weren't a precision weapon, but they excelled at wreaking havoc on their targets.

They started their descent into the long-dormant caldera. The recon drone had spotted a lake a few kilometers from their location, and there were several outcroppings along the sides that allowed them to break up their descent into manageable chunks. Finally, the jungle wasn't as thick as it had been, and they were able to see the sky above them through the thinning canopy.

"Look at what the recon drone just found," Kyle said.

Noah brought up the video feed. There was a massive break along the walls of the caldera, and the deep fissure looked as if it reached all the way to the bottom. Noah couldn't imagine how it had happened, but given the amount of flora, it must have been a long time ago.

"That's going to complicate things," Kyle said.

Specialist Denny looked at him. "Complicate it more? How?"

"Because the wildlife we encountered before are likely down there as well," Noah said.

Specialist Denny divided his gaze between them for a second and didn't respond.

When they reached the bottom, wildlife sounded throughout the area and shallow streams flowed nearby. Several large shadows flew overhead, and Noah ducked reflexively. He wasn't the only one. He looked up and glimpsed the pale underbelly of the flying whales, wondering where they nested. He doubted this was one of their nests. It was too exposed to other creatures, but perhaps being the size of a behemoth meant that didn't matter.

Noah tried to initiate a comlink to the emergency beacon

and got a reply. "Two hundred meters ahead of us," he said and frowned.

"What?" Sean asked.

"It's above us, like they're in a tree," Noah replied.

They started walking.

"I thought you said the beacon is coming from the Pathfinder suit," Kyle said.

"It is."

"Then why would it be above us? You're telling me they spent six months in a tree?" Kyle asked.

Noah had been wondering the same thing, but he didn't have any answers. He quickened his pace.

"On your left," Sean said quietly.

Noah looked and saw a single Uvai at the base of a tree. Its roots went into the stream nearby.

"I should collect a water sample," Kyle said.

Sean intercepted him. "Not this time."

"But it's right over there—"

Sean hardened his gaze. "If you take a step in the direction of that Uvai, I'm going to have Staggart carry you on his back the rest of the way."

Kyle looked toward the CDF soldier and then back at Sean, holding up his hands in a placating gesture. "All right, I don't need to get a sample right now."

Sean motioned for Kyle to go ahead of him, which the young scientist did.

They kept a quick pace but were careful to watch their surroundings. Noah kept expecting to see a group of broadheads or those other ambush predators they'd encountered. The branches above them were widely spread, and those predators would find it difficult to sneak up on them here. He wondered if it was too much to hope for that there was nothing harmful to them in the old caldera.

Sean gave him a questioning look, eyebrows raised.

"I was just thinking that at least we don't have to worry about this old volcano erupting while we're here," Noah said.

Sean shook his head. "You know what? Some things are better left unsaid."

Noah snorted. "You don't really think a volcano is going to suddenly become active because I spoke about it?"

"No, but that doesn't mean something equally as bad couldn't happen."

They reached the waypoint location. There were multiple small streams nearby that looked barely a meter deep. Noah looked around, searching for a Pathfinder suit.

"I don't see anyone," Kyle said. "Could it be the same interference with our nav system we had before?"

Noah shook his head and gestured above. "No, this is the place." Three trees grew together, their branches intertwined. "A good hiding spot," he said.

Sean peered upward. "Yeah, I think you're right."

Noah went to the base of the tree and jumped. His suit jets pushed him upward, and he grabbed onto a thick branch. He pulled himself up and found that it was wide enough to stand on. Sean followed, and Noah leaned down to help him up. A tangle of branches had grown around the area in front of them, creating a platform. In the middle of it all, a gray helmet poked out.

Noah peered into the gloom. It was Lars.

He started to step forward, but Sean held him back. "Wait!"

"For what?"

Sean gestured above and Noah looked up. Three meters away from Lars was a Uvai. At first glance it looked as if it had grown out of the side of the tree, but it hadn't. The vine-like roots made it look as if it had pulled itself up there and was keeping watch over Lars.

Thump. Thump.

"Did you find him?" Kyle called up from the ground.

Noah and Sean shared a glance.

Thump. Thump.

27

"Please tell me you hear that," Sean said.

Noah nodded. "I hear it."

The Uvai was perched close to Lars. Thick brown vines that looked to be part of the tree had grown around Lars's Pathfinder suit, appearing as if they were holding him against the tree. Were they holding him prisoner, or had they simply grown around the area because Lars had been there for so long?

Thump. Thump.

"What does it mean? What does that sound mean?" Sean asked.

Noah took a step toward Lars. "You want me to guess? It could just be an acknowledgement."

"Or it could be a warning," Sean replied. He lifted his weapon a little.

Thump. Thump.

Noah took another step and disabled the safety on his rifle. Better safe than sorry. "We're here for our friend," he said, gesturing toward Lars.

There was no response.

Sean exhaled. "How would it even understand us?"

"I can only take care of my side of the conversation, Sean. I'm kinda out on a limb here, literally."

Thump. Thump.

Noah stepped closer and his shoulders became tight. He felt like Sean was a few seconds away from shooting the Uvai.

"I hate this," Sean said. "I don't have a clear shot."

He had to stay behind Noah on the thick branch.

Noah's gaze went from Lars's helmet to the Uvai above him.

A thick red root the same color as the Uvai snaked through the branches, slithering toward Lars.

Noah inhaled sharply. He jerked his weapon up and fired. High velocity darts severed the Uvai's root and it tumbled to the ground.

A deep, roaring vibrato came from the Uvai, startling Noah, and he squeezed the trigger again. As the burst of darts penetrated the Uvai, crimson spores emerged from the wounds. A loud screeching noise sounded, and the Uvai fell away.

"Go!" Sean said and pushed Noah toward Lars.

The platform of branches widened, and Sean pushed past him.

Noah stared at the rifle in his hands. "What have I done?"

Sean began tearing thick vines away from Lars, using the combat suit's brute strength.

Noah heard the others call up to them, but he couldn't hear what they were saying. He'd shot it. He shot at the Uvai. He'd been worried that Sean was going to do it, and then he'd gone and done it himself. It had reached toward Lars's helmet. He didn't know what it was going to do. He had to do it. Didn't he?

"I need a hand here!" Sean said.

Noah snapped out of it and rushed in to help Sean.

"Look at them all," Sean said.

There were layers upon layers of vines holding Lars in place, but they were finally able to clear enough of them to uncover his body. Lars was sitting on a thick, moss-covered tree branch with his back against the tree.

Noah tore away the vines that were holding his arms down and opened the wrist computer on Lars's Pathfinder suit. Power levels were critical. He pulled a cord from his own suit and connected it to Lars's. Then, he enabled the charge function to transfer power from his own suit to Lars.

Sean continued to cut through the remaining vines.

Noah checked Lars's biometrics. "He's been here for six months."

Emergency reserve power could be trickle-charged from solar, but with the amount of tree cover here and all the overgrowth around Lars, it hadn't worked.

"How long will it take to charge his suit enough to revive him?" Sean asked.

"Not long. He's not in stasis. It's more like a medically induced coma," Noah said.

He looked into Lars's helmet and could see a thick, dark beard. His Pathfinder suit showed signs of wear on the arms and legs that had left it with a brownish tinge.

Loud knocks sounded throughout the area, echoing all around them. Some of them seemed distant while others were much closer.

"We've got to move him. Let's bring him down to the others," Sean said.

They lifted Lars up and carried him away from the tree. Sean attached a tether from his combat suit, and they lowered Lars to the ground. Then they both jumped down, using their suit jets to slow their descent.

Screeches sounded from high above them.

"I don't know what you did up there, but you set them off," Sergeant Staggart said.

Kyle was lowering Lars to the ground while the CDF soldiers stood ready, keeping a careful watch all around them.

Noah looked around, expecting to see the Uvai he'd shot on the ground, but it was nowhere to be found.

Kyle looked at him. "What happened up there?"

"I shot one of the Uvai," Noah said as he checked Lars's suit computer and initiated the revival protocol.

Kyle's mouth hung open a little. "You shot one. I thought you said not to do that."

"I thought it was going after Lars," Noah replied.

"It *was* going after him," Sean said.

Noah didn't know what the Uvai was going to do, but they had more important things to worry about.

Lars inhaled loudly and began to cough. His eyes shot open, and he looked at them. He blinked several times and his gaze darted to Noah and Sean. Then he squeezed his eyes shut for a second.

"This isn't happening. Not again, damn it!" Lars said.

"It's us, Lars," Noah said. "We're really here."

Lars looked away from them. "That's impossible. You can't be here," he said and glared at them as if they were the enemy. "You can't be here!"

Sean squatted down so he was eye level with Lars. "We're here."

Lars shook his head, and his face twisted into a haggard expression. "No, it would have taken you ten years to get here. Life support from my suit would have run out way before that. You're not real. Stop it. Stop doing this!"

Lars tried to stand, but he was still weak from the semi-stasis he'd been in, and Sean held him down. "Hold on a minute, buddy."

Noah placed his hand on Lars's shoulder. "Lars, I figured out FTL. It only took us months to get here, not years."

Lars frowned as if he was starting to believe them, but then he shook his head, not trusting his own judgement.

"We lost contact with the *Ark II*, so we came to investigate."

"Someone from the ship should have come already. Mancuso was next. He should have come," Lars sputtered.

"There was a lockdown. We couldn't access the ship, so we retraced your steps by pulling data from the observer satellites. We found your shuttles and then traced your emergency beacon here. Where are the others?" Noah asked.

Lars shook his head and looked away.

Noah gestured toward Kyle. "Come over here. Let him see you."

Kyle had been hovering nearby, and he came to stand in front of Lars. "Hello, Mister Mallory. I'm Kyle Regan, field biologist on the *Infinity*. Everything they've told you is true. We traveled over three lightyears in about forty days."

Both Noah and Sean stepped back from Lars, and Kyle helped him stand up.

Lars stared at Kyle for a few seconds. "I don't know you," he said, glancing at the others and then back at Kyle. "I don't know you. I've never seen you before. You *have* to be real. You're really here." He smiled, looking more relieved than happy. He turned toward Noah and Sean, his eyes gleaming. "It's true. You're all really here!"

Noah smiled and nodded encouragingly.

Loud knocks sounded in great pulses that seemed to cause the ground to shake.

"Lars, we don't have a lot of time. Where are the others?

Where is the rest of the away team that came here with you?" Noah asked.

Lars's eyes darted back and forth. Coming out of a medically induced coma wasn't easy. When it happened to Noah, he'd been out of sorts for months. They didn't have that kind of time.

"Focus!" Noah said. "I know it's hard. You're still waking up, but we have a shuttle on its way here right now. We're going to get out of here, but not without the others. Where are they?"

A deep, roaring vibrato came from all around them as if they were surrounded. It was as if everything in the ancient caldera was coming to life.

Lars's eyes widened. "It's too late. They're going to attack. They attacked us before. The attacks always follow that sound. They're calling…"

Sean peered at Lars for a second and then looked at Noah. "He's out of it, Noah. Try a comlink to the secondary signal."

Noah raised his wrist to access his wrist computer, and Lars grabbed his arm.

"No! They can detect comlink signals somehow. It's what drew them to us," Lars said.

Noah looked at Sean. They'd been using comlinks the entire time they'd been on the planet. Even when there was interference with establishing a connection, they'd been trying to use them.

"We can limit comms," Sean said. "Tell us where the others are."

Lars looked around trying to get his bearings. Then he opened his own wrist computer and a map appeared on his holoscreen. "It's this way," he said, gesturing away from them.

Several shadows flew overhead, and Noah looked up.

"It's those flying whales again," Kyle said. "Look how many there are. They're circling."

The large creatures were flying above the trees. There were so many that Noah quickly lost count. Then, he glimpsed something move among the treetops. It was hard to see, but something was definitely moving up there. Several of the soldiers called out a warning.

Screeches from above broke through the knocking crescendo of the Uvai. They'd heard them before. The entire canopy of treetops seemed to come alive all at once as hundreds of pale, domed-shaped heads peered down at them.

"Run!" Sean shouted. "Head to the waypoint."

Noah grabbed Lars's arm. "Come on."

"Oh my God!" Kyle shouted.

They started to run in a cluster, pairing up. Noah looked up at the lower branches where large screechers were howling at them. Their bodies were sickly white, and they had thick, domed-shaped heads with prominent brows. Noah remembered how they'd slammed their armored skulls into the flying whales, penetrating thick skin to tear out flesh. Their leathery wings folded in such a way as to allow them to stand on all fours as their powerful tails lashed back and forth behind them.

Suddenly, the predators began to lunge toward them like a wave of screeching white death from above.

28

The CDF soldiers changed their ammo configuration to use larger, denser darts that would cause more damage and fired at the dive-bombing screechers.

Noah brought forth decades-old training and fired his weapon in controlled bursts while running. He wasn't that accurate, but with so many creatures attacking them, it became hard to miss.

His heart raced and there was a pounding in his ears as fear threatened to overwhelm him. He saw Sean firing his weapon; a beacon of calm, lethal precision as he barked orders to the soldiers. They followed Sean's commands, trusting their commander. They had to keep moving. Dying screechers crashed into the ground around them as they ran, but more swooped overhead, snapping at them with powerful jaws big enough to take their heads off, armored or otherwise.

They moved as quickly as they could, only slowing down to fire their weapons at the screechers, which flew among the trees with a speed and agility Noah might have appreciated if he hadn't been terrified they were going to kill him.

Then the screechers changed their tactics. Instead of dive-bombing them in a random pattern of attack, they began to coordinate and come at them in groups. Noah fired his rifle on full auto in a futile attempt to stem the tide of death swooping toward them, screaming as he fought for his life.

Sean was suddenly by his side. He adjusted the power output of his AR-74, setting it to full plasma mode. Noah heard a high-pitched whine coming from the rifle, and then Sean aimed it at the creatures barreling toward them from above. When he squeezed the trigger, a bar of blue-white fire so dense that it was nearly a solid object lashed across the distance to the cluster of screechers and slammed into them like an enormous lance. The screechers howled in pain as the plasma burned through their thick, rubbery skin and flash-boiled the blood inside. Sean swung the plasma lance in wide arcs, killing the creatures by the dozens, and the rest finally broke off their attack.

Screechers' bodies crashed to the ground, their mangled bodies steaming.

Noah had seen a plasma lance used before, and he knew it depleted nearly the entire ammunition pack.

Sean reloaded his rifle. "Come on, we need to keep moving."

A comlink from the shuttle registered with both Noah and Sean.

"We can't make it through to you," Gil said.

A video feed was added to the comlink session, and it showed that the skies above the caldera were packed with flying whales, circling overhead.

Lieutenant Rhoades joined the comlink session. "Colonel Quinn, we've tried to reach out, but each time we get near those creatures, they try to slam into us. We've had a few close calls already."

The comlink was staticky from the interference. "I propose using the combat drones to punch a hole for us to reach you."

The combat drones were based on Krake technology. Once activated, they burned at the surface temperature of a main sequence star, and they were almost unstoppable.

"We'll be crushed by those things," Noah said.

Sean nodded. "I'm transmitting our coordinates to you. We're almost to the waypoint. Don't kill any of those things above us. Avoid it if you can."

Noah glanced back and saw Kyle looking after Lars. Two CDF soldiers were behind them.

They reached a semi-clearing and stopped. The screechers flew above them, but their attack had stalled. There must have been limits to how much the Uvai could control the screechers, or maybe they'd been conditioned to avoid vast clusters of Uvai.

Ahead of them were six mounds roughly two meters tall, covered in the crimson vines of the Uvai. Dozens of their broad, knobbed heads surrounded the area for more than thirty meters around the mounds. Lars's waypoint had them going directly to the mounds. The rest of the *Ark II* away team had to be there.

"They can't be alive in there," Sergeant Staggart said. "Colonel, there's no way they're still alive."

"They're alive," Lars said.

"He's right. They never penetrated Lars's suit. See the marks?" Noah said.

Sean looked at Lars and then back at the huge cluster of Uvai.

The Uvai vibrato increased in tempo, drowning out the sounds of even the screechers' howls. Answering howls came from the Uvai in a modulated imitation.

The skies above them flashed and Noah looked up to see bright, elongated spheres crashing into several large trees until the attack drone eventually hit the ground. Towering trees fell as the drones burned through them as if they weren't there.

"Danger close! Danger close! Take cover! Take Cover!" Sean shouted.

Then the screechers began to attack.

Noah heard Lieutenant Rhoades on the command channel telling them that they'd lost control of the attack drones. They'd been drawn to the ground where they buried themselves, penetrating deeply until they disappeared from sight.

They were surrounded by screechers, some of which galloped toward them from the ground while others attacked from above. Noah watched as Sean and the CDF soldiers tried to defend them, but they were getting pushed back. Kyle and Lars squatted on the ground, trying to stay out of the way.

Sean screamed something at Noah, but he couldn't understand what he said. The Uvai were doing their utmost to kill them, that much was certain. If Sean, Noah and the others were the invaders, the Uvai were simply defending their home. Noah understood that all too well. All he wanted to do was to rescue the away team and leave the planet. If he could just communicate that to the Uvai, would they let them leave? Were the Uvai just evil? They'd used the creatures of this world to attack them ever since they arrived, and they'd attacked the *Ark II's* away team, too. They viewed them as a threat, and Noah couldn't fault that logic. He'd been able to communicate with them once, and they'd shown him a humanoid form with the *Ark II* mission logo. Would they listen if he tried to communicate with them again? He glanced up at the sky, wondering if he could even get close enough to make that happen.

They'd created a humanoid form using their spores, which

meant the Uvai could see them, and they could definitely hear them. This was ample evidence to support that they had all the other senses. He needed to show them what they intended, and maybe he could get them to stop the attack.

Noah stood up and ran toward the cluster of Uvai, hearing Sean shouting for him. A screecher howled as it flew toward Noah, but he darted ahead anyway, feeling as if the creature's powerful jaws were moments from biting down on him. The cluster of Uvai were just ahead, and Noah dove to the ground, sliding between the large fungi. The screechers swooped upward and broke off the attack. Several crimson roots slithered toward him, and Noah danced away. He activated his holoscreen and showed the recording of the Uvai-created humanoid. The roots coming toward him slowed, and Noah moved closer to the mounds. The away team was only twenty meters from him.

Crimson spores began to fill the air, and Noah heard Sean ordering the soldiers not to fire on the Uvai.

Roots darted toward him and wrapped around his ankles, but Noah didn't try to move, remembering that Lars's suit had been marked where the Uvai had touched him. Then he thought about the dead broadhead he'd encountered and exhaled forcefully. The Uvai were trying to figure out what they were. That had to be it. The materials that made up the Pathfinder suits were exotic and must seem artificial to them.

Screechers howled from above as they made another push toward Sean and the others. They were going to die if he didn't do something.

Noah lifted his wrist computer. He inhaled deeply several times and held his breath. Then he opened his suit, and stepped onto the ground, exposing himself to an atmosphere that would surely kill him, but he hoped he had enough time to save the others.

29

The air stung his eyes, and the howls of the screechers nearly deafened him. The air was hot, humid, sticky. Noah held his breath and stepped toward the Uvai. His eyes teared up, and he blinked hard. A cloud of spores floated toward him, and Noah reached out his hand. His skin felt tingly, and he tore off his shirt.

Crimson vines wrapped around his legs. It didn't hurt. He felt an almost gentle pressure, but the vines were rough, like honeycombed rock hollowed by the sea. He tried to open his eyes, and the painful stinging became worse. He looked down at his body amid a torrent of tear-stricken blinks and saw that he was covered with spores. His skin burned as if he'd been bathed in acid, and he cried out in pain, expelling some of the breath he held.

Noah sank to his knees and reached toward the knobbed head of the Uvai. The burning decreased as the vines secreted a cool liquid that seemed to neutralize the acidic sting he'd felt before. His lungs longed for breath, and he opened his mouth involuntarily, gasping desperately. The air tasted bitter and thick, and he couldn't catch his breath. As he gasped for breath, his vision started to tunnel, closing in around him. Noah shut his eyes and thought about Kara, her large brown eyes watching him in that way of hers. She smiled and he was home because home was wherever she was. Other images came to his mind like separate holoscreens—visions of his journey here and seeing the *Infinity* for the first time. A lifetime of memories crowded to the forefront of his mind, from stepping off the shuttle on New Earth for the first time to when he'd met Kara on Titan Space Station. He'd seen hundreds of worlds through the spacegates, some stranger than anything he could have imagined, while others he recognized as being Earth-like. Familiar faces of his friends appeared, who he loved like family. He felt a tinge of regret at the thought of not being able to explore the galaxy, but his sacrifice would be worth it if he could save his friends.

Noah's thoughts seemed to stretch to oblivion as he faded into unconsciousness.

THE JUNGLE BECAME QUIET. Sean watched the screechers fly away, scattering in all directions as if whatever force kept them there had suddenly released its hold. The Uvai were silent as well. Sean spun around, searching for Noah. He'd run toward the cluster of Uvai, but Sean had lost sight of him.

Specialist Denny helped Sergeant Staggart to his feet. Their combat suits were covered with the dark blood of the screechers. The soldiers scanned the area, anticipating another attack, but none came.

"He's in there," Lars said.

Kyle stood next to him, peering at the Uvai across the clearing.

Sean stood a short distance from the nearest Uvai. "I can't see him."

"I saw him go in there. He headed toward the mounds," Kyle said.

"I saw him too, but I still can't find him," Sean replied. He stepped toward the Uvai.

Thump. Thump.

The sound came from all of the Uvai in the entire area, and not just from the cluster around the mounds.

Thump... Thump.

A longer pause between them now.

Sean took another step toward the cluster of Uvai, trying to find Noah.

A cloud of crimson spores vented out of the Uvai, and a path formed ahead of him. As the roots of the Uvai pulled away, the path led right to Noah. He lay face down on the ground. He was out of his envirosuit, and he wasn't breathing.

Crimson spores coalesced to form multiple humanoids, all of whom gestured toward Noah.

Needing no further prompting than that, Sean ran to Noah. He dropped his weapon and lifted Noah, carrying him over to his envirosuit and shoving him inside. As the suit activated and closed around Noah, Sean grabbed Noah's helmet and pulled it over his head. The auto-locks engaged and sealed. Then he saw the suit function indicator switch to green as atmosphere was restored inside. Sean grabbed Noah's wrist computer and engaged the suit's medical interface. His biochip showed a status of cardiac arrest. A mouthpiece extended from the side of the helmet and went into Noah's mouth. Sean heard the slight hiss of oxygen being forced into Noah's lungs. The medical interface flashed a defibrillate function, and a controlled electric shock caused Noah's body to jerk.

Noah began to move, and he coughed. The mouthpiece retracted into the side of the helmet. He squeezed his eyes shut, taking long blinks. His eyes teared.

"Can you hear me?" Sean asked.

Noah blinked several times and looked at Sean. He nodded.

"Just breathe, Noah."

Noah nodded and took several deep breaths.

Sean saw movement nearby, and the thick layers of vines that covered the six mounds began to unravel as if a complex knot was being pulled apart. Sean's eyes widened.

"What is it? What's happening?" Noah asked.

"The away team," Sean said, not quite believing what he was seeing.

"Their suits need power," Noah said and tried to sit up.

"Sergeant," Sean said, "get them emergency power." He gestured toward the away team. "And don't touch the Uvai," he added.

A path formed to the away team as the Uvai moved back. It was one of the strangest things Sean had ever seen. It wasn't a single Uvai that moved but all of them at once.

Noah sat up and then regained his feet.

Sean looked at his friend. The skin on his face, neck, and chest was reddened. It looked as if he'd gotten a rash.

"What did you do? How did you get them to stop?"

Noah licked his lips for a second and looked at the humanoids standing nearby as the spores maintained their formation. They looked to be waiting.

"I touched them. I let them touch me. They tried to penetrate the envirosuits and couldn't. I think they didn't understand what we were," Noah said.

Sean frowned. "And now they know what we are? That's crazy."

"More than they did before. They know we're flesh and blood like the other creatures on this planet."

"Are we safe?"

Noah chewed on his bottom lip for half a second. "I don't know. For the moment. I think they're giving us some space. They're intelligent, Sean. Like us."

Sean wasn't sure about that. The Uvai were obviously intelligent, but that didn't mean they were alike at all. "How do we communicate with them?"

Noah blew out a breath and brought up a holoscreen, expanding it so it reached the ground. Then an animation appeared, showing a shuttle landing in a crater like the one they were standing in. Next, humans inside envirosuits climbed onto the shuttle, and the shuttle flew away.

One of the humanoids dissipated as the spores formed a small shuttle flying away. The spores refined the display by showing it leaving the crater. The animation was repeated several times.

"I think it's confused," Sean said.

Noah nodded. "I think you're right. I think it wants to know where we're going."

Sean added to the animation on the holoscreen, showing the shuttle flying to their ship in orbit near the alpha moon.

The Uvai's animation stopped, and the spores settled into a cloud for a few moments. The rest of the humanoids dissipated, and the spores created a more elaborate scene. First, they formed a moon, and then an accurate representation of the *Infinity* that Noah had just shown them. They added shuttles to the scene, while a part of the planet was created by other spores. Then the shuttles flew back to the planet. As they closed in on the planet, the scene changed to show the caldera again, but this time it was more detailed. There were Uvai on the ground and trees nearby. There were even flying whales in the skies. The shuttle flew among them, coming to land near the group of Uvai. They then added small humanoid figures coming out of the shuttle. Vines emerged from the Uvai, and the humanoids extended their hands until they were joined together.

The whole elaborate scene took about a minute to play out, and Sean couldn't keep his mouth from hanging open.

Noah looked at him. "I think that's an invitation."

Sean nodded and pursed his lips in thought. "Only one way to find out for sure," he said.

He accessed his combat suit controls, and the armor surrounding his hand and forearm opened. He did the same for his other arm and then used his hands to push up his sleeves. He extended his hands toward a Uvai. A crimson vine extended into the air and wrapped around Sean's hand. It was warm. The vines secreted a viscous liquid that made the skin on his hands tingle.

"It feels like when you have your hand near a power core," Sean said.

"Their touch has an electric current," Kyle said. "I wish these suits allowed us to expose our hands, but they don't. The only way this is going to work is if I step out of the suit."

"Don't!" Noah said. "We'll come up with a better way."

The *Ark II* away team was brought back to consciousness.

Noah made another animation that showed their ship leaving a planet with a ring around it, giving a visual representation of New Earth. He then had it traveling through space until it reached this planet with its two moons.

The Uvai seemed to absorb it. They even went so far as to recreate the animation using the spores.

Sean looked at Noah. "Find out why it attacked us."

Noah pinched his lips together in thought. Then he created an animation that showed the various creatures they'd encountered attacking them as they walked through the jungle.

The Uvai didn't reply right away, and Sean was beginning to wonder whether they understood the question. This mode of communication had its limits, but he believed that over time they could refine it. Perhaps they could even improve communication so that it was as easy as interacting with the Ovarrow.

The spores formed a jungle landscape with groups of broadheads and ambush predators, along with many other creatures both big and small. The amount of detail the Uvai used was precise and impressive. The landscape included depictions of the Uvai themselves. It showed broadheads fighting each other sometimes, and other times they grazed. The scene then changed to show the ambush predators succeed in hunting the broadheads and other times where they were thwarted by them.

"It's showing us a natural balance," Kyle said. "See how the cycle repeats across all the different species. This is unbelievable."

Some of the creatures Sean hadn't recognized disappeared. More scenes showed creatures competing for various resources, and throughout each scene the Uvai were there.

Then it showed a scene where a shuttle landed in an area Sean didn't recognize. Humanoid figures exited the shuttle and it looked as if a camp was being set up. The scenes were highly detailed, as if the Uvai were sharing a vivid memory.

"Do you see the common theme they keep showing?" Noah asked.

Sean didn't and said so.

"The Uvai try to balance nature. They try to keep their world in harmony. When they encountered the away team, they didn't understand what they were. Their observations show them to be destructive. See what they did with the shuttle?" Noah asked.

The scene showed a shuttle spinning and the jungle burning.

"We'll need to have this analyzed, but I think the Uvai thought we were here to hurt them, like a disease that it sought to better understand and drive away."

Sean nodded, understanding. "And now?"

"I think they're open to a second chance. Let's see," Noah said.

He created an animation that showed them boarding a shuttle and leaving as they did before, but this time they left a device behind. When the Uvai approached, a holoscreen appeared. Noah created a scene aboard the ship that showed humans watching the screen and the Uvai through it.

The Uvai quickly recreated the scene but with the Uvai creating their own animations.

"That answers that. You're really good at this," Sean said.

Noah shrugged. "I don't know for how much longer. I'm running out of ideas for animations."

Sean nodded. They were exhausted. "How about one more that shows our shuttles coming here to pick us up. Can you make it show the Uvai and other animals clearing the area so the shuttles can land?"

Noah created the animation.

Sean sent a comlink to the shuttles and had them fly to the area. A few minutes later, they landed nearby.

The *Ark II* away team was guided to the shuttles, along with the rest of the team. Staggart and the other soldiers were quite eager to get aboard. Only Sean, Noah, Kyle, and Lars remained with the Uvai.

"One more," Noah said.

He created an animation of the planet and the continents.

He showed the continent they were on by depicting it with the caldera and the Uvai. He then added more Uvai across the region and stopped.

The spores floated toward the holoscreen and added more and more Uvai. They covered the entire planet.

"They're everywhere. They span the entire planet!" Noah said.

Sean watched in amazement but knew they had to leave. "Time to go, Noah."

Noah nodded and closed the holoscreen, walking toward the nearby shuttle. He stopped and waved toward the Uvai. The spores formed a solitary humanoid figure that waved back at them.

Sean peered at the humanoid figure and then glanced at Noah. "I think you've made a friend."

Noah frowned for a second and then his eyebrows raised. The figure looked exactly like Noah, even including the length of his hair.

Sean made a thoughtful sound and Noah looked at him. "I think they made you look even better. Who would've thought they'd already pick up on appealing to our vanity? Interesting."

Noah's mouth opened, and he looked at the Uvai again. "No, they didn't. I'm tired, Sean. Stop messing with me."

Grinning, they climbed onto the shuttle and left.

30

ONCE THEY LEFT the planet's atmosphere, Noah received an update from the *Infinity*. Kara had found a way to end the lockdown, and the ship was docked with the *Ark II*.

Lars and the rest of the *Ark II* team were on *Pathfinder 2* where CDF medics were examining them.

Noah sat in the shuttle, feeling as if he hadn't been still for days. It felt glorious to come out of the envirosuit and get cleaned up, rubbing a damp washcloth on his face and neck in near ecstasy. It amazed him what he could put out of his mind. Even the little bit of washing went a long way toward easing his tension.

"I never thought I'd be so happy to get out of that thing," Kyle said, gesturing toward his envirosuit. It had collapsed into storage mode.

"I didn't think you wanted to leave," Noah replied.

Kyle shrugged. "I didn't, but we're not equipped for a long-term stay." He regarded Noah for a few seconds. "Do you think they'd let me stay on? Be part of the colony? I don't want to miss a chance to study the Uvai and the rest of the planet."

Ezra had been sitting nearby, and she looked at him. "You really want to stay here?"

Kyle nodded enthusiastically. "Don't you? There's so much work to do, so many things to learn. We discovered a new mineral here that somehow interferes with subspace comms. I detected traces of it on the Uvai. It could be part of them."

"We *think* it interferes with subspace, but we don't know for sure," Ezra said.

Kyle smiled. "Don't you want to find out? See whether it does or not? How many planets here have it? Is the lack of it the reason comms worked in the outer star system?"

She hesitated.

"You don't have to decide anything now," Noah said, knowing the decision wasn't one to make without careful consideration. "There will be other trips here. It doesn't have to be an all-or-nothing commitment anymore."

Ezra smiled and nodded, looking relieved. "That's true. I hadn't considered that. In that case, I'd definitely sign up for a rotation, but will there be a colony here?"

Sean came over to them. "Would you give Noah and I a few minutes?"

Kyle and Ezra both walked away, giving them some space.

Noah sat, leaned back in his chair, and sighed.

"Feeling better?" Sean asked.

Noah nodded. "My chest is a little sore, and I need about ten showers, but yeah, I feel fine. The medical nanites are doing a full check."

Sean nodded and glanced toward the others to be sure they wouldn't be overheard. "We need to debrief the *Ark II* team."

"Of course."

"I don't think you understand. This was a massive failure. Saul Ashworth's actions almost killed five thousand people."

Noah frowned and glanced around for a second. "It's probably more complicated than we think it is."

"It doesn't matter. This situation spiraled out of control and there needs to be accountability."

"I'm not following. I mean I understand accountability, but what are you saying? Are we going to bring Saul back to the New Earth and put him on trial?" Noah asked.

"That's not my decision, but it might come to that when we report this."

Noah tore open a protein ration bar and bit into it. It tasted like strawberries and cream. It wasn't bad, but it wasn't great either.

"I guess a decision will be made once we find out all the facts," Noah said, finally.

They returned to the *Infinity* and went through decontamination and medical evaluation. The process took hours, but at least they got to take showers and have a hot meal. Those little creature comforts went a long way toward making them feel better.

It was nice to be in a fresh set of clothes, but what was better than all of that was seeing his wife again.

"I can't even be mad at you," Kara said.

Noah watched his wife, his eyes drinking up the sight of her.

"Especially not when you look at me like that," she said.

"I really didn't know how this was going to play out. To be honest, I'm still getting it straight in my head," Noah said.

Kara nodded and smiled a little. "I don't know what the Uvai did when they touched you, but Claire couldn't find anything different about you."

Noah shrugged. "That's good. I wasn't really thinking about

that when... you know. Mostly, I was thinking about the things that were important to me, about my life. I don't know if they sensed that somehow."

"Maybe they didn't like how you taste so they didn't consume you," Kara replied.

Noah rolled his eyes and grinned.

"Why is Sean insisting on this debriefing right away?" Kara asked.

They'd been back on the *Infinity* for about eight hours, and the *Ark II* team had been given temporary quarters aboard. Sean insisted that the debriefing occur before they were allowed to return to the *Ark II*.

"We need to find out what happened. Too many things went wrong, and Saul Ashworth's continued leadership is being called into question," Noah said.

They headed for the large conference room near the bridge. The *Ark II* team was being escorted to the room by CDF soldiers.

Noah shared a look with Lars. They all looked much better. They'd been able to get cleaned up and the men had shaved their beards. Nails had been clipped. Being in a medically induced coma only slowed down bodily functions—not quite the same as simply being asleep for six months. The growth experienced by Lars and the others was somewhere in the middle.

"You all hold the record for the most consecutive amount of time in a Pathfinder suit," Noah said.

Lars grimaced and shook his head. "That's not what I really want to be known for," he said and sat down in one of the chairs around the conference table.

The rest of the *Ark II* team arrived.

Saul Ashworth was an older man, tall and lean. His hair was metallic gray, and his eyes were dark. He, like the rest of his team, were still in shock over what had happened. Being rescued by people from New Earth hadn't even been a consideration in their minds.

Sean sat next to Noah and gave him a nod.

"It's time we get this meeting started," Noah said. "Each of you will get a chance to speak. This session is being recorded and it will be transferred back to New Earth."

Saul leaned forward. "I'll go first," he said. "I know we've already said this, but I can't thank you enough for everything you did to find us. All of us owe the crew of the *Infinity* our lives. This is one of those times when a simple thank you isn't enough. We'll have to come up with something appropriate as a way to honor what you've done," he said and paused for a moment. "I'll try to answer all your questions. No doubt you're wondering how we ended up in the situation we found ourselves in. Before we go any further, I want it on the record that I take full responsibility for everything that happened. I was mission commander, and the decisions that were made were mine. Five thousand lives were in my hands, and I'm still coming to grips with the weight of it all."

"Understood," Noah said. "Please continue."

"When we arrived in the Zeta-Alpha star system, we received the data from the exploratory probe that had come here first. We'll go into detail later, but I'm going to give a high-level overview first. When we learned about Zeta-Alpha-5 and the properties of the planet, we weren't sure whether it made an acceptable colony site. We were the first early risers," he said, gesturing to the rest of his team. "I decided that we should take a small scouting mission down to the planet and perform an evaluation. We'd only intended to be there for a week at the most," Saul said and paused while he gathered his thoughts.

"We didn't understand what had caused the loss of subspace communications. We hadn't encountered any advanced or hostile alien civilization, but we couldn't be sure. There were so many things we weren't sure about, and there were many options to be considered—even leaving this star system altogether. I ordered a lockdown put in place for the *Ark II* as a protective measure to prevent access by an alien force. I never imagined that anyone from New Earth could have made it here. It's just something none of us ever anticipated. We had a failsafe that would revive the next senior officer in the event that our mission became overdue. First, Officer Truman Mancuso was to be revived. He could then revive more colonists and investigate what happened to us. We filed mission reports about what we learned on the planet each day so Truman would have current information."

"Truman Mancuso died while being revived from stasis," Kara said. "Dr. Hathaway examined the record and his body. He suffered complications of the revival process."

Saul grimaced and shook his head. Then he rubbed his eyes. "He was a dear friend." He poured a glass of water and drank it. "You retraced our steps on the planet. The reports will fill in the gaps, but our encounter with the Uvai was similar to yours, if a bit gentler initially. But it spiraled out of control, and we were cut off from our camp."

Lars cleared his throat. "They captured us. I climbed the tree and tried to contact the *Ark II*, but communications were spotty at best. I don't know why the Uvai didn't kill us. Based on what we've learned from your accounts, I think they wanted to study us."

Saul nodded. "We had nowhere to go. We couldn't fight anymore. Our only chance was to utilize the Pathfinder suit's function for extended short-term stasis. We hoped that enough people would come out of stasis to rescue us."

Sean leaned forward and stared at Saul. "Why didn't you

revive more people before you went down to the planet? This whole situation could've been avoided if you'd done that."

Saul regarded Sean for a few moments. "I didn't think we were going to stay here—not really—so reviving more people would've been pointless."

"Your decision created a single point of failure that would have killed everyone on the *Ark II* if we hadn't come," Sean replied.

Saul looked away for a second and then lifted his gaze to Sean again. "You're right, Colonel Quinn. Those would have been the results of my actions had you not come here, and there's very little I can say that will change those facts. It's a forgone conclusion that I regret those actions," Saul said and looked at Lars, "and that I didn't follow the advice given to me."

Noah looked at Lars, as did many of the others.

"I did give that advice," Lars said. "However, I... *we...* all went along with the plan. Complications while coming out of long-term stasis are so rare that no one could've anticipated it." Lars looked at Sean. "Those of us who've had people under our command have learned that there are times when despite our best efforts and intentions, we find ourselves in situations that spiral out of control. It was a bad call, but it didn't seem bad at the time."

"Colonel Quinn," Saul said, "I'd like to know what your intentions are. How long do you plan to prevent us from returning to our ship?"

"I have to report these events back to COMCENT," Sean replied.

Saul nodded. "As well as you should. I would never dispute that. However, I'd like you to consider what holding me and my team here will accomplish. The decision of whether or not we colonize this star system still resides with us."

Silence stretched for a few long moments.

Noah cleared his throat and looked at Sean. "Saul is right," he said.

Sean regarded Noah with a thoughtful frown.

"However," Noah continued, looking at Saul, "we have good reason to question the decision-making that's been done. Our authority here is limited, but it's not nonexistent."

Saul blinked several times, and then he shifted in his seat. "What do you propose?"

"A bit of a compromise. We'll file our reports with COMCENT. At the same time, we'll assist you in reviving more of your senior leadership. Then you can decide as a group what you'll do as a colony."

Saul pressed his lips together for a moment, and Noah looked at Sean.

"That's fair," Sean said.

Saul looked at the other members of his team. Lars gave him a nod. "Captain Barker, I accept and welcome your proposal."

OVER THE NEXT FEW WEEKS, they did exactly that. They revived twenty colonists spanning multiple disciplines, and an in-depth review was organized. During that time, they learned the limits of the subspace interference, which extended just under halfway to the sixth planet in the star system. A communication station was deployed there and would act as a hub for the colony. The reports they sent back to New Earth were reviewed, and Governor Mullins endorsed Noah's proposal.

Noah walked onto the *Infinity*'s hangar bay. Kyle and Ezra were there with several storage containers.

He strode over to them. "All packed and ready to go?"

Kyle smiled and nodded. He stuck out his hand and Noah shook it. "I'm going to miss this ship, but the opportunities here are too good to pass up."

"I'm sure you'll make the most of it," Noah said.

He'd come to like both the young scientists, but staying on Zeta-Alpha-5 really was a great opportunity for both of them. "It's not often that an opportunity comes to put you at the forefront like this."

"It's not forever," Ezra said. "I hadn't considered that they'd establish a lunar colony instead of a planet-side one."

"I think it's the best choice, for whatever that's worth," Noah said.

"I agree. It gives us some space from the Uvai. You never know whether they'll decide they don't want us on the planet… their planet that is," Kyle said.

"Have you met the lead scientists you'll be working with?" Noah asked.

They both nodded.

"We had to interview with them," Ezra said.

"We did, but it felt more like a formality. Right now, we're the foremost experts," Kyle said.

"How long do you think it will be before more people from New Earth will come here?" Ezra asked.

"Will you be coming back here?" Kyle asked.

"Yes, I'll be back. I'm just not sure when. There are some production issues with making more I-Drives, but we'll work those out. It could be another six months at the earliest before another ship arrives. But we've got the relay set up, so it's not like you'll be completely cut off from us back home," Noah said.

He expected that there would be regular voyages between the two colonies as time went on, and this was just the beginning.

Kyle and Ezra, along with Dr. Lachlan, would be staying

with the lunar colony, and they walked through the docking port to the *Ark II*. They wouldn't have to stay aboard ship long. The outposts being built on the alpha moon were almost finished. Seeing the autofactories being deployed from the *Ark II* made him remember his early days on New Earth. No, it wouldn't be long before the lunar colony was up and running, and there would be plenty of mysteries to keep them occupied.

Sean walked over to him. "Feeling nostalgic?"

Noah nodded. "A little bit. Reminds me of when we arrived at New Earth."

Sean nodded. "Yeah, it does. At least they won't be completely cut off from us. No one will anymore, thanks to you and Kara."

Noah snorted. "Are you going to become clingy now?"

Sean grinned. "I miss my cuddle time with Oriana."

Noah laughed. "I can't help you with that. One thing I can promise is that the trip back home will be much shorter than it was to get here."

"How much shorter?"

"Less than a month."

"A month? I thought you were trying to impress me."

"All right, fine. Twenty-four days."

Sean nodded, pursing his lips. "Well, color me impressed then."

"I aim to please."

31

The *Infinity* transitioned back into normal space fifty thousand kilometers from New Earth.

Noah stood on the bridge and looked at the video feed on the main holoscreen. External feeds showed a bright blue planet with a ring around it in the distance, and it put a smile on his face. Sometimes the best part of a long journey was coming home.

"Captain," Jessica Yu said from the comms station, "we're being hailed by COMCENT."

"Put it on the main holoscreen," Noah said.

The head and shoulders of Connor Gates appeared on screen. "Welcome back, *Infinity*."

"It's good to be back," Noah replied.

Connor smiled. "I bet. I've read the reports, but I look forward to hearing all about it in person."

Noah inhaled deeply and sighed. "She still has that new-ship smell. Do you want to take her for a spin?"

Connor grinned. "One of these days, but not today. I'll see you at the lunar base."

They flew the *Infinity* to the lunar base, where they gave control of the helm to the space dock to guide them the rest of the way.

"Mister Markovich," Noah said, "change our readiness status to docked. Secure all moorings."

"Aye, Captain," Markovich replied, and an announcement was broadcast to the ship.

Noah walked off the bridge and headed for the docking port. Just outside the bridge, Sean and the platoon of CDF soldiers lined the corridors. Noah's eyes widened as they all stood at attention and saluted him.

Noah felt the edges of his lips lift, and he returned the salute. As he walked past the soldiers, Sergeant Staggart caught his eye.

"Thank you for getting us home, Captain," Staggart said.

"You're welcome. Thanks for keeping us safe," Noah replied.

Sergeant Staggart smiled a little. "We don't usually get a choice in our assignments, but if you ever need someone to watch your back, we'd be proud to have the opportunity, sir."

As the soldiers in the corridor broke into deafening screams of appreciation, Sean walked over to him, and they continued down the corridor.

"I knew you'd win them over," Sean said.

Noah snorted. "It was touch and go there for a while."

Over the next few hours, care of the *Infinity* was turned over to a relief crew, and Noah and Kara were escorted to Connor's office. Oriana had already met them on the space dock and hadn't left Sean's side.

The door opened to Connor's office, and Noah saw Connor and Lenora speaking with Ethan.

Ethan wore a serious expression. "But he was my brother."

Connor nodded. "He was."

"And he died a hero," Ethan said.

"He did," Connor replied.

Noah could hear the slight rasp in Connor's voice when he answered. Connor had left a son behind on Old Earth when he'd been shanghaied onto the *Ark*, and when they'd suspected that a calamity had decimated Old Earth, it hit Connor hard. Although he didn't have a choice about coming to New Earth, he still carried the guilt of leaving his son behind. Over the years, he'd made his peace with it, but Noah knew it was always with him.

"We'll talk about it more later. I promise," Connor said.

Ethan nodded and turned toward the door. His eyes gleamed when he saw Noah.

"Uncle Noah!"

Noah leaned down to hug Ethan. "What have they been feeding you? I swear you almost broke me in two."

"What was the Zeta-Alpha star system like? Did you encounter any aliens? How long did it take you to return home?"

Noah smiled. "I'll tell you all about it. We also have tons of video recordings."

"I can't wait to see them," Ethan said, "but I have to go to school now. The afternoon session starts in fifteen minutes."

Noah smiled and arched an eyebrow toward him. "Well, what are you doing here then?"

Ethan laughed and headed for the door.

Noah heard Ethan shout a greeting to Sean just outside Connor's office.

Lenora came over and hugged both him and Kara. "I'm so glad you're back," she said and looked at Kara. "How are you feeling?"

"I'm much better now. Thank you for asking," Kara replied.

Lenora turned toward Noah. "I'm so proud of you."

Lenora had always been like an older sister to him. He hugged her again. "Thank you."

Noah looked at Connor. "I thought I'd have to go right down to Sierra for a briefing."

"I persuaded Mullins to let you get your bearings first. We'll be going to Sierra tomorrow," Connor said.

Noah looked out the window of Connor's office and saw a heavy-cruiser-class ship that had a nearly complete I-Drive around the middle. "You just couldn't wait to put that on one of your ships."

Connor chuckled. "It was only a matter of time. We tried to finish earlier but had a few setbacks. A lot of people were worried about you when we lost contact."

"I wish I could say there was nothing to worry about," Noah replied.

"The Uvai, a planetary-spanning intelligent fungi," Connor said.

"That really doesn't do them justice. After the terror, the whole experience was really quite amazing. We've received some reports from the second colony, and they're having regular contact with the Uvai. I don't know if I'd say it was easier communicating with them than the Ovarrow, but I will say it was definitely different."

Connor nodded. "I think they made the right choice to establish the colony on the moon rather than on the planet."

"I do, too—at least until they have a better understanding of the Uvai and can negotiate with them for a settlement site," Noah replied.

Connor regarded him for a moment, arching his eyebrow. "Listen to you. If I didn't know better, I'd say you're looking to become governor."

Noah shook his head. "No, thanks."

"That's how I felt when people proposed the same for me. But still, you handled yourself really well. The situation could have been much worse, and I'm not just referring to what happened on the planet."

"I think Saul Ashworth will do better from here on out."

"I'm glad to hear you say that. Reviving more of the senior leaders was the best option. They need to govern themselves, and we'll update our own charters for future colonies. I don't ever want there to be a repeat of what happened at the Zeta-Alpha star system."

Noah looked over at Lenora for a second. She was speaking with Kara across the room.

"Is she upset?" Noah asked.

Connor's gaze went to Lenora for a moment. "A little. Lauren and Ethan are getting older, and she's worried that they'll leave us behind one day. Thanks to the I-Drive, they now aren't limited to another place on New Earth."

Noah frowned. "I hadn't considered that."

"She left her family behind on Old Earth, her parents and siblings, to join the Ark Program," Connor said.

"Oh, I see. She thinks the precedent has been set."

Connor nodded. "I worry about it, too. It comes with being a parent. We'll just have to wait and see."

Noah nodded. "The galaxy is a big place. There's a lot to explore."

Connor regarded him for a long moment. "Indeed, it is, and thanks to you and Kara, we'll be able to see a lot more of it."

AUTHOR NOTE

Thank you so much for reading. *Infinity* is the 13th book in the First Colony series. This series has been home to my imagination for a long time. Helping me to stay motivated to write these stories has been the enthusiasm of the readers who've reached out to me and the people who took the time to review my books. I sincerely hope you enjoyed this latest book in the First Colony series. Almost inevitably, I get the question about whether this will be the last book in the First Colony series. No, it won't. I think there are a lot more stories to tell in this series and more characters to explore.

Writing *Infinity* gave me the opportunity to return to the exploration root of the series. The invention of FTL opened up many doors for future stories, and *Infinity* was the first step along these lines. What would happen if we had the ability to travel faster than light? What or who would we encounter out there? What obstacles would we need to overcome? Why would we keep pushing the boundaries of what we're capable of? These are some of the things I think about, along with how would the characters from the First Colony series react to the situations that come from those previous questions.

There will indeed be a 14th book in the First Colony series, and it's something that I've been working toward for a long time. It's not a question of whether or not the colonists will return to Old Earth one day. The question is, what's going to happen when they do?

I continue to write stories in the First Colony series because I enjoy it and because people keep reading the books. The best way for me to gauge whether people want more First Colony stories is by people reading the books and perhaps leaving a review, or recommending it to a friend or a group. Word of mouth is crucial. I take a lot of pride in my work because I think the quality of the story matters, as well as your experience reading it.

Thanks again for reading my books. Please consider leaving a review for *Infinity*.

The series continues with the 14th book!

First Colony - EXPEDITION EARTH

If you're looking for another series to read consider reading the Federation Chronicles. Learn more by visiting:

https://kenlozito.com/federation-chronicles/

I do have a Facebook group called **Ken Lozito's SF readers**. If you're on Facebook and you'd like to stop by, please search for it on Facebook.

Not everyone is on Facebook. I get it, but I also have a blog if you'd like to stop by there. My blog is more of a monthly check-in as to the status of what I'm working on. Please stop by and say hello, I'd love to hear from you.

Visit www.kenlozito.com

THANK YOU FOR READING INFINITY - FIRST COLONY - BOOK THIRTEEN.

If you loved this book, please consider leaving a review. Comments and reviews allow readers to discover authors, so if you want others to enjoy *Infinity* as you have, please leave a short note.

If you're looking for something else to read, consider checking out the following series by visiting:

https://kenlozito.com/federation-chronicles/

https://kenlozito.com/ascension-series/

If you would like to be notified when my next book is released please visit kenlozito.com and sign up to get a heads up.

I've created a special **Facebook Group** specifically for readers to come together and share their interests, especially regarding my books. Check it out and join the discussion by searching for **Ken Lozito's SF Worlds**.

To join the group, login to Facebook and search for **Ken Lozito's SF Worlds**. Answer two easy questions and you're in.

ABOUT THE AUTHOR

I've written multiple science fiction and fantasy series. Books have been my way to escape everyday life since I was a teenager to my current ripe old(?) age. What started out as a love of stories has turned into a full-blown passion for writing them.

Overall, I'm just a fan of really good stories regardless of genre. I love the heroic tales, redemption stories, the last stand, or just a good old fashion adventure. Those are the types of stories I like to write. Stories with rich and interesting characters and then I put them into dangerous and sometimes morally gray situations.

My ultimate intent for writing stories is to provide fun escapism for readers. I write stories that I would like to read, and I hope you enjoy them as well.

If you have questions or comments about any of my works I would love to hear from you, even if it's only to drop by to say hello at KenLozito.com

Thanks again for reading *First Colony - Infinity*

Don't be shy about emails, I love getting them, and try to respond to everyone.

ALSO BY KEN LOZITO

FIRST COLONY SERIES
GENESIS

NEMESIS

LEGACY

SANCTUARY

DISCOVERY

EMERGENCE

VIGILANCE

FRACTURE

HARBINGER

INSURGENT

INVASION

IMPULSE

INFINITY

EXPEDITION EARTH

FEDERATION CHRONICLES
ACHERON INHERITANCE

ACHERON SALVATION

ACHERON REDEMPTION

ACHERON RISING (PREQUEL NOVELLA)

ASCENSION SERIES

Star Shroud

Star Divide

Star Alliance

Infinity's Edge

Rising Force

Ascension

Safanarion Order Series

Road to Shandara

Echoes of a Gloried Past

Amidst the Rising Shadows

Heir of Shandara

Broken Crown Series

Haven of Shadows

If you would like to be notified when my next book is released visit kenlozito.com

Made in United States
Orlando, FL
26 March 2024